KITTEN

Medium Manor: Book 2

Brandy Rife

ISBN-13: 9798345231746
ISBN-10: 1477123456

Cover design by: Collin Foster https://
www.featheredhaberdasheryco.com/

Library of Congress Control Number: 2018675309
Printed in the United States of America

This is for all the Good Boys who are out there looking for their Good Girl.
To the Good Guys who get the naughty and freaky girls, and they aren't afraid to shoot a motherfucker over her safety and to save her life.

CONTENTS

TRIGGER WARNINGS

Slow burn, Abduction, Murder, Violence, Sexual Assault, Human Trafficking, Guns, Drug use, Alcohol use, Ghosts, Public sex, Bondage, Explicit sexual situations, Strong language, Depression/Mental Health/Counseling, Mentions of cheating, Divorce, Consensual Non Consent, Talk of pregnancy, Breeding kink, Pegging, Same Sex with consent M/M.

This book ends with a HEA. I got you.

Hi Friends!

I encourage all my readers to listen to the music compiled in the playlists to enjoy the mood of the moment notated in the book.

I listen to music the entire time I am writing, dancing and swaying in my seat. I hope you enjoy my selections.

Happy listening!

Devin's Playlist

Dangerous Hands/Austin Giogio

Horns/Bryce Fox

Swim/Chase Atlantic

Something In The Orange/Zach Bryan

ANGEL/Toby Mai

Prisoner/Rachael Lake, Aaron Levy, Daniel Ryan Murphy

Way Down We Go/KALEO

Not Enough/Elvis Drew, Avivian

Do It For Me/Rosenfeld

Glitter & Gold/Barns Courtney

Lose My Breath/Rhea Robertson

Half of Forever/Henrik

Freak Like Me/NoMBe

Play With Fire/Sam Tinnesz, Yacht Money

The Devil Wears Lace/Steven Rodriguez

Work Song/Hozier

FEEL/Beneld, BURY

Pretty Boy/ Isabel LaRosa

Never Let Me Go/Florence + The Machine

Oak's Playlist

I Don't Need Your Name/Rosenfeld

Idfc/Blackbear

IF I/Limi

In Over My Head/Moonshine, Sam Gray

Ain't No Love In Oklahoma/Luke Combs

Raise Hell/Dorothy

Real Life Sux/Justus Bennetts

Swing/Savage, Soulja Boy

Lil Bit/Nelly. Florida Georgia Line

Eat Your Man/Dom Dolla, Nelly Furtado

In The Rave/Double Bass Players

Cravin'/Stileto, Kendyle Paige

Like You Mean It/Steven Rodriguez

Slow Down/Chase Atlantic

PLEASE/Omido, Ex Habit

Easy To Love/Bryce Savage

Fire/Barns Courtney

Tonight You Are Mine/The Technicolors

Scared to Start/Michael Marcagi

Chapter 1: Devin

College is so hard.

I've been here at Clemet University for about 5 and a half weeks now since we started school at the beginning of September. Before school began, I had spent the majority of the summer working. Clemet U is near a bigger college, Clemson, and Clemet is full of kids who can't afford the higher tuition at the bigger schools in the state. For me I'm at the smaller college because I could only get a few scholarships and per my parents' divorce, my dad must pay for my tuition and books. He is not paying a dime more if he doesn't have to. He's so cheap.

I was supposed to go to Clemson, but my dad refused to pay for the more expensive school, so I had to change schools right out of high school. He said I either go to a community college or not at all. I took what I could get from the bastard.

The schools are basically the same anyhow. Lots of students have gone to both, so I hear. For example, they do 1 or 2 years at Clemson, then come to Clemet to finish the degree, or vice versa.

I don't really understand why this happens, but I have been told by lots of people at my job this is a common thing around here. At least I will get to go to college. That's more than some and I am grateful for my piece of shit father to be forced to pay for it.

I found a job at a cute and quaint café along Main Street in downtown Clemetville, the town I live in. It's called Book Nook. I love the atmosphere and the people who come in. I have learned so much about coffee and tea. All the spices and flavors that go into the concoctions.

And the fact that the shop is lined with bookcases full of books is an added bonus. Books everywhere! It's my own personal heaven.

The café borrowing system runs on an honor system, like a library, but no one keeps track of who takes what. I've been told it's a system that's been in place since the early 2000s and is legendary around these parts.

If you find yourself needing to get rid of some books, just bring them to the café and place them on the shelves. The only rule is no textbooks. Other than that, it's a free for all on what kind of books are there to choose from.

Physically looking for a book? Please don't ask me to find it in there. Needing a book rec? Yes, let's talk, hope you like smut.

I have an eclectic taste in reading material, but smut has my heart. Some days I want to come home from an especially hard day of school or work, and just get lost in a good sexy story. This is why I don't go out. I would rather lay in my bed or curl up on the couch with a good book on my e-reader.

I live in a 2-bedroom apartment in town with my long-haired cream-colored cat, Luna Love, and my new roommate, Clover. I found this apartment on a social media app as an ad. I got super lucky Clover is a good person as I was kinda scared at first. We hit it off immediately at my interview.

Hey, you never know anymore! I used to watch a lot of true

crime shows too. Ask me about murder, I can talk about it. Ask me about Hollywood stars or what new trendy streaming show is making the rounds, I'm out. I have learned Clover on the other hand loves watching tv and any free time she has is spent with her phone streaming something.

Clover is a strikingly beautiful girl of 20 years old, with amber eyes the same color as a fine whiskey, and bouncy curls that have blond and tan streaks I'm jealous of. Her rich brown, sun-kissed skin always looks like it's glowing.

Clover goes to school at Clemson. She is a year older than me and has been living in this apartment since she got out of high school. Her mom Toddy routinely stops over to clean our kitchen and do Clover's laundry.

Her mom is Indian, and her dad is African American, which are blended perfectly into Clover's features. Her mom is also beautiful. You can't tell that lady is almost 45. They could be sisters. Her mom migrated over to the US when she was 20 and immediately fell in love with Clover's dad. They are such a cute couple when they stop for a visit.

It's bizarre to me her mom still comes and cleans up after her, but that's their family dynamic, not mine. But I always make sure the kitchen is clean, so her mom doesn't have a lot to do. Plus, my mom would have my ass if I left the kitchen trashed all the time.

My time here is sometimes spent cleaning up after Hurricane Clover. I don't mind because I am only paying $400 a month in rent. That's unheard of! I have to pay my living expenses; my dad is not responsible for that, so it has to be as cheap as I can get.

I want to keep this place because I love it here and it's a really nice place over some bougie shops in the heart of downtown Clemetville. Plus, I'm like 3 blocks from my work. I can walk there on nice days.

I definitely won the roommate lottery, that's for sure.

Being her roommate is smooth and easy if you look past the chaos. And she absolutely adores Luna Love. I was afraid to say anything about Luna when I interviewed for the roommate position, but I'm glad I did. Lots of people are allergic to cats or the cats end up stinking the place up. Luna is not like that, and Clover and her parents were excited to have her here.

I love that Clover loves her. They have a good bond. Luna doesn't take to strangers easily, but that hard ass fell for Clover like immediately.

My cat is my emotional support animal. I've had her since I was 14, when I convinced my dad to let me have her. Luna is the sweetest little girl, and she loves anyone who will give her attention, pets, or hair brushings. It was no question; I was taking her to college with me. She got me through my breakup, my parents' divorce and the summer I spent alone for the first time in my life.

My mom invited me to come live with her, but I like it here. I really love living with Clover and working at my job. I'm just not ready to leave yet.

Mom moved away from the area beginning of summer, to a place 2 hours away, and I miss her terribly. We were so close before she left. She is my biggest champion and best friend. I do talk to her through text every day and send her Snaps of my life here, we video chat when we can.

When Mom moved, I felt so alone. Still do a lot of the time. My brother lives close, but he is one town over. My brother is going to graduate early this year from Clemet. I'm really proud of him. One day I hope to get there.

If I don't get my ass in gear and get used to this new life I won't be making the Dean's List like him.

While I didn't have school this summer, I loved going and

spending one of my weekends off work with my mom. Granted it was once going to her house, and she came here once and stayed with me, but it's better than nothing. Our schedules with work were just too screwy to get more time in.

n"What do you have planned on your fancy night off?" Clover asks me, interrupting my life thoughts. I need someone to pull me out of this funk. Clover helps a lot with the loneliness I feel most days.

I inwardly sigh because even in her silk robe, she looks like a tiny model. I am not a small petite girl like her by any means. I got some of my dad's height, topping out at 5'9". Let's just say I am not hurting to reach items on the top shelf like Clover or my mom.

"I am going to read. My mom is 2 books ahead of me on our To Be Read list." I held up the current book, waving it around, "This is just picking up and getting juicy, and I have a nice bottle of wine waiting on me."

"Don't be a recluse. Come out to my bar. I'll only charge you half price," Clover teases and wags her perfectly arched eyebrows at me.

"When do I ever go out to bars?" I tisk.

"You don't go to enough in my opinion." She levels me with a look and one hand on her hip.

I look at her over my glasses, "Look, some of us don't like to participate in noisy and loud social interactions with smelly, drunk people."

"MmmHmm," Clover just flips her hand at me and flounces off to the bathroom to finish getting ready.

Eww, bars.

I have been to a few around town, and I am not impressed. There is a big sports bar across the alley from the coffee shop.

It's called Here Kitty Kitty, but everyone calls it Kitty's. It's always thumping with bass every time I take the trash out and I hear people laughing on the back patio that is a few steps from their back parking spaces. From my glances, you can only fit a few cars in the parking in front of the patio and the rest of the parking is on the side of the building in a much larger lot.

The patio has a fence around it to keep the chaos contained but it never fails, there's always something going on over there, seemingly every other weekend there is a fight.

That is the sports bar Clover waitresses and bartends at. It can get really wild in there.

It's where most of the basketball and football teams hang out. It's where the cheerleaders and half the female population hangs all over the players and any other hot-blooded males they can find. Not my scene.

I get up out of my nest on the couch and go into the kitchen for my wine. I'm halfway through my glass when Clover appears with a cotton candy pink crop top with a low cut for her cleavage, and a pink and black plaid skirt. She has it topped off with her clumpy black penny loafers.

She must be bartending tonight if she's showing that much boob.

Her make-up and hair are on point! That pink bow in her hair is a cute touch but those thigh high white school girl stockings with pink bows…chef's kiss!

Sometimes it's hard to swallow around Clover. I wish I could look half as good as her. She's gorgeous. She has an exotic look to her, and she always plays up her mixed heritage.

Slathering on her pink gloss she looks at me in the mirror, "If you change your mind, make sure you come find me." She puts her hand up and blows me a kiss. I catch it and take a bite out of it like I'm biting jerky.

It always makes her chuckle, "Bye, Dev."

"Bye, girl, have a good night."

I raise my glass to her and walk over to throw all the locks when she closes the door. It may be a small town, but we don't take any chances.

I have a healthy dose of paranoia. One, I watch murder shows. Two, it comes from having a mom that talks to ghosts.

Spooky shit.

She says people never know if a ghost is humping you, but my mom can tell you. She can see and talk to them like it was someone sitting across from you. I am used to it since it's been around my whole life.

I've always thought her unique trait was a gift. She brings happiness to so many people by relaying messages from the other side.

She would say spirit told her or her gut was talking. This was normal in our house. She was always being called to someone's house to move on spirits, or speak to them. Mom has always felt she was giving family members a precious gift one last time.

I've gone on a couple dozen house calls with her. I watch her in amazement. The things that come out of her mouth that no one should know about, but the homeowner knows exactly what it means. My mom has been validated by so many people. She's legit.

I have never once wanted her gift. I would hate to see even more people than I already do.

I'm not much of a people person.

Except when I am at work. I love talking about books and my newfound love for tea. I've always been an iced coffee girl at heart, but all the new flavors of tea I get to try has me forgoing my coffee for a seeped tea. Hey, it's still a caffeine fix either way.

"Luna, come sit with Mommy while I read." I fluff up the blanket and my pillows just as Luna comes tearing out of my room and flies up onto the settling blanket. She loves snuggling with me.

"That's my good girl." Luna purrs her contentment for me.

Chapter 2: Oakley

Senior year at college seems to be a breeze so far.

My class load is fairly light. I really dove into college my first 3 years and took classes in the summer too, just so I could cake walk through my senior year. I knew I was taking a full-time position at my dad's company so I needed to free up as much time as possible.

I wanted to be able to do as I pleased this last year.

I am able to work remotely and it's flexible enough for my evening class schedule. I could be working at 11 pm or 7 am, depending on how my class schedule is for the day.

My work flexibility could be based on my last name. Being a Grayson has its perks when working for Grayson Enterprises and all the subsidiaries. Either way, I am happy to have a job. I don't want to live on my dad's money forever even if one day it will all be mine. I already have a sizeable trust I can draw from whenever I want, but my dad insists he pay for a lot of stuff still.

He's already footing the bill for me to go to Clemet. I deliberately chose a smaller school. My dad is not happy about it as he wanted me to go to Clemson, like he did.

Look, I don't care who hands me a degree, I just want the piece of paper. Whichever school is fine by me. My future is already planned, I just wanted this one thing, the degree, for me, so he conceded.

My dad loves to buy me things and take care of me still, even though I'm a grown man now; that's his love language, he loves giving gifts.

Take for instance, my car. No one else on campus is driving a Maserati. My friends have Hondas and Toyotas. Nope. I asked for a Hyundai SUV and my dad got me a Maserati SUV. That was his compromise.

I have no use trying to impress people. I don't care enough about what people think of me to buy all the fancy shit they do. I feel like my dad does it to set the standard with his business associates. It's his inside joke with himself.

I have watched all my life people try to emulate my dad in both personal and professional life. He has always been my role model, and I couldn't of had a better father.

Dad is a titan in his industry, I have to hand it to him. He has built an empire. His workaholic ways have passed onto me unfortunately. I just focused all that energy on accelerated classes and getting the best grades I could. I haven't missed a Dean's List yet while at Clemet.

Coming up the driveway to the apartment complex in Clemetville where I live, I mentally tally up the chores I need to do before I head out to meet my buddies, Sam and Xavier (everyone calls him X), over at Kitty's.

I pull up to the complex and see Tristan coming out of his apartment. I grab my backpack from the passenger seat, and head over to the walkway by him. Tristan is the local apartment complex plug. I only buy weed from him, I'm not into anything else. Occasionally, I like to smoke and get high. It's not an everyday thing for me.

Holding out my hand I say, "Hey man, how's it going?" Trying not to tower over him, I don't step up onto the curb. He's about 5'10 and I'm at 6'1, 205 pounds.

I know I can seem intimidating and I'm really not trying to be. Tristan has told me a couple of times while we smoked, 'You look like one of those guys that plays the evil villain that women fantasize about." I'll take it.

I have my dad's dark black wavy hair, his bright blue eyes and naturally tan skin. I have long, dark lashes framing my eyes that I have been told by numerous women that they are jealous of them. I get my dimples from my mom though. She was beautiful from the pictures I've seen of her.

I never met my mom. She died in childbirth and my dad, our housekeeping Sarah, and her husband Myles helped raise me. I would love to get to know her but I have come to terms that will never happen.

Tristan takes my hand and pumps it, "Not much bro, you?" Stepping back he looks at me expectantly.

"About to go out to Kitty's with X and Sam, you wanna come along?"

"Nah man, I'm about to go meet my girl for supper. Thanks, though."

I scratch my chin and lean closer to him, "I'm going to need to reup."

Tristan smiles and pats me on the arm, "Already got you homie, it's under your door mat."

I laugh, "Alright. Thanks, man. I'll CashApp ya soon."

He bounces off the curb, raises his arm and says over his

shoulder, "I'll catch you later, you good. Drink one for me."

I wave at him and trudge up the stairs to my own apartment, picking up the bag of weed from under my doormat. Unlocking the door I walk into the complete deafening silence.

Sometimes I miss the sounds of home. Sarah and Myles in the kitchen humming or bickering playfully, Dad up in his office talking on the phone.

Here it's always silent. Not that I mind. I like silence but I also like having a constant background noise at times. That must be why I have music on all the time.

I prefer listening to a healthy mix of genres when I do have my music on. I have a couple playlists I run through, but my favorite is one on Spotify is named Oak's.

I hang my keys on the hook and set my bookbag on the counter when I walk into the kitchen. "Alexa, play Oak's playlist."

Music starts playing through the apartment, starting with 'I Don't Need Your Name' by Rosenfeld. I think to myself '*Good one, Alexa.*'

Heading into the master bedroom I pull my shirt over my head and make my way into the bathroom. I turn on the shower and set out a towel. My body is stiff today. I roll my neck and lift my shoulder to work out some of the stress.

Dropping my pants, I turn to look at myself in the mirror. Maybe I should start going to the gym again. I haven't been running consistently. I've grown lazy the past few months.

I'm not built badly, but I'm also not stacked like a football player. I can't complain. I have a lean build, just not a thirst trap like women are fawning over nowadays. That's my dad. That man spends too much time lifting weights. And it shows. No thanks, I will keep my almost dadbod build. I'm comfy in good places and hard in the places it counts. I have definition, just not a 6 pack you can see with precision.

I feel like I'm just a regular average guy.

I step into the shower as 'idfc' by Blackbear starts playing. I let the water cascade over my head, running down my body. I sigh and think about the last time I got laid. It was 6 months ago, I got tested right after it. I trust condoms, but not whole-heartedly and I like regular testing. My dad taught me that.

I have a girl on call, Mystic, she lives upstairs, but our schedules haven't been able to sync up in the past 6 months. We will text and see if we are busy, but she's a stripper in a club to get her through college, so she has a wonky sleep schedule as it is. It's just not been working out. I think she got herself a boyfriend honestly.

I'm good though. I have porn and a hand.

My favorite place to jack off is in the shower. I love feelings the water running over my cock and down my balls. I also love the ability to clean up easily.

After washing my body and rinsing, I squirt out some of the mint and menthol soap on my hand and slather it around my cock. The menthol makes my dick and balls tingle, and it heightens the feeling in the stroke.

It's getting harder to picture any good sex scenes either from porn, or from my experience. I'm just not interested in getting laid here lately. This is just a release.

I rub my cock up and down, slowly while it gets harder. I stretch and pump, repeating until it's rock hard.

One hand up on the gray tiles holding me there, the other is sliding up and down my slippery cock. I rub the head of my dick in the palm of my hand and close my hand around it, moving all around the tip.

I reach into my mind and bring forward the memory of pussy.

I'm a pussy man. I could stare at that beautiful thing all day long. I love running my tongue and fingers around the folds, and the smooth, soft skin way up in there. I love how it clamps down on me and literally pulls cum out of my cock. But having my face up in it, that's where it's at.

I eat pussy like a champ.

I picture a pretty pink opening and my tongue in there, pushing in and out. I imagine sucking on a clit and putting my finger in slowly.

Sliding across my dick quicker, I pump in earnest and fuck my hand harder. I tip my head back and my breathing picks up.

Remembering the smell of pussy on my face is what drives me over the edge. Spurts of cum land on the wall and floor, quickly washed away by the water.

I lay my forehead on the tile and get my breathing under control. My legs feel like jelly, but I finish rinsing off the excess soap and cum.

I get out of the shower as 'If I' by Limi is playing. A black towel is tied around my waist as I rub lotion all down my arms and over my chest. I head to my walk-in closet when I'm done to pick out something to casually wear tonight. I'm not going to try and pick up women. I just want to hang with my guys. It's been a difficult week at work and school.

Grabbing a pair of darker blue jeans, I slide them on over my navy-blue boxer briefs. Holding up 2 shirts, I choose the royal blue one. It's my favorite color and bonus, it almost matches my eyes.

I smooth down my shirt and spray on a couple spritzes of Y by Yves Saint Laurent. It's my favorite smell and it lasts a long time, unlike some of the others I've tried. I don't do my day unless I have my cologne on.

Running my fingers through my hair, I smear the styling cream through my locks. I have a nice fade up to a longer on top style. I go to a supreme barber, and he is amazing with my hair. I just got my fresh fade 2 days ago.

I smile in the mirror and feel like my look is complete. It's still warm enough, I don't need to grab a jacket. South Carolina fall is still summer basically. Grabbing my phone off the charger, I see I have a missed text in our group chat between me, Sam, and X.

Sam: X it's your turn to be DD, don't forget.

X: Did not forget.

X: Not gonna be like you and get 'accidentally drunk' either.

Sam: ONE TIME!! Jesus. Are you ever going to let me live it down? It's been 9 motherfuckin' months bro!

X: LOLOLOL NEVER

I chuckle at their banter. So, this one-time Sam was our DD, we went to a bar the next town over. Sam found some of our other friends and helped them drink a pitcher of beer, forgetting he was the DD. He was last seen chasing these 2 girls around the dance floor until we caught him out back in the parking lot kissing some guy. We finally got him away and shoved him into the back seat of the car.

We watched him sit there for a moment before I got into the driver's seat and turned to look back at him. He was way too drunk to be left to his own devices.

You never know what trouble he will end up in. Sam is bisexual and has come on to me a few times when we were drinking or high. Admittedly, I am bicurious, and me and him have kissed a handful of times, but it's never gone further than that. He wants to but I've been holding back. Not sure why.

X says it's college and anything goes. He said try everything because you never know when you will get the opportunity again. He has a valid point.

"Hey Sam, how's it going?'

Sam just looks out the window and raises a hand at me while he nods his head.

I had no idea how much he had to drink, but there was no way in hell I could let him drive. X opened the passenger door and dropped into Sam's car. "You good, man?" he says as he looked over at me.

"Yeah, I had 2 beers over the past 3 hours. I've pissed most all of it out, I didn't feel like drinking." It's a good thing too. We would have been fucked. Nine miles from our town and this jackass would have stranded us over trying to drink and get pussy or bob on a dick in the parking lot.

That moment will forever be etched in our memories and Sam will never not be teased that he forgot he was the designated driver. We do get a little leery when it's his turn, but so far the past 9 months, he's been good. It was just that one time.

Me: OMW horsecocks.

X: About time.

Sam: I been pregaming. You got the smoke?

Me: Yep

Sam: Tristan's shit?

Me: Yep

X: <sad face emoji>

Sam: DD, motherfucker!

X: Like I need you to remind me, of all people.

Sam: Fuck you X

Me: LOL <laughing face emoji>

The weather is perfect and it's a clear night. 'In Over My Head' by Moonshine, Sam Gray starts playing.

Ugh. It reminds me of my ex, Riley. Fuck, I dodged a bullet there.

She somehow found herself tripping on a dick attached to an up-and-coming attorney in the big city when it was 'girl's weekend'. That was last winter and I haven't heard from her since.

We dated for a year and had some great times. She never said anything about us moving in together, marriage. She loved her space, and we gave each other breathing room. Obviously too much.

Riley always wanted big city lights and endless pockets. Once I got away, I realized what a gold-digging bitch she was. The sex wasn't even fire, it was just comfortable and available.

It always annoyed her that I didn't want more of that lifestyle. I'd rather be here in my 2-bedroom apartment living next to an old lady named Mable who lives with a couple of cats and knows all the skinny on people, the stripper Mystic upstairs, and Tristan the plug. All of them hated Riley.

It was nice to have someone for sex on call whenever, someone to talk about my day, listen to music or watch tv with. I miss the friendship. We were great friends when she wasn't being a pain in the ass.

Friend or not, I still dodged a bullet. I'm not even bitter anymore. I'm just indifferent. She was someone to pass time with in college. But something about getting cheated on. Man, that betrayal. It eats away at you.

I feel the pull more and more to settle down. Then I think I might be going a little crazy because it's my last year of school and I have a corporate job now. Who the fuck wants to settle down at 23? I don't want to be alone forever. I'm tired of being alone all the time. Seems like it's my life story.

Sam and X live together, and both have offered to get a 3 bedroom so we could all live together. One problem is I like my solitude mostly. Second, they are constantly having people over and partying. There is no way I am throwing a party at my apartment complex. I couldn't do that to my neighbors. That's why primarily young people live in their run down complex.

Getting out of my car in their parking lot, I see their neighbor, Monica. She's in her early 30's, hot as fuck, and is completely obsessed with her wife.

"Hey Monica."

"Hey Oak, how ya doin?"

"I'm good, how are you and Emma?"

"We are great. Gotta run, see ya around!" she says while getting into her car.

I rap my knuckles on their door on the third floor and Sam answers it, smiling. "Hello fine sir, we have been awaiting your arrival." I nod to him as I walk through the door. I don't have it in me to put up with Sam's shit tonight.

X is in the kitchen getting a snack, he waves to me with a mouth full of potato chips. I nod at him and ask, "I didn't bring my bowl or papers, can I use yours?"

He wipes his mouth with the back of his hand, then points towards his bedroom and tells me, "Sure, man, its under the bed on the far side."

These fuckers live like college kids but aren't even in school. There's a weird smell, a couple pizza boxes, fridge full of beer and alcohol, dirty dishes on the counter.

I could never live with these two. Fuck that. I'm not a clean freak but these two can't clean up after themselves for shit and I sure as hell ain't doing it.

"That strange smell is back," is all I say as I head down the hall to his room.

Sam yells, "Goddamn it. We just cleaned. What the fuck!"

Coming back into the kitchen, I set the smoking tin on the table and sit down. I look up at Sam and say, "You asked me to tell you the next time I smelled it and I'm telling you. Do what you wish with the information."

"You know damn well I will be cleaning tomorrow because I don't want to be known as the stinky fuck," X says as he throws away his empty bag. "Get your shit under control, Sam."

Out of the two of them, Sam is by far the messier one. He is like chaos smashed into a fuckboy body. It's like his mom never got through to him about keeping a clean room. Or the importance of a clean house.

I continue breaking up the weed and grinding it. X takes his bowl off the table and packs it for us. He walks back into the kitchen and grabs something off the top of the fridge. He tosses me rolling papers and says, "Go ahead and roll a few for the night at the bar."

I get busy rolling a few for the road.

'Ain't No Love In Oklahoma' by Luke Combs is playing when we walk into Kitty's. You can hear all kinds of genres in this bar. That's why I like it best. You never know what's coming up next, but I guarantee it will make you want to move your body.

We arrive properly toasted and thirsty. I go up to the bartender and grab two beers and a Coke for X. I take them back to Sam and X, looking around to see who all's here.

Bringing my attention back to X, "I see Sam is already trying his luck. Guess he don't need this beer. More for me." I see Sam's tall, brown-haired head disappearing in the crowd, chasing after 2 girls. He has never learned the art of pussy coming to you.

"He tries too hard," X shakes his head. "What about you? You gonna find you some girl to take back to your place tonight?"

I take a swallow of my beer and survey the room. There's a few I would consider, but I am not in the mood tonight. "Not feeling it, man."

"What? Damn. The almighty flirt that's Oakley Grayson is not in the mood to fuck?" X tips back his Coke and comes back to face me. "You alright, man?"

"Yeah, why?"

"I don't know, turning down pussy for like months on end? Come here and let me see if you got a fever." He goes to put his hand on my forehead, and I bat his hand away. "You just seem you're in a depressive mood the past few months. Now you don't want to fuck. Is this about Riley or Sam again?"

X has been my best friend for years. We share everything. Even women when the time calls. He's my ride or die. I told him about me and Sam's kiss and X was cool with it.

I can tolerate Sam in small doses when he drinks. Like going out to the bar tonight, I won't want to deal with him in an hour. Usually, he is off networking or trying to pick up girls or guys, so he isn't around. His game is terrible, I can't believe it when it actually works.

Sam was overjoyed when Riley left. He thought he had his 'in' and then I went hard as a motherfucker with drinking, smoking and banging pussy for like 2 months after she split.

Just a self-destructive phase, thinking I was worthless and not enough.

X threatened to call my dad. He was truly scared I was hurting myself. I put my big boy britches on and got my shit together, and put her and her bullshit behind me.

I turn to X and give a half smile, "Nah, fuck that bitch. I think I'm just hitting the numb indifferent stage. It's like I'm bored with life suddenly."

X side eyes me while taking a drink of beer, he finishes swallowing and puts the glass back on the table. "Ok, I don't know what you mean, but I'm listening. Just don't wallow in misery though. I'm going to need my wingman back soon." He shoves my arm and chuckles.

I tip my beer at him, gulp down the last swallow, and ask if he wants to go out back and smoke. Quick scan of the bar, Sam is nowhere to be seen, so we head out without him. His loss.

Maybe getting stoned will help liven up my mood.

I light up the joint and pass it over to X. After holding it in, I blow the smoke out and ask him, "Have you ever craved something more out of life? Like you just one day realize you are existing, and not experiencing?"

He passes the joint back to me and on exhale says, "Yes, I know that feeling. I crave finding the one that's out there for me. Until then I'm going to plow through as much pussy as I can. It's just practice so I can be my best for her." He pats me on the arm with a chuckle, "Seriously though, sometimes I feel like I need more, Like go back to school, but I can't afford it right now. It's not in the cards for me. I keep applying to corporate offices hoping to get an office job. I can't keep temping forever. I been feeling restless"

"That's part of it. I guess I miss Riley being around. Like I miss going and doing the things we did. Fuck, I don't remember the last time I went out to eat at a restaurant. Shit like that. I think I miss having her as a friend honestly."

"Now granted I haven't had a serious relationship like you had, but I can see how that is depressive. I'm gonna tell ya, dude, I thought y'all were gonna move in together and eventually get married after college. I thought it was headed that way."

"Yeah, I don't know about that. I realize now it wasn't all that serious, and she never made me have that passion you are supposed to have for your significant other." I knock the cherry off the joint and pocket the roach. I look at him again, "It wasn't like she was a great person; it wasn't even good sex, it was just someone to occupy time. Now that I don't have that, I get bored. I don't really feel like she was 'the one', if you know what I'm talking about."

"Well, it's been 10 months since she's been gone, man, and we've had a pretty good time integrating you back into single life, but what you need my friend, is a tolerance break from your stressful job, or someone to turn your world upside down." He claps me on the shoulder. "Take a few weeks and check out. Go on a vacation, my man. When's the last time you did that for yourself? Just get your shit aligned and we can pick up where we left off. I won't even bust your balls about not going out."

He puts his hands in his front pants pockets and looks at me expectantly. Like I got answers.

"Yeah, maybe that's what I need. Get my head straight although I know exactly what I want. I'm hoping it's just a funk."

He puts his arm over my shoulders, and we go back inside while he says, "You just let me know what you need, and I will help anyway I can."

I smile at him and say, "Thanks, man."

We get back into the bar as 'Real Life Sux' by Justus Bennetts finishes playing. Just as 'Swing" by Savage and Soulja Boy comes on, I head to the restroom.

The place is starting to heat up from so many bodies here on this Friday night. I pass a sign for Kitty's Halloween party with a costume contest during the Fall Festival that's in 2 weeks. Maybe I will feel better and come to that.

The whole town has a 'Fall Festival', but all the businesses have been preparing for weeks now. Advertisements are all over the town for it. There are pumpkins on every corner uptown. The reign of pumpkin spice has come, friends. Hail to the Pumpkin King and all that shit.

After waiting in line, I finish my business and wash my hands, I look up and see myself in the mirror. I look really tired. I have some dark circles around my eyes. I haven't been sleeping all that good. I think all this is coming from work being extra stressful lately.

I have a huge project for a big client that I am devoting hours to with my team, and we are a little over halfway through it. I have deadlines looming and I'm starting to stress about it. I do not have time for a meltdown.

I walk out of the bathroom as one song ends and 'Lil Bit' by Nelly and Florida Georgia Line starts playing. I squeeze my way through the mix of people. I feel a hand on my chest trying to stop me. I look down and see a petite blond.

She's so small I would be afraid to break her.

She smiles up at me and yells over the music, "You want to dance?"

I smile down at her, knowing I have a dazzling smile that can disarm most women, I lean down to her ear, "Thanks but I'm heading out right now." I see her nod her understanding and I remove her hand from my chest and keep walking.

I reach X's side, and he raises his eyebrows. I shake my head. I lean over and say, "I'm just going to catch an Uber back to my place and head out. I can get my car tomorrow."

"Are you sure?"

"Yeah, no worries. I just want to go home."

"Ok, I will check on you Monday."

I knuckle bump him and turn to go outside. I pull up my rideshare app when I get out there and order me a ride.

Hopefully I don't get a chatty one.

Chapter 3: Devin

For fuck's sake! The past couple weeks have flown by. Time flies past me so quickly because I'm always working, and school is kicking my ass.

Halloween is coming up in a week, and I have to grab a costume for the fall festival the town is putting on this weekend. I need to figure out what I'm going to dress up as first. I was hoping to get out of it so I wouldn't have to do this, but there's no getting out of it per my manager.

I head into the seasonal costume shop with low expectations. Immediately, I'm overwhelmed as I look around at the amount of costumes and decorations stuffed into this place. They have everything it looks like. I will have plenty to browse through.

The first couple of racks I pass are all kids costumes. Pass on that.

I find the area some would call the slutty section. For the most part, this is going to be a pass for me too. I doubt they have anything to fit me. Hell, I'm not a small woman I don't think. I've always felt I was bigger than most women. Maybe it's because I am taller than every woman I've ever known.

I have some pretty curvy hips and ass, but not the fullest boob area. I've accepted that I will never have some big boobs like my momma, but my barely C cup is managing just fine. With the proper push up bra, I've managed.

I got my dad's height unfortunately. Coming in at 5'9, I tower over my mother. I know that it may not sound too tall to others, but for me it's always been an insecurity. It's the big difference between me and my mom. I do get my curves from her and my red hair is a shade darker than hers. We have the same green eyes and fair complexion, but I have a few more freckles than her. I am a carbon copy of her, besides my junk in the trunk and height.

When things were good in our house, my dad used to call me Red Jr. because I looked so much like her. Then I became a teenager, and he was already off to conferences, working late, and business trips. I have thought for a while now that's when my dad started cheating on my mom, when I went into middle school. That's also when my mom and I were getting closer.

I barely talk to my dad now. Not since I caught him cheating on my mom with his co-worker. In their fucking bed. That was an unfortunate event in my life. No one wants to see their parents having sex, but they sure as shit don't want to see a parent cheating on the other, especially wearing a cowboy getup.

If only I would have stayed in school that day, but no, I had to get the flu and come home. He thought no one would be home at that time. You could tell they expected no one by how loud they were. Also, the fact that they never bothered to shut the fucking door, and my room is across the hall from my parents' room.

There was no way to get to my room without seeing it.

Traumatizing. Scarred for life.

Besides trying not to throw up, it took me a nanosecond to

recognize that is NOT my mother he's fucking.

Double gross.

I immediately went downstairs and called my mom. She came home and caught them too. All hell broke loose when the mom bomb detonated. It's like all the pent-up boredom and frustration spewed out of my mom at him full force with the fury of a royally pissed off redhead.

Then my mom filed for divorce. I am really happy my mom didn't stick around for his shit anymore. Fuck that guy. She deserves better. My dad is a piece of shit.

Now he pays for me to go to school, because it's in the divorce agreement, and I still want nothing to do with him. He tries to text me and tell me he wants to see me, he loves me, and he's sorry. I am not forgiving him. He can go to hell for hurting my mom.

I hate cheaters. Just like my ex. Man, fuck cheaters.

That's all guys my age do anymore it seems. My mom has always told me I am too mature for my age, therefore I can't find a boyfriend worth my time. I just turned 19 but she says I have the mentality of a 35-year-old. I like to think it's just common sense and the duty of responsibility.

My high school boyfriend Aaron cheated on me with one of my close friends, Talya. I gave him my virginity and he gave me trust issues. Go figure.

There were fun times, and I knew we weren't going to run away and get married, but damn, I didn't expect after 7 months of dating him he would go behind my back and fuck one of my friends. I'm mad at her ass too. I've talked to neither since I broke up with him 2 months before graduation after finding out.

Talya was never a good friend, and Aaron wasn't a very good

boyfriend. My mom hated him and her, too. That should have been my first red flag. If moms don't like someone, there's a good reason. Trust your mom's gut.

It doesn't help that I read so much smut that I'm jaded to guys now. My book boyfriends need to step out of the book and fuck me already. I swoon and get deliciously wet when I read my books. Sure I have to take care of myself, but oh to be fucked by one of them.

Smut has made me have unrealistic expectations for men, I think. I can't help it; I have darker tastes now thanks to researching things from my books. I yearn for something more than my ex could give me. A quick bland fuck in his room. Like 3 minutes long. I didn't even get off. I just sat there and blinked like 'It's over?'

There has to be better out there.

Men give women orgasms, right?

Granted I've only had sex a few times, but I feel with the right person, I would be willing to explore all kinds of things. Even fucked up ones. I've read up on so much stuff I've come across in the books and I want to try it all. I want to know what it's like to be in control, to own my sexuality and enjoy it.

I want someone to show me all the things I've been missing.

My mom and I read these dark romance books together and have our own book club with just us. Together we talk about what we've found out, who is fucking who, and when's the plot finally making sense. I don't care about a plot, I am a horny smut slut so give me all the steamy scenes. I mean, yeah, a plot is good, but it doesn't have to be something deep and mysterious.

We have so much fun talking about our books. That was until she just told me her very own book boyfriend stepped out of the book and fucked her in the kitchen on her island, and it rocked her world.

I did not need to know all that.

I love my mom, she's my world, she's my bestest friend, but I can't be talking to my mom about her sex life. I have to have some boundaries.

I am super happy for her though. She was glowing the last time I was there. We shared a bottle of wine, and we talked about all kinds of things long into the night. My mom is my cozy blanket I wrap around me and be who I am. She accepts every whacky thing I come up with and supports me in every venture. This is why my heart hurts so much being away from her.

Snapping back to the task at hand, I mindlessly browse through the 'sexy' costumes and dismiss them all. Not my style. Also, none my size. I see all the other curvy women came and snatched the extra larges up first.

Nothing on me is petite though. I am not ashamed of my body, I'm pretty proud of it actually. I am not so much defined, as I am what you call bootilicious. I don't diet and I don't work out. Mom says I'm lucky currently, but it might catch up to me one day.

Clover told me I have the most banging body and to watch out because she's into women, too.

I wasn't sure if that was a compliment or a threat.

And it made me think, would I fuck a girl? I've never been presented with the option, so I haven't given much thought to it.

I pick up a cat costume and hold it up. It's a red pleather half mask with cat shaped eyes and perky ears on top. There is a long red tail to attach with a safety pin on the back of me. I can throw on some black leggings and a black T-shirt. I have the perfect crop top for it. Yes, I could get down with this costume.

She can't say I didn't try or didn't dress up, so bam, there's that. Easy Peasy. Bonus, it's in my price range too.

I can be Luna's evil stepmom.

I wistfully look at the sexy, sparkly costumes. I'm not against donning the sexy costumes, it's just not something I would do. One, I've never been in anything remotely sexy. Two, I don't know how to be sexy. Three, I don't want the attention.

The less people that notice me the better.

I am not a people person. I ignore most people, except for when I'm working. All of a sudden, I'm Chatty Cathy then and my inner demon that's an extrovert comes slithering out to discuss books and characters. Some nights I go home with a sore throat from talking all night.

I have so much fun at my job though. There is always a good vibe, and the people are the best.

My manager Pam is the sweetest lady. She is part-owner with her best friend who has a corporate job somewhere in the city. It is a very popular and busy coffee shop and Pam makes sure no funny business goes on.

We sometimes get a rush right before 9:30ish on a Friday or Saturday night because of the rowdy drunk people at the bar across the alley. We close at 10 and the bar behind us knows it. They also know that the baked goods that are about to expire for the week all go half price at 9:30.

I stand in line and look at the display of fake eyelashes. Something I have never tried. I see a set of purple metallic ones and take them off the hook. Doesn't hurt to try. If I fuck it up, Clover can fix it. She is amazing at makeup.

I normally wear bare minimum makeup. No foundation or coverup as I don't like how it feels on my skin. Just mascara and liquid eyeliner on top, and some mauve or a pink shade of lip gloss or lip stain. That is the effort I put in. I know how to put makeup on, I choose not to. Most of the time it's because I'm running late, or I don't have the energy.

This should be enough. It's a costume and it shouldn't impede performing my job. And it's still a little sexy. At least by my standards.

◆ ◆ ◆

After dumping the stuff at the apartment, I head over to meet my best friend Nicole at the sandwich shop on the main strip.

I have to work tonight, like every Thursday night, so I just park in the back of the café like normal and walk the block or so to meet her. I haven't seen her in 2 weeks. I get to video chat her and we gab through text, but something about getting a hug from your best friend is magical.

As I walk into the shop, I see her sitting at a booth in the back. She stands up when she sees me and opens her arms for a hug. Of course, I wrap her up in my arms and try not to tear up. It's been an emotional 2 weeks thanks to my geometry and American Government classes, and that's how long it's been since I could see her.

We pull away and sit down. She smiles at me and says, "Sooo, what's new?"

I shrug my shoulders and tell her, "Not much. Same old shit. What's going on with you?"

Her eyes light up and she says, "I got that art scholarship for a summer program in Atlanta that's super hard to get into." She clasps her hands together and squeals.

My mouth drops open, "Oh my God, that's so amazing for you! I know how hard you have been working. Wow! I'm happy for you. Congrats!"

Nicole looks so proud, as she should be. It's an elite program with only 12 attendees. She has talked nonstop about it.

"Thank you! I found out today. I've been bursting at the seams to tell you," she says with a smile. "I can't wait to spend my summer in Atlanta and see the city." She sighs and looks out the front windows.

Our little town is a far cry from being big city life. We are mostly country people with a town smack dab in the middle, and another town a few miles over to the west. We have to travel an hour to get to a city big enough for a mall. We are lucky to have rideshare and food delivery services.

"I'm sure you will have a blast." I tell her.

Just then the waitress comes over with 2 waters and takes our order. Nicole twirls a dirty-blond lock of hair and says, "Are you going to the fall festival?"

"I wish, I have to work that Saturday night. And we are open until midnight that night, which sucks balls. Which also means I won't get out of there until 1 probably. Thankfully, it's a Saturday and I won't have classes the next day." I take a sip of water, "What about you?"

Nicole nods her head and says, "I started talking to a guy so maybe I will be going with him. We are going out tomorrow night for the first time. He's really nice. At least in text he is."

"I'm happy for you! I hope it works out but be careful. There are too many girls disappearing around here for my comfort. It's scary."

"True. We didn't watch all those episodes of Paula Zahn for nothing." She winks at me. "I will be fine. You still have Find My Friends and you know my movements and I know yours."

"I'm happy you found a guy you are interested in. Can't wait to meet him."

"Have you been talking to anyone?" she looks at me imploringly.

I snort and say, "No, definitely not. I don't have the time or energy for a man in my life right now."

"So, what I'm hearing is your vibrator is getting a work out," she giggles.

I almost choke on the water I'm sipping. "Don't be dirty in the sub shop." I can't help but giggle too. Only because it's true.

"Girl, I know. This dry spell has been killing me."

Nicole and I have very different sex lives. I've only slept with one man, never been ate out, never had an orgasm with a man, and never been bent over and railed like I've always wanted. She, on the other hand, has made it a point to fuck her way through life and love every second of it. Good for her. I am not looking for a one-night stand or into slut-shaming. Go girl, get you some dick.

I truly meant it when I said I have no energy.

I need a week of sleep.

"I'm sorry you are suffering from a lack of dick. I'm sure you can find a willing victim soon." I tell her.

I also know Nicole lets them do anything. She is down for whatever. I tell her all the time she should take lessons from the books I read. I could probably fuck like a champ now that I've been exposed to so much more in the form of literary porn.

Ahhh, the dirty, filthy words that make my panties wet and my nipples tingle.

I don't want to be one of those women who settle for vanilla sex when there are so many exciting things to do out there. I think that's what happened to my mom. She settled, then accepted. Now from what I she tells me she is living her own smut book.

My mom has a better sex life than me. Comical.

I want to try so many things. I want to feel it all. But I have to have a connection with someone in order to think about having sex with them. Nicole says I'm demisexual but I don't know.

"Might as well speak about the elephant in the room, have you heard from Aaron lately?"

Just then the waitress brings our food and sets it down. I wait for her to walk away before I look up at Nicole and say, "No, thank God. I still have him blocked."

"Good. That guy was an asshole. I mildly tolerated him at best."

"I'm aware. I should have listened to you and my mom." Nicole made it known every time she could that she thought Aaron was not good enough for me.

"Can you get off for Halloween? There's a party the seniors are throwing out in a field."

"What day is it?"

"Saturday."

"The Saturday after the fall festival? Like next weekend?"

"Yep."

I think for a minute. "I believe I have it off because I'm working the fall festival and closing the shop."

"Excellent! You're coming with me then. It's settled." She seems pleased with herself over this. I just got roped into social interactions I avoid.

"I guess I can go for a little bit. I'm not staying out all night with you though," I say as I point my fork at her.

Taking another bite of my sandwich, I listen to her, "You have to wear a costume. They won't let you in without one."

"It just so happens I bought a cat costume an hour ago."

"I should have known you would pick something lame like that."

"Well, what are you going as?" I pin her with a stare, one eyebrow cocked.

"Playboy Bunny."

I snort, "Yeah, I figured."

"I dare you to wear something showing off your boobs for the Fall Festival. Show a little cleavage. I'll come into the shop to see if you did. Live a little, Dev." She wiggles her eyebrows at me.

"I do live. I don't see why I need to show off my assets. I don't want to share them with anyone. I sure don't want people staring at my tits while I'm taking their order or setting a cup on their table." I dismiss the idea, but she continues.

"I don't think you have the balls to do it. You hide that spectacular body under leggings and long t-shirts. Show it off a little, girl! You have it to flaunt. I'm just saying, it will help your tips." She points a fry at me while taking a gulp of her water, "You wait and see. You'll be hearing me say I told you so."

I blow a tendril of hair out of my face, "I will think about it."

She claps her hands and laughs, "I can't wait to see it. People are going to be drooling over my best friend." She keeps nodding her head and pointing fries at me.

I just shake my head.

We finish our food and say our goodbyes. I take off walking to the café and she goes the opposite way. This part of Main Street has a lot of closed stores. There's not a lot of people out tonight but I didn't expect there to be for a Thursday at 5. I pick up my pace and scurry to the café. Pam gave me an extra 2 hours to shop for a costume. I'm normally here at 3 since my last class ends at 2:30pm.

I was being serious about being spooked. Four girls have gone missing between the 2 campuses. There are so many rumors, and everyone is on edge. It's all over the news. The main rumor I keep hearing is sex trafficking. It's a high possibility too. That shit is everywhere nowadays.

Like I told Nicole, you just never know. Trust no one.

If my mom hears about the missing girls, she will freak out and beg me to come home to her.

I have upped my awareness of my surroundings, not gone out alone at night, and make sure I keep my location on at all times for Nicole, Mom, and Aunt Jilly.

I reach the café and pull open the door and prepare myself for my shift with a deep breath. I plaster a smile on my face and start telling the regulars hello.

Chapter 4: Oakley

The Fall Festival crept up on me today. I'm in disbelief where the time went. Oh yeah, long nights and deadlines at work.

I only had time to run this morning to the costume shop and grab a mask. There wasn't a lot left to choose from. It has a black hood, lights up with red buttons for eyes, and a has a light up wiggly line for the mouth with matching red light.

Hey, it's the best I could do.

I finish tying my black biker boots and stand up. Looking at myself in the full length mirror I think to myself *You look like a robber.* I have a black V neck t-shirt on, black jeans, and black gloves with the fingertips cut off.

My shirt hugs my arms and shows off the black, red and gray angels and demons sleeve I have on my left arm. It's flying angels fighting demons with swords and shields, and there is a big shield over my heart. There is a devil on my back that covers my entire shoulder blade.

It was a gift from my dad for my 18th birthday. I love how it looks. It goes up onto my shoulder and around my chest and back. It has pulled pussy to me many times.

For the most part, I have gotten over my slump. It really was the pressing deadlines. The project lasted weeks and finally wrapped up yesterday and I am grateful for that. Now maybe my life could go back to normal.

I snap the chain to my wallet on my belt loop and shove my wallet in my back pocket. Grabbing my mask, I walk out the door and to my car.

I park at Kitty's side lot and walk a block over to the live band on the makeshift stage at the edge of Main Street. I'm meeting up with a few other Seniors and X. I was told Sam was going straight to the bar.

I bet he will be wasted by the time we get there.

I meander through the crowd, zigging and zagging through the throng of people until I find our group about 30 feet from the stage, off in a grove of trees.

Pulling out the joint I brought, we light it up and pass it around. A few others pull theirs out too. X looks at me, chuckles and says, "Ya know, you look like one of those thirst traps from social media."

"A what?"

"Those dudes who run around in masks, showing off their body but not showing their faces. It's a chick magnet move. Girls eat it up."

"By a guy in a mask?" I'm still not believing this.

"Yeah, these guys have tons of followers. You could be one right now." He gestures up and down me, "All I'm saying is don't be surprised if you get some clingers tonight wearing that mask."

"If you say so."

I spin around and talk to a few of the guys that come up to me about our party next weekend. We don't have too much to plan actually. Just drive out to the field, park, bring alcohol and weed, and dance around the bonfire. Typical fall night in South Carolina.

Turning back to X, I elbow him and say, "It's after 10, do you want to head over to Kitty's?"

He puts out the 3rd joint that was rotating around us. The other 2 joints are still circulating somewhere. I'm sure everyone can smell us in the parking lot behind the stage. We don't give a fuck. Legalize the shit already.

X and I walk past the closed stores and boutiques on Main Street, and take the side street back between buildings, then hang a left. The bar's back entrance is up ahead and I see a few cars parked there. It stays pretty dark back here but it's the fastest route from Main Street. It's lit by one streetlight, that flickers in and out randomly. I suppose some would say this area give serious creeps.

We are walking the last couple of steps to the entrance of the fence that surrounds the place, I notice a couple cars parked by the dumpster across the alley. I notice because one of them is halfway out in the alley. It will be a tight squeeze to get through. Some asshole didn't give a shit if anyone could get through.

There's always going to be daddy and mommy's all American boy slinking around the corner to act like a spoiled, entitled bitch who does shit like that. We run those uptight assholes out of Kitty's all the time. Thinking they are God's gift to women and have to ruffie a girl to get her to put out. When we find those guys, we tend to beat the shit out of them.

Sliding my mask back down my face and making sure the lights are turned on, we walk in as 'Eat Your Man' by Dom Della and Nelly Furtado is blaring throughout the place.

Kitty's is a sizeable bar. It's a sports bar on one side and a dance club on the other. The bar and club take up the entire bottom floor of the building. A long time ago the building was used as a department store. Takes up the whole block.

Kitty's is the only club in the town or the surrounding towns. It's the biggest bar within 30 miles and definitely the rowdiest. It attracts all ages and all walks of life, but it's 18+ for the dance club. You never know what you will see in the club side. The booze and drugs flow fine over there, and the women are usually easy to take home and just as fine.

If you are going to Club Kitty, you are looking for drugs or sex. Sometimes both. I have taken my fair share of college girls home from this bar over the past 3 years. It's just too easy. I didn't need to ruffie them either.

I take 10 steps into the place and already the first girl steps in my path. She licks her lips and smiles. Placing one hand on her hip and the other on my chest, she leans in and says, "Do you need someone to ride your dick tonight?"

Her strong perfume wraps around me, as I step back and look at her. She's alright but I need to pass right now. I just got here.

"Maybe later, I want to hang with my boys and drink. I'll keep you in mind." I pat her arm and step around her. Jesus. That was fast.

I walk up to the bar and order a rum and coke for X, and I order me a Four Roses on ice. That bartender X likes to look at is here.

She is like half Indian and half African American X says. That mix on her is gorgeous. He has a big crush on her and he will do anything for a reason to speak to her. He comes up here when it's not busy so he can talk to her.

Just because she may be off limits to me, doesn't mean I can't look at the goods on display. I hand her money and take the drinks. I smile at her and walk away.

I elbow X and nod my head towards the bar, "Your girl is working tonight."

He nods at the bar, smiles slyly at me and says, "I know. She gave me her schedule last night when I was up here. She asked if she would see me here tonight. Also put her number in my phone and we been talking all night and day."

I put my hand up to my chest and grin, "Oh, ok, it's like that then. Cool, bro. I hope it goes well." I clap him on the shoulder. I hope it works out.

Turning to the dance floor, I survey the room while 'In The Rave' by Double Bass Burgers is playing. The lights are flashing and moving around everywhere. The dance floor is already filled with moving college girls. It's like fishing with a net in a minnow pond.

Another couple of girls walk past and look at me, giggle, and walk away, looking back. I look over at X and he just shrugs.

I hold up my glass at him and toast to a good night. I have a great buzz going on. It feels so good to relax. I finish my drink and lay it on the table. I point out on the huge dance floor and bounce my way there with X following me.

Yeah, we dance.

We have spent the past couple hours dancing, shooting pool and hanging out with our friends. It's been a blast even though I stopped drinking after I had 2 beers. We are on the last joint we brought, still haven't seen Sam. He might have left with someone for all we know.

Standing on the back patio of the bar, we pass the joint back and forth between us. The patio is packed with smokers. Some legal, some not so legal, like us.

The music isn't as loud back here, and you can have a decent conversation. The thump of the bass always reaches out though. It's soothing. When you're outside it sounds like the heartbeat of the bar.

"So my dad has a girlfriend."

X's mouth drops open, "No way! Mr. I Stay Single. Wow. The sex god has taken a woman." He is really familiar with my dad and a lack of a steady woman in his life.

"I know. I was shocked when he told me."

X has grown up with me. He was at our house often through elementary and high school. He's been my best friend since I could remember. When I moved here 4 years ago, he moved too.

We both know about Dad's sex room and his weekend trips to Columbia for 'conferences'. Yeah, we know they are BDSM parties with rich people.

His sex room is badass. X and I stumbled into it one night while dad was gone. It's state of the art, tricked out in black and blue and has everything you could possibly want for fucking. This lady must have a golden pussy is all I'm saying.

"I didn't think I would see the day that man would be in a relationship."

"He said this woman might be 'the one'" I air quote.

"Holy shit. That's bold speak for Quinn."

"I think it might be serious." I nod.

"Who is it?"

"Get this, it's his new neighbor," I chuckle.

"Your dad seduced the neighbor," he grabs his belly and laughs, "How am I not shocked at that. That man has game."

"Apparently, they are happy. Been dating since July. That's all I want for him. He has been alone for too long." I take a swig of water, "If he likes her, I will probably like her too. He doesn't fall for bullshit so she must be alright."

"Does she know your dad is filthy rich?"

"I imagine so since she lives next door and can see where he lives. It's a dead giveaway. That house looks like a castle and is as big as one."

"True, that place is giant. Cool ass house, just really big." He drinks some of his drink, "I just don't want to see someone take advantage of him."

"I don't think that's what's happening honestly. He wouldn't allow it. He's too smart. I talked to Sarah, she said she thinks dad is in love. Said he's been a lot happier in the past few months."

I see X's eyes bug out as his neck snaps over to look at me, "Oh, it's that kind of serious then."

"Yeah."

"Ok, I want to meet her too. I want-"

Suddenly a muffled scream is ringing in the air. I turn around towards the alley, and through the dim lighting, I see a tussle going on. Someone is fighting another. I can make out the shadows moving frantically.

I am running down the few stairs and jumping over the gate. I run through the smaller parking lot and across the alley. I see it's a man with one arm wrapped around a woman's neck and the other hand over her mouth.

She is fighting with everything she has. Kicking, elbowing, scratching. She's trying to do it all but he's too big.

He never heard me coming up behind him, so when I grab his

hoodie and yank him back, landing a blow to his face; it knocks him on his ass. He scrambles to get up, backing up like a crab.

I look over my shoulder real quick and see the girl is moving towards the front of the dumpster.

This piece of shit was trying to steal her. I was sure of it.

There are people starting to move this way from the bar. He notices and runs for the black van with the open door that is parked in the alley. I totally missed it as I ran over.

I wasn't quick enough to catch up as he dove into the moving vehicle. Of course, the van doesn't have visible tags, and they were all wearing balaclavas.

X comes to a skidding halt in the alley as the van turns the corner. I look at him and then run back over to the dumpster to check on the girl. She's not standing there. I run up by the front of the dumpster and she is there, crouched down, hiding.

I must scare the shit out of her, because when she sees me, she jerks away towards the wall. I take a step towards her with my hand out. She stands up and presses herself up against the building, arms out to her sides.

I realize I still have my mask on. Fuck. No wonder she doesn't want to take my hand.

I rip my mask up on my head, and hold my hands up, "I'm not the bad guy. Are you ok?"

She looks like she's in shock. I see her blink a few times and lick her lips. Her appearance settles in around my vision, her bright, wide eyes, her wild red hair billowed around her. The black tank top that shows a nice view of her breasts, but those black leggings on the most perfect set of hips and legs I've ever seen. All dressed up as a cat.

Dick, now is not the time to come to life. We are scaring this poor girl as it is. Down, boy.

I look over at X and he calls up to me, "Everything good?"

"Yeah, we good."

I turn back to her and lift both my hands in surrender again, "Hey, my name is Oakley, and I was just over at the bar and heard you scream. Do you know who was attacking you?"

She shakes her head but is still staring up at me.

"What are you doing back here in the dark?"

I see her look longingly at the back door propped open about 15 feet away. "I work at the café."

"I didn't realize it was open this late."

"It's not normally."

I look her up and down for anything hurt and say, "Hey, seriously, are you ok?"

She takes a deep breath to calm herself and nods, "Yeah, I'm good. I better get back to work" She wrings her hands and tries to slip past me, "I really appreciate your help."

And just like that she slips into the back door.

What the fuck just happened?

Chapter 5: Devin

Oh my God, I think someone just tried to kidnap me! What in the holy fuck just happened? It was all so fast.

I am screaming in my head. My heart is racing. My whole body is shaking.

I tried to fight them off, but they were just too strong. I couldn't get a good strike lined up. Thankfully I got that scream out when I bit their hand and they moved it.

Then the masked man comes to my rescue. Someone tell me why when I saw him it aroused me. Like my panties are very moist.

For fuck's sake Devin, you about got kidnapped and you are wetting your panties like a dog in heat over a masked man.

I blame my books for this reaction. What a thing to think about right now. I am seriously deranged.

My guardian angel is somewhere cracking a bottle of tequila open and clocking out.

First, he fights off my attacker.

Second, he's a masked man with a nice body.

Third, he seemed to actually care if I was ok.

Fourth, he's a masked man.

I have no idea who he is I think as I pull out my phone to call Aunt Jilly.

She answers on the first ring, "What's wrong, honey?"

I let the first tear fall, "Aunt Jilly, someone just tried to abduct me." Aunt Jilly is my mom's best friend, practically her sister, she is like another mother to me.

I hear her getting out of bed. I rush out, "I don't want to tell mom, she will make me come live with her. There was a guy, he came to my rescue. The attacker left. It's a lot."

"Ok Devy, oh my God, right now we won't tell your mom, but what the fuck is going on over there? Where are you?"

"I'm at work. Today was the Fall Festival. We stayed open late. I was taking the trash out."

"Are you the only one there?"

"Yeah, I am," I whisper.

"Do you need me to come down there? I will, ya know."

"No, no. I think I'm ok. They left. It was so scary Aunt Jilly." I let out a small sob.

"I know honey, I am so glad you are safe. I don't know what we would do if you disappeared. Thank God that guy came to your aid!"

"I am grateful for him, but what was embarrassing is he was wearing a light up mask and I just stared at him as he's asking me questions. I mean, I was in shock, but I don't even know if I told him thank you, for fuck's sake."

"Did he give you a name? Introduce himself?"

"I think so. I don't remember his name if he did. Dammit. I was a little out of it there for a couple minutes. I can't believe this happened!" I try hard not to break down.

"Ok honey, the main thing we have to do now is make sure you are safe. Are you almost done working? Do I need to come guard you?"

"I only had the trash to take out, that was all that was left. I was coming back in to grab my backpack and phone. Then all that happened. Should I call the police?"

"I think you should, yes. They need to be on the lookout for this type of stuff. Report it so they can stop it from happening to another girl. You know those girls are missing, maybe these were the people taking them. Jesus, Dev. I am so glad for that man."

"I am too.' I breathe out. "I'm not as shaken now. I think I can manage to stay here long enough for the police to come. Thank you, Aunt Jilly. I just needed to hear someone to make me feel safe." I walk over to the front door and make sure it's locked. "I should be good. You don't need to come down here. I will get off here and call the cops now." I sniffle.

"Anytime, sweetness. You text me and let me know when you get home. I mean it!"

I walk back to the back door and make sure it's locked, "I will Aunt Jilly. Thank you again."

"And Devin, we can't keep this from your mom forever. She deserves to know. You were in danger, and this was a very close call. Don't keep this from her, even if she tries to make you come live with her."

I sigh, "I know. I just don't want to do it right now. I have enough to deal with at this moment."

"Ok honey. Let me know how it goes with the police. Love you tons."

"I will. Love you too."

I end the call with her and take a look around the café. I can see the streetlights from Main Street shining in the front windows and doors. I can see the deserted street and realize I am most likely one of the only people on this street right now.

That guy saved my life. And I acted like a complete fool.

In my defense, I was under duress.

I place a quick call to the police, and they assure me they will be there in a few minutes, as officers are around the area because of the festival and partiers.

I stand against the counter and bite my thumb nail. A knock comes on the front glass door that makes me jump.

I see it's 2 officers in uniform and I rush over to let them in. They introduce themselves and I get busy telling them what happened. I write out a statement and sign it and they offered to walk me to my car.

I let them know I would greatly appreciate that. I gather my things as one officer steps outside the back door and says, "I'm going to come back around tomorrow and suggest to the owner a bright back light in this area is necessary. It's too dark back here and with the bar right there, it's amazing anyone heard you. You got lucky, little lady."

I reach my car and unlock it. I tell the officers thank you and before I get in the car I chance a look over at the bar. I see a silhouette of a man that has a red light up mask, standing on the bar's back patio. He waited for me to get in my car! That's so sweet.

I quickly duck down into my car, shut the door, and lock the car. As I'm pulling away, I take another look. He is still standing there on guard in his mask.

And I don't even know his name.

Chapter 6: Devin

I am still up when Clover gets home at 2:30 am from her shift at the bar. She is surprised to see me sitting on the couch with a book and Luna.

"Hey girl, what are you doing up still?"

"I had a really rough night…." Then I tell her what happened. She immediately rushes over to me and hugs me.

"Fuck, girl, I am so happy you are ok."

"Thanks. It was pretty scary. It's definitely made me more paranoid. Like I thought I was on guard before, but now it will be worse. What if they come back for me? Was I targeted?"

"That is terrifying to think about. I want to believe you were random. They thought no one would notice because," she counts off on her fingers, "the bar is loud and full of drunk people not paying attention, the café doesn't have a back door light, and no one would have questioned someone parked in the alley because of the festival."

"Good points. Still, very bold of someone. These people have to be stopped." I put the pillow propping my book up on the coffee table. I reach over to hold her hand, "Please tell me you will be more careful."

"Most definitely I will. You can count on that. I think we need to get some self-defense weapons."

"That would have been great but are we going to have to carry all of that on ourselves at all times? Because I didn't have my backpack, only my apron. What good will weapons do if we aren't carrying them all the time?"

"Fair enough. We will just have to see what all is out there and anything discreet enough to put in our aprons. I will start wearing mine again at the bar."

She squeezes my hand. "How are you feeling now?"

"I'm really tired but wired at the same time. If that makes any sense."

"Is there anything I can do for you before I take a shower and go to bed?"

"I don't think so. I appreciate you just being here."

She leans over and hugs me again, "I'm really glad you are here too." Then she leaves me to head to her bedroom and shut the door.

The apartment is quiet again and I idlily run my fingers through Luna's fur. I think back to the masked man.

He was tall, he had a nice body. Not like built or stacked but still defined. I was mesmerized by his chest and arms as they heaved from his actions. Watching him lay that motherfucker out was exhilarating.

He seemed like he genuinely cared about my wellbeing afterwards. I was shaken but that surprised me. Not many college guys around here concern themselves with mousey girls like me. I expected him to see if I was ok then walk back over to the bar.

I sure didn't expect him to wait on the patio until I left.

I jolt awake and whisper, "Oakley."

I was having a nightmare about the attempted kidnapping.

I sit up and for a minute I panic because I don't know where I am. I look around and realize I'm in our living room on the couch. Right, I took one of Clover's sleeping pills.

Fuck! I said his name. I remembered his name!!

In my nightmare he came in and grabbed me to haul me away. He cradled me to his chest and ran his hand down my wild hair. I remember plain as day him saying 'My name is Oakley.'

Oakley is my masked stranger.

Hot masked stranger.

Who knew I would have that kink?

Thinking about him makes my tummy flip and knees weak. Maybe it's trauma attraction.

Either way, he was still hot as fuck.

I get off the couch and go use the restroom. I'm still groggy from the pill. I look at my watch and see its just after 6 am. So, I've only been asleep a few hours.

I wash my hands at the sink and look up at myself in the mirror. Before I have a chance to really look at myself, I see there is a girl standing behind me. I let out a startled gasp and whirl around.

She isn't there.

I know what I saw goddammit!

I turn back around and look in the mirror again. but no one

besides me is there. What in the fuck was that?

I must be going crazy from stress, or this sleeping pill has hallucinogenic effects. I swear someone was standing behind me. My heart is racing out of my throat. Am I still dreaming?

I walk on shaky legs over to the couch and pick up my phone off the coffee table. I pick up Luna, cuddle her like a baby, and trod to my bedroom, shutting the door. Maybe I can get a few more much needed hours of sleep.

Chapter 7: Oakley

Since I didn't have that much to drink, I don't have a hangover. I just needed to hydrate more, therefore a trip to Dunkin' was in order. Good thing it's in walking distance.

On my way up to my apartment, I see Mystic coming down the stairs. Her long blond hair is up in a high ponytail and she's in workout clothes with a gym bag over her shoulder. She sees me and smiles, "Hey Oak, how's it going?"

She looks up at me with her sunglasses on and I see my reflection. I try not to look bored. I change my expression and say, "Hey Mystic. I'm good, how are you?"

Mystic isn't that big. I could literally pick her up and throw her. I was afraid to be too rough with her. It made for a lot of holding back on my part and I was never truly satisfied with Mystic.

She was convenient when I needed release. We have no feelings for each other. It's just sex.

"I'm great. I'm glad I ran into you; I want to let you know I started seeing someone."

"Oh, ok, that's cool, good for you. I hope everything works out well, I won't text you anymore. No worries."

"Thanks, Oak. Good seeing ya," she continues down the stairs to the parking lot. And just like that I lost my booty call.

She's been gone for a while, friend.

Entering my apartment, I kick off my shoes and start stripping as soon as I reach my bedroom. I get in the shower now since I came in too late for one last night. My mind wanders to last night.

I did notice in all the flurry of activity is that the girl is gorgeous. She was afraid but I think she was in shock. I mean it was a pretty traumatic event. She almost got abducted. Fuck.

These disappearances are getting ridiculous.

She was putting up a hell of a fight, I'll give her that. She just needed the right traction to do any damage. I know my hand hurts from cracking him in the face.

Hands down, would do again.

My dad raised a man that tries to protect others. I would have fought her own family if they were manhandling her like that. Nobody should have to put up with that treatment.

The way she stared up at me in awe, like she couldn't believe I showed up. Then I went and scared her further. I want to apologize for scaring her, but I don't even know her name.

But I do know where she works!

I just want to talk to her again. The need to make sure she's ok is strong. We don't even know each other but I feel strongly I need to see for myself.

Maybe I can go to the café and see if she's working. I want to stare into her eyes, see the fire that was there last night, I seen it through the fear. Underneath the terror, she's feisty.

She looked like a feral kitten, ready to attack and looking for a way out. I wanted to pick her up and hold her, making sure she was truly ok. My cute, feisty, little kitten.

After the scuffle, her boobs kept rising and falling, distracting me. How could I not notice her perfect, perky tits?

I'm like any other red-blooded man, BOOBS ARE DISTRACTING.

She had on a really nice shirt, I liked how it showed off the swell of her breasts. I'd like to put my hand down it and cup them to my face.

Annnd my dick shows up to this convo.

Thinking back to how pretty she was, it makes my dick jump. This bastard hasn't wanted anything in months and suddenly a random girl we are playing hero to is making it throb.

I'm going to hell.

Just go with it.

I would love to run my hands down those curvaceous hips and bring my hands right up under her ass, then bury my face in her pussy.

I'm absently stroking my cock, and I wonder how she will taste. She looked so innocent and tempting at the same time. I bet it tastes like the finest peach, sweet and juicy.

I grab the menthol soap, and I stoke my cock up and down. Running my fingertips over the tip, feeling my precum, my breathing picks up. The water falling over my chest and hitting my dick feels so good.

I lay my head back against the grey tiles. I pick up my pace, my hand knows this action like an expert. I rub my forefinger over the ridge of my dick, right where the head comes together underneath. I like how it tingles. It's the fastest way to make me cum.

I place my foot up on the edge of the tub. I take my other hand, flex my stomach muscles, and cup my balls. I think about how it would feel to be inside her.

My kitten is down on her knees in front of me with her lips around my cock… her head is buried in my crotch…..I have my fingers in her hair, pressing her head down on my cock until she gags…..she runs her tongue around the head on my dick and sucks it like a lollipop..

I cum all over the tiled wall and release the breath I was holding.

I have to find out more about her or my mind won't rest.

I clean up, shut off the water and step out. As I'm drying off, I hear a message hitting my phone. I put the towel around my hips and go in the kitchen to check it.

X: Hey man, you alive?

Me: Yeah, been up since 8, already been to Dunkin's.

X: I feel like I'm dying.

Me: Should have stuck to the weed lol

I grab me a bowl and a spoon. I pour Lucky Charms into the bowl and add milk. Breakfast of champions.

After I eat my cereal, I go get dressed. I put on a dark gray long-sleeved shirt and dark blue jeans. I throw on my tennis shoes and run my fingers through my hair. It's going to do what it wants anyways, but I do run some product through it in hopes that it will make the waves stay in place.

The idea of going to the café in search of finding out about my kitten is getting better as the minutes tick on.

This is also called stalking, Oak.

No, not the same. We just want to find out more. That's all.

Stalkers just want to find out more too.

Not having this internal argument with myself. I am not stalking her. Final.

I open my panoramic roof and 'Cravin'' by Stileto and Kendyle Paige is playing. I put on my shades and back out of my spot. It's a nice October day. Fall is in the air.

The drive across town is relaxing. It truly is a quiet little town. Clemetville is your regular sleepy town. That's what draws me to it; however, I plan to move to a bigger city once I graduate. Even this little town is better to me than going back home. I felt so isolated.

I find a parking spot out front of the café. I look up at the shop and see there's a decent amount of people in there already. Pulling open the door, I step through, taking my sunglasses off.

I don't think I've ever been in here. It's cute. Quaint. It's bigger than it looks from outside. It smells like coffee, French vanilla, and old books. I notice there are books lying around everywhere. They seem to cover every surface. There are shelves on all the walls, and they are full of books too.

There are tables scattered about. The chairs to the tables are mismatched. There is a few overstuffed loungers placed about. The counter is off to the left, parallel to the opposite wall.

The windows in front of the shop are covered in suncatchers, stained glass ornaments, and plants. There are rainbows floating across the walls from the prisms in the windows.

Why have I never come here before? It seems really peaceful. Oh yeah, I don't read...or like coffee....or tea.

I'm here for pussy. Erh, I mean a girl. Jesus fuck.

I see there are a few people in line so I step in behind them and look up at the menu. How stupid will I look asking for a water and then sitting here looking around, not reading like everyone else is? I have to get a better cover story. Now I'm starting to get paranoid because I'm stalking a person.

It's not stalking mother fucker! We are checking up on a victim.

Suddenly, I see smoothies on the menu. That's it. There's the story I need.

The girls in front of me move away and I approach the counter. Pretty blond says, "Hi, what can I get for you?"

"Hi, I umm, wondered if the manager was here."

She smiles at me and says, "Yes, Pam is here. May I tell her who you are?"

"Oh, yeah, she doesn't know me. I have something to discuss with her about the incident last night." I sound nervous. Fuck.

Get your shit together, Oakley!

I give her my disarming smile, complete with dimples. She dips her head and smiles, "I'll go get her for you." She flounces off to the office but looks over her shoulder back at me and hides her smile again.

A middle-aged lady with sandy blond hair and brown eyes comes up to me, "Hi, I'm Pam. How can I help you?"

"Hi, I wondered if I could talk to you about what happened last night."

Pam looks puzzled. "What do you mean?"

I'm confused for a minute. Does this woman not know what took place?

"About the almost abduction of one of your employees?"

Her eyes get really big, and she says, "What? I know nothing about this. Yeah, me and you need to talk. Come on back here, hurry."

I go to the Employees Only area and she lets me behind the counter. We go to her office and close the door.

"Start from the top then."

I tell her what all happened last night, and I saw the cops walking her employee to her car and she drove away.

"Devin never said anything, she didn't leave a note or anything."

SCORE! Devin! My kitten's name is Devin. Very pretty name.

"I'm sure you can verify all this with a call to the police."

"I plan to call them, right after I call her." Pam picks up her phone and scrolls through her contacts. She hits call and I can hear it ringing. It picks up but it sounds like voicemail, I get to hear the angel's voice again, "Hey this is Devin, I can't answer right now, so send me a text instead. Thanks."

Wonder if I can talk this lady into giving me Devin's number or address?

No, man. Act right.

Pam looks over at me and says, "I've called twice and she's not picking up." She looks stressed. "Do you think she might still be sleeping since she had a late night?"

"That does seem like a logical excuse. It was almost 1 in the morning when she left." How am I supposed to know if she sleeps in. Maybe one day I will know.

I faintly hear 'When You Say My Name' by Chandler Leighton playing out in the sitting areas. I look around the office while Pam tries again. Devin. I have a name. It's a start.

Pam draws my attention back to her, "Well she isn't answering. How did she seem last night?'

"Well ma'am, she was scared, rightfully so. In shock too, but told me she was good, and then ran into the building." I can't tell this woman she looked like a frightened kitten ready to slice a bitch if they came near her.

Fucking ninja kitty.

Hi ho! I am the Masked Man and this is my Ninja Kitty, fear us!

She rubs her forehead, "Thank you for bringing this to my attention, and thank you so much for coming to her rescue. I will have a light installed back there today."

"Oh, you are welcome. That's a good idea."

"Is that all you came for, is there something else I can help you with?"

"I was just checking on Devin, but I see she's not here."

"No, she has Sundays off usually. She's my best girl so she gets spoiled first." Pam smiles gently. "I'm glad you were out there when you were." She pats my arm that sits on the desk.

I stand up, "No problem. Glad I could help. I better take off." I tip my ball cap at her and open the office door.

"Wait! What is your name?"

"It's Oakley. See ya now."

I slip out of the café and didn't even need my cover story. Well played, nerd.

I start the SUV up and nod along to 'Friends' by Chase Atlantic.

Soon, Kitten.

Chapter 8: Devin

My first semi-conscience effort is stretching like a cat in the sun, and groaning in pleasure. I open my eyes and see sunlight filtering through my curtains.

Holy fuck! How long did I sleep?

Fuck it, it's Sunday and I'm off work.

Reaching over for my phone, my neck protests in pain. Then I remember someone tried to steal me last night and had me in a tight headlock. Just a painful reminder I wasn't good enough to fight him off of me.

I unlock my phone and see all kinds of messages and 4 missed calls. Three from Pam, and 1 from my mom.

One text from Nicole: **Love the shirt with that peepshow! Bravo!**

I call my mom back first after I use the restroom. I flip open Spotify, start my playlist called 'Devin's' and it softly starts playing 'Dangerous Hands' by Austin Giorgio in the background while I call my mom back.

"Hey baby! How are you?"

I love hearing my mom's voice. It makes me start to shake, thinking about never hearing it again.

"Hey mom," I say softly.

"What's wrong baby?" She sounds worried.

"I have something disturbing to tell you.."

I tell her about last night events while fixing my coffee, and she is crying by the end of my story. Of course, I knew she would try to talk me into coming to her house. I hear 'Horns' by Bryce Fox haunting me from the speakers as I make my mom cry.

Aunt Jilly was right. Mom needs to know.

I feel awful hearing my mom cry. Like I did something bad.

I need to rationally think of this and not feel guilty for making her cry. Mom is just scared and playing the 'what if' game in her head right now. Fuck, I played it until four this morning.

"Mom, hey, Mom it's alright. Shhh, hey, I'm ok." I try to use my calming tone with her.

"Thank God that young man came along. It makes me sick to think of what might have happened if he wasn't there. What did you say his name was?"

"I didn't say because I don't know it." I'm going to hell for lying to my momma. I don't want her tracking down this guy somehow and sending him a new watch or gift cards, or some other shit, like I know she will.

"That's a shame. Well, maybe you will see him in one of your classes."

"I don't even know if he's a student, Mom." I flash back to him in the dim light from the bar. "I didn't really see him that great, so I doubt I will recognize him if I did see him."

"I would love to hug him."

"I'm sure you would, Mom."

"Ok honey, I will let you start your day at noon," she giggles. "I'm really glad you are ok, Devy."

"Me too Mom."

"Thanks for telling me. I love you whole lot bunches."

"Love you too."

We hang up and I call Pam and explain the night to her too. She is very worried but assured me she was putting in a new light back there and putting up security cameras. I told her I appreciated it a lot.

Then she says, "The young man that helped you stopped here looking for you."

I gulp as my air gets caught in my chest. "He came there?"

"Yes, he's the one who told me what happened. He came to see how you were doing. Very nice guy."

I can feel her sly smile through the phone. I swear she's in cahoots with my mother trying to get me to date.

"Yes, he was very nice. I appreciate him coming to my place of work to check on me. Thanks for letting me know, Pam."

"No problem. I have to go call some security companies to price cameras. Take care of yourself, kid. I'm glad you are ok, kiddo."

Hanging up with Pam, I put my cup in the sink. He came to my work today!!! That is kinda scary and sexy.

I take the speaker with me to the bathroom so I can shower. The perfect song has been playing, 'Swim' by Chase Atlantic.

Warming up the water, I yank my hair out of the ponytail, and I step into the steamy shower and get my hair wet. I start humming along with the end of this song, then 'Something In The Orange' by Zach Bryan starts playing.

I have to wash all the sweat out of it my hair. Yesterday was a rough shift. We were super busy. There was always a line to the door or past it. We sold out of every baked good. I have no idea what they opened the café with this morning.

It had to be because the dessert food truck backed out of the festival at the last minute, so they all came to us for sweets. Even the ones stored in the walk-in refrigerator were put out last night. Pam is going to have to make a rush order.

I work this whole week so I can have the weekend off. I will go to the Seniors party with Nicole, but I won't stay out all night and that's my boundary with her. When I want to go, I will go. She won't try to convince me, and she usually respects it.

Maybe I'll see my masked man. I don't know what I would do with him.

He's a complete stranger and I don't accept strangers well. I am too paranoid of people. And the night of the Fall Festival proved I need to be worried.

One of the reasons I can't date is because I'm secretly afraid of guys. There I said it. I watch too many shows.

Finishing rinsing my hair, I soap up my washcloth in my favorite soap. Peach and vanilla. I hope they never get rid of this smell. I love it.

I turn the shower off and get out as 'ANGEL' by Toby Mai plays. I stand there naked and get in my basket, lifting out my hair oil. I bend over and run my oiled up fingers through my wet hair.

I have a thick mane of hair that reaches my elbows. It has the same waviness as my mom's. Most days I throw it up in a messy bun.

Today I want to go shopping for some new long-sleeved shirts and a new pair of tennis shoes to work in. I want to go to this new lingerie shop I heard of. I'm going to spoil myself for a minute.

Drying off I picture my hair done how its supposed to be; big, bouncy curls. Fuck it, just do it. It's not like I ever do it, and I have time right now.

Grabbing my diffuser, I bend over and get to work.

I walk out of my room carrying the speaker playing 'Prisoner' by Raphael Lake, Aaron Levy, and Ryan Murphy.

"Good morning and afternoon, Clover!"

"Ugh. Sunlight."

She busies herself making her coffee. "Did you sleep alright?" She turns to look at me.

"Yeah, I did, thanks again. I got up and went to my bed finally." I fold up the couch blanket and throw it across the back. I fluff the pillows and set them where they go on the cushions.

Luna runs past me as her automatic feeder goes off. Stay out of that cat's way when she hears that food drop. She acts like I'm starving her. Her vet said she's just fine, and I routinely have to remind Clover that Luna is limited on the treats. Clover says fat bottomed girls rule the world and baby Luna can have anything she wants because she's a rockstar.

Clover is almost as obsessed with Luna as I am. She posts her all over her social media with bows and flowers in her fur. Since Clover works at the bar, she has a lot of followers. My cat is famous around here.

"Where are you going all dolled up?" She raises an eyebrow at me over her steaming cup as she leans against the counter.

I smile and say, "I'm going shopping at the mall. For me

because I want to treat myself. Do you want to come along?"

"How long do you plan on being gone?" Clover has Sundays off because the bar is not open.

"A few hours. I have homework to catch up on."

"Ok, cool, me too. Can you give me 20 minutes to get ready?" She starts moving towards her room after dumping the rest of her coffee in the sink.

"Absolutely."

I go back into my room to rub some lotion on my hands. Season change is playing hell on my cuticles. Constantly washing dishes at work doesn't help either.

I steal a look at myself. I took the time to put make up on too. I have some nude and gray eyeshadow lightly dabbed on and my eyes are lined with liquid liner. My wings perfectly drawn on with the 9th wipe off and try again.

I have a pair of stretchy skinny jeans on and a maroon long sleeved crop top. I have a pair of tan boots on. Very autumny. I put in a pair of fall leaves earrings I picked up from a polymer clay artist at a small craft fair.

I spray more Caroline Herrera's 'Good Girl Supreme' on me, it's my favorite scent. I pick a maroon lipstick and put it on. I rub my lips together and approve of the color choice as I blow kisses to myself in the mirror.

I look hot today.

Clover comes walking out of her room with a pair of skinny jeans and a pink sweater that hangs off one shoulder. She has thrown her hair up in a ponytail and donned some mascara and lip-gloss.

"It's not fair you are so beautiful and us peasants have to be stuck with this."

I snort, "Are you fucking kidding me right now? You are too gorgeous, and you know it."

She puts on her sunglasses and says, "Maybe that's the key, I do know I am, but you won't accept you're naturally beautiful. Now come on, we don't have all day. Shop, shop!"

By late afternoon, we have been wandering around the mall for the past few hours, and we have numerous shopping bags as proof. I don't have the same spending limit as Clover, so I have a few less bags than her. Her parents are rich, and mine do not support my shopping habits.

I'm sure my mom would give me money if I really needed it. And sometimes there is a random hundred dollars that appears in our joint checking account. I have saved those up for this shopping spree, plus I've been working overtime. Hence the reason I'm so tired all the time.

It's not like I have anything to do besides reading and school. I am the most anti-social person I've ever known.

"Do you want to get something to eat?" Clover asks while looking around the restaurants at the food court. "Do you want to eat here or get something somewhere else?"

"Umm, I am fine with whatever and yes, I am hungry."

I see Clover take a step forward and suddenly, she beelines to the right. I follow her direction with my gaze and realize we are not going to a place to eat; she is stalking prey.

I follow behind her as she walks up to a tall man with olive skin, dark hair and dark eyes, a shadow of a beard, and a Clemson hoodie on. He is intently texting on his phone with a smile on his face.

Suddenly, I hear her text notification go off.

Did this guy just text her? Who is he?

Clover stops in front of him with her flirty smile and says, "Fancy seeing you here."

He looks up shocked and smiles real big, "Hey Doll, I just messaged you."

"I heard." Again, her cheshire flirty smile.

OK, I'm tracking. This is a new guy.

This guy is staring at her like she's the last woman on earth. If I didn't know better, this guy would lick her feet clean if they were muddy, that's how smitten he is.

Clover turns to me and says, "Devin, this is my newest prey, Xavier or X as he likes to be called. X, this is my roommate, Devin." He holds out his hand to shake my hand, and I take it for a moment and shake his back as my phone starts ringing.

"I have to take this, it's my mom." Clover nods her head and turns back to X. I turn away and take a step away to answer it so I'm not rudely talking in front of them.

"Hey Mom."

"Hey baby! How are you feeling this morning?"

"I am better. I got a good sleep, and I feel rested. I'm out shopping at the mall with Clover right now."

"Oh! Well, don't let me interrupt girl time! I just called to check on you. Do you need shopping money?"

I put my hand over the receiver and say in a low voice, "It's cool, Mom. No, I don't but thank you for the offer. However, I think I just met her next ex boyfriend," I chuckle.

"Oh yeah? Alright, I will let you get back to having a friends day. Have fun baby! Love you lots."

"Love you too Mom. Bye."

"Bye babe."

I turn back around and there is a very tall man with black hair in front of me now, and he's staring at me intensely. My eyes flick up to his blue eyes. They look like the ocean and a girl could really drown in them. I know how cheesy that sounds, but it's true.

He has the most beautiful blue eyes framed by dark, long lashes. I am immediately jealous of those lashes. Imagine not having to wear mascara.

His chiseled jaw and full lips are beautiful, and it looks like he hasn't shaved in a day, so he's got dark scruff. This man is sex and beauty in human form and he is delicious.

He is drop dead gorgeous.

Involuntary thigh clench.

It's not fair guys can look this yummy and it just be natural.

As I stand and stare at him, ripples just run through my pussy like I'm a needy whore. I am truly awful.

Will need a visit with BOB (battery operated boyfriend) because my mind is garbage today.

His dark wavy hair looks like he just ran his fingers through it when he pulled on his dark gray shirt. Wavy hair that will tickle when you run your fingers through it.

I feel my heart skip a beat. This is too much. This reaction to a stranger is not normal for me, but I am drawn to this man like moth to a flame.

His chest and arms are defined by the tight shirt and his sleeves are rolled up to reveal a large black, red and gray tattoo that takes up his whole forearm. Enough to make me wonder where it leads when his shirt is off.

He is holding a drink in a nice firm hand that would cup my

ass cheek perfectly....*Why the fuck are you thinking this about a stranger!*

Jesus, Devin. Simmer down before your blush gives you away.

Then he makes my heart skip a beat when he gives me an irresistible smile, his eyes seemingly act like he recognizes me. He licks his lips and says, "Kitten?"

I am so confused by this. Who does he think I am? I know no one that calls me Kitten.

Of course, I keep standing here like an idiot, staring at him, with my brows furrowed now.

Clover says, "Devin, this is X's friend, Oak."

Recognition dawns and I breathe out, "Oakley."

This is the man who saved my life. This is the sexy masked man that made my pussy cum to with all kinds of naughty thoughts. He is just as breath-taking with the mask off in the daylight now.

"You two know each other?" Clover asks, puzzled.

Oakley is the first to break the staring contest between us, he looks at Clover and says, "I am the masked man that saved a kitten in the alley."

I lick my lips and suddenly I am thirsty, why? I don't know. It feels like my knees are going to give out. My palms start sweating as my heart continues its quickened pace. This is a heightened visceral reaction to him, and I am quite frankly reeling from it. It confuses and excites me at the same time. I have never reacted to someone like this.

This man is too beautiful to be interested in mousey ole me so stop staring, Dev! I have no idea why I'm letting him get to me like this. He is out of my league. Oakley saved me because he's a nice guy. Nice, hot as fuck guys are not interested in girls like me.

Then why does he stand there looking at me with devilish eyes and a promising smile, like he will lay me down on one of these food court tables and eat me for lunch while I pass out screaming from pleasure...

Get your shit together, Devin!

I am horrified as I feel the reddening creep up my chest, up my neck, then to my face. My face is giving away my reaction to him. The smirk on his face says he knows where my thoughts were. His smug expression says he's pleased with my reaction.

And he looks like he wants to pounce on me any moment.

"What, wait, you're THE Bruce Wayne? The masked man swooping in to save the damsel in distress? Holy fuck. Small world." Clover looks shocked.

Coming out of my stupor because, yeah get your shit together, I look over at Clover, clear my throat and say, "I remembered his name when I woke up this morning."

And immediately I'm mortified because that sounded exactly like I was dreaming of him. Which I was, but he doesn't need to know that. The rest of them don't either.

Earth, swallow me up right now!

Oakley is still staring at me like a wolf does to prey.

X stands there with his eyebrows up, looking between me and Oakley. "Hey man, cool you found her." He pats his arm. X looks over at me and says, "You're all he's talked about." Which shocks me. He then looks at Clover and asks, "What are y'all out doing today?" He's giving her a sly smile, that she is definitely returning.

I have a feeling these two will be fucking any time soon, if not already.

Clover bats her eyes, "We were just going to get something to eat. Do y'all want to come along?"

I could choke on air as she says this. Anxiety is wrapping its cold fingers around my neck. She's trying to kill me.

Alright, I may fantasize about men, lots of men actually, and read dirty books with a passion, but I really do not pull off flirty very well. I pull off quiet, clumsy girl in leggings and a messy bun very well, though. Do I want to flirt with him? I mean where's the harm if he's willing to flirt with me.

Gah! I don't even know how to flirt!

Oakley looks at me and grins, "Sure, I would love to, if it's ok with you." Why does he have to have the most sultry, sexy, and seductive voice. And that southern drawl.

Involuntary thigh clench.

I need dry panties ASAP. These are ruined.

I blink around everyone as they look at me expectantly. "Sure."

My Stranger Danger reflex has yet to kick in around him so there's that.

"Where to, ladies?" X offers to take Clover's bags and carry them. She hands them right over and slips her arm through his.

"Let's go to The Cheesecake Factory, that's Devy's favorite."

The urge to be invisible gets stronger.

Oakley lifts one eyebrow and leans in, "Devy?"

I give him a look right back, "Yes, it's my mom's pet name for me. It sticks with everyone else, too." I challenge him to laugh at me.

He shrugs a shoulder, "I like it, but I prefer Kitten more."

Before I can say anything, he offers to carry my bags. I have a split second to make up my mind and take advantage of his chivalry, or be the independent bitch and carry them myself. He takes the choice from me as he reaches for the bigger, heavier bag, "Here, at least let me carry one of them."

I allow him to take the bigger bag. It's not like I think he's going to run off with a shopping bag full of women's clothes and lace panties and lingerie. Just please God, don't let him drop the bag and dump the contents. I bought me new see through bras and panties and I would be mortified to see him picking those up.

Chapter 9: Oakley

How fortunate I let X drag me to this godforsaken mall.

She is exquisite. I am dumb struck by how beautiful she is.

I can tell I threw her off her game; however, she didn't look like she was going to shank me this time. Almost like she was awed by my radiant smile and starstruck. I'm not famous so it must have been the smile. I chuckle to myself.

That's me, bringing the ole razzle dazzle with cheese.

She willingly hands me over the last bag. I usher my arm in front of us. She takes another look at me and starts walking, following X and Clover.

We exit the mall and hang a left to the entrance of the restaurant. I hold the door open for her and she quietly tells me 'thank you' as she passes by. I get a whiff of her perfume as the air rushes up to me. Ahh, jasmine and vanilla with something fruity. I can't pinpoint it exactly. Fuck. It smells amazing. I follow that scent like a bloodhound up to the reception desk.

We are seated instantly because it's in the middle of rushes. We are here at an odd time of day. It's past lunch, but not quite dinner, but the dinner crowd will be in soon. There are plenty of tables open right now though.

They put us in a booth. I come up to the table and turn to look at Devin, "Do you want inside or outside?"

I see all the conflicting thoughts going on behind her eyes as she looks up at me. I see her start to panic but immediately see her shoulders straighten, she steps up to the table, "I'll take the outside."

She thinks I will put up a fuss and doesn't think I will slide in. Normally I will refuse, but I feel like she needs to be in charge here, and she feels the need to have an escape plan. I can't blame her after last night. This is why I oblige this request.

I place her bag by the wall and slide in. I turn to look at her and put my arm out to get the rest of her bags, "I have plenty of room over here for them."

"Oh, ok then. If it's inconvenient I can keep them over here."

"Nah, it's good, hand them here." I take the offered bags and place them beside me. There is a reason I do this. It will make me have to sit closer to her.

I admit I found her on Facebook. I searched every Devin until I found one that fit her description in this area. It also helped she has her work listed as the Book Nook. That's how I recognized her standing in the food court.

I went stalker mode. *This isn't stalking.* It's researching.

I found out about her cat Luna, about her mom and the fun things they do together. I learned about her high school years, and I know she just broke up with her boyfriend right before she graduated.

I learned she has a best friend Nicole, who lives around here, but does not go to college. And this area is where Devin's from. She is going to Clemet University for nursing and she's a freshman.

It's amazing what people will put out on social media, even if it is really old information. She's posted nothing within the last few months.

When she's mine, I will make sure she locks that shit up tight. Can't be having anyone come stalk my Kitten.

I have to be her #1 stalker.

That thought came out of nowhere. I have never been a possessive man. That is not a normal thought for me. But I still feel that pull inside me to make her mine. It jerks my dick to think of her as mine.

Maybe I just needed the right woman to pull out the possessive trait.

I look over at Devin as she's searching the menu. She smooths her hair back over her ear. I see her profile and really assess her.

She has long lashes that appear to be real and not the fake ones girls are wearing now. Lucky her. She has a cute little nose, slightly upturned. Her lips are plump and look entirely kissable with her shiny lip gloss on.

I can imagine how beautiful her lips look wrapped around my cock as she's on her knees in front of me.

Starting to get uncomfortable in these jeans.

Is the room getting hotter, too?

I pull my shirt away from my neckline and steal more side eye glances of her. Her jawline is softly defined, and she has a slender neck. Devin is tall, I would say from 5'9 to 5'10, somewhere in there. She wasn't completely dwarfed to my 6'1.

I don't feel like I could break her. She has a sturdy build, with amazing curves everywhere. Her boobs are a nice handful, not too big or too small for my preferences. They look perfect.

But those hips. Her waist tapers from her ribs to her hips like an hourglass. These type of women do exist and she's walked right out of a guy's wet dream.

Jesus fuck. That's the most incredible ass on the back of her. I made sure to walk behind her so I could stare. I absolutely love that she is so curvy. Part of the reason I wasn't attracted to Mystic as much was she was too skinny for me. I don't want someone I can break or slap their ass too hard and they fly off the bed.

That ass will be a handful and then some. Fuck, I can't wait to bite her ass cheek.

Oh, it's happening.

She just doesn't know it yet. She has just became my new fascination.

I steal another glance at her and see her small smile forming.

She totally knows I'm checking her out. Maybe I'm just as nervous as her.

The waitress comes over to take our drink order. I am curious to know what she drinks. She orders a sweet tea light ice. I thought for sure she would order a girly drink.

When the waitress leaves, Clover looks at me and asks, "So, how did you know she was in trouble? X told me one-minute you guys were talking, the next minute you took off and launched yourself over the fence to run over there."

I sit back on the booth with my arms on the table. "Well, that's pretty accurate of what happened. I heard her scream in the dark." I look over at her. She's got her head bowed slightly. Looking back at Clover, "I didn't know what I was walking into. I just knew something bad was happening to someone and I had to help."

"She was up until 4 am shook up."

I see Devin's mouth pop open and whisper, "Clover!"

I look over at her beside me and she slowly brings her emerald gaze up to mine. "Are you ok now?" I ask her.

She nods her head and softly says, "Yes." I look back over at Clover as she continues, "I'm just glad you decided to step in like a knight in shinning armor. Thank you for saving my friend." She places her hand on mine and pats it.

It's my turn to blush. "You're welcome. My pleasure." Turning to Devin I say, "I had no idea what the darkness hid that night, I mean you were beautiful in the dim lighting out there, but out in the daylight, I have to say, you're stunning."

I hear X take in a sharp breath.

He knows this is not my normal flirting style. Mainly because I'm dead fucking serious about her and I'm not using the smile on her. I want her to know I'm sincere.

Her neck jerks over to look at me. Her wide green eyes tell me she has no idea how beautiful she is. Devin downplays herself because she wants to be invisible. But I see her. And I like what I'm seeing.

Our late lunch passes by too fast for me. The conversation was good. Devin relaxed when she was served her shrimp fettuccine. She looked over and told me she sometimes gets hangry and it's best she shut up until she gets food. I let out a laugh at that.

We were all laughing and getting to know one another, and Devin opened up more during our meal. That is until Clover dropped a secret. I learned from Clover my little kitten loves to read dirty books. Clover called her a smut slut. Very interesting.

Devin was staring daggers at Clover while she was telling me all about her book loving friend. I ate it up. Sounds like my kitten might be into some freaky shit. I'm here for it.

When Clover and X start talking among themselves all secretive and petting all over each other, I bump Devin's arm and say, "So, if there was a person who's never read a smut book, what would you suggest they start with?" I smile at her.

She gets a surprised look on her face. "Well, I, uh would first ask what trope they are interested in."

"What's a trope?"

She wipes her mouth with her napkin and sets it back in her lap. She reaches for her drink and says, "It's what you are interested in basically. Are you interested in BDSM, threesomes, possessiveness, domination; what kink are you wanting?"

Suddenly, the inner Devin comes out. I can see her passion peeking out about reading these books. I want to read one.

I want to see the hype. I want inside her brain.

"What if someone wants them all?"

I see her halt sipping tea up her straw. Then her throat moves up and down with her gulp.

I concentrate on her full lips wrapped around a straw. I would be lying if I wasn't picturing them around my cock. These lips are going to be the death of me. She pulls the straw from her mouth and licks her lips. I could moan.

My pants are cutting into my cock more and more by the passing second. I'm running out of room in these pants. My dick don't give a shit.

I see this motherfucker can't act right where she's concerned.

Her chest rises, "I guess I would start them on some popular books to see which trope they fit into most."

"And which one do you fit into?"

She stares at me before slowly smiling. "No," she shakes her head with a chuckle, "You only find that out if I want you to." She wags her forefinger back and forth with a cocky smile as she turns to face the front once more.

I watch her sit back in the booth, sipping her sweet tea.

I lean closer so only she can hear, "What if I want to find out?"

She is now choking on her sweet tea thanks to me. She is sputtering and coughing so I pat her on the back and Clover is jumping out of her booth to come around the table.

"Honey, are you ok?" Clover puts her arm around her.

Devin's coughing subsides and she pulls the napkin from her red face. She looks at Clover and tells her, "I'm ok. I'm fine. Went down the wrong pipe."

Clover steps back and says, "You gave me a heart attack. I wouldn't mind kissing you but mouth to mouth with my garlic breath is a no go for me, girl."

X pulls her face over and kisses her lips and says, "I don't taste any garlic. Seems just fine to me." Clover leans into his arm and wraps her arm around his.

Devin takes a deep breath and looking over at me, she cuts me a dirty look with her narrowed eyes. She does not disappoint, "We'll see. You have to earn it."

Ok. My kitten wants to play hard to get. I got nothing but time to win over her.

Our cheesecakes arrive but we are so stuffed we can only eat a few bites. The waitress comes and boxes them up and comes back with our checks. Before everyone can get out their cards, I hand mine to the waitress and tell her run it for everyone. Everyone tells me I don't have to do this. I know I don't. "It's ok.

I want to." I look at Devin, "Consider this our first date."

Devin gives me a deadpan stare. I just give her my cheeky smile.

Clover pulls her face away from X's and says, "Welp kiddos, is it time to go?"

Devin stands from the booth, I slide out, and right up to her. She jumps back out of my space. She was busy looking at the cheesecakes and I snuck up on her.

I turn around and reach for her bags. I am not about to let her carry any of them to their car.

Something about her makes me want to chase her down, and not let her get away. I have never chased a woman in my life; I've never had to. Pursuing a female is something new to me. Not to sound egotistical, but women usually throw themselves at me.

She reaches out for her bags, and I shake my head 'No' and remove them from her reach. I watch in amazement as her face tells everything she is feeling. She is the worst poker player.

I see the stubbornness flash in her eyes and then the resolve to maintain control sweep across her brow. She simply says, "I appreciate it," and starts walking out behind Clover and X. I am ok with this, as it gives me a great view of that ass.

I practically run into someone because I can't take my eyes off her. I don't think I've ever been this interested in a girl so quickly. I wasn't this excited to get to know Riley or any of the other women I've been with. A big part of me wants to be around Devin as long as possible.

We almost reach Clover's car, and Clover walks up to Devin and talks softly to her. Devin looks alarmed, and her eyes flick over to me. Clover is still talking softly to her and rubs her arm. Devin nods and looks down at the ground. Clover is beaming when she turns around and walks towards me and X.

Devin looks up and her gaze finds mine. I don't know what's wrong, but she is on guard again.

Clover stops in front of X and says to me, "X is going to take me back to his place using my car, do you mind giving Devin a ride back to our apartment, Oak?"

Now I understand where the body language is coming from. I vow right here to do my best to make her feel comfortable around me. I would never hurt her.

But she doesn't know that.

I like how my kitten has a sense of self-preservation.

"Yeah, that's no problem at all." Clover grabs X's hand and waves at Devin as they get into Clover's car.

Devin looks like that scared kitten again. She's just standing in the parking lot, a car length between us, looking after Clover pulling out. She pulls her gaze back at me.

I slowly walk up to her with her bags, my eyes never leaving hers. I give her a smile, "Hey, it's ok, I'm not going to hurt you. I would never. I didn't save you to hurt you myself. Only if you want me to that is."

She looks at me and narrows her eyes. I prepare myself.

"I want to be clear; I don't know you; I'm not sleeping with you."

"Yet."

"What?"

"You aren't sleeping with me, yet."

I see her nostrils flare. She crosses her arms and thrusts her hip out. Oh no, she has the stance of a woman about to argue.

"Although I can appreciate your bravado, I'm not like all these other college girls who have sex with any guy they meet, or who saves them in my case, or on the first date. You have to earn it."

"How do I earn it?"

Her mouth drops open. She shakes her head and chuckles. "How do you think you earn it?" She bites her plump bottom lip.

"I date you. I get to know you and let you get to know me."

"That's a very good start, only the brave would ever attempt it," she smiles as her shoulders straighten.

"Ok, then I accept the challenge. I want to date you."

Her bewildered expression tells me she thought I would walk away or laugh it off, that I wouldn't pursue her or comply. She has no idea what she's been doing to me. I hardly believe it. *What the fuck am I doing?*

I can't let her slip away and the feeling I have when I think about her dating anyone else is not normal for me, but it's strongly there, pulsating inside me. I still have this fierce need to protect her.

She holds up a finger, "Ok, but first, why do you call me Kitten?"

I chuckle and look at my shoes for a moment, shaking my head slowly. I look back up at her with a half smile and say, "Because you were dressed as a cat and the first time I got a look at you, you reminded me of a scared kitten ready to strike at anyone coming near you."

Dawning of the meaning is written in her eyes. She gives me a small flirty smile. "So does that make you the big bad dog chasing the cat?"

She's perfect.

I finish walking the car length between us and stand right

in front of her, in her space, I can smell her perfume, "Absofuckinlutely."

Devin has the most intriguing shade of green eyes. They are paler green in some areas; other areas are a deeper shades of green like you would see in a forest canopy. They are like looking into the woods and finding solace with Mother Nature. They have a calming effect on my nerves and for a few moments, I can't look away, memorizing their pattern..

I move past her, never taking my eyes off her, and say, "My SUV is over there, Kitten. Come with your new boyfriend."

I see her form a genuine smile and cock her head, but she follows me. I have to stop and take in this moment as she walks up to me. I did this to her. I made her happy. And she's not putting up a fight over the boyfriend thing.

Yo! Heart, you are falling a little too fast, boy.

Anxiety is gripping that same heart. I can't believe she said yes! Well technically she said 'Ok', but same difference. I'll take it.

I have a girlfriend.

Just like that I'm dating a woman.

And I don't mind at all.

Great fucking God, she is wonderful. Witty, intelligent, sweet and she's independent to a fault. She's perfection wrapped in red hair and smoldering emerald eyes.

I lead her through the parking lot towards my SUV. She keeps up and continues to follow me looking around. Probably making sure there are witnesses seeing her leave with me. I know how girls are obsessed with murder shows. They have every right to be. As a man, I recognize the world is not safe for women. One of the reasons I jumped in. Too many crazies out there.

I hope everyone sees her leave with me. You can't miss her. She's too pretty not to notice. I would for sure have noticed her if our paths had crossed previously. I've not seen her around campus or town.

We arrive at my SUV and I put my foot under the bumper to open the back door.

"You drive a Maserati?"

I look over at her. She's looking at me some sorta way. I can't figure it out.

"Yeah. It was a present from my dad."

Her face falls a little as she looks away and says, "Oh."

I set the bags in the back and hit the button to shut the hatch. I step up to her and put my hand on her left cheek. She doesn't shy away, but she does stiffen, then looks up at me. "What happened there? What was that reaction?"

She looks off over to her right at the other car. I softly say, "Hey, look at me. Please." She looks back at me. I do not remove my hand cupping her face. It feels too good. "Talk to me. I'm supposed to be learning all about you, help me. Use words."

I see her sigh. She says, "I'm sorry. I mentally judged you and my hope depleted there for a minute."

"Why? What did you judge me as?"

Devin crosses her arms over her chest in a defensive pose. I rub my thumb across her cheekbone. "Please tell me."

"One of the assholes at school. The rich, stuck up, better than everyone people I go to school with. They drive cars like this."

I let out a laugh and say, "I can see that. No Kitten, I am not like those assholes. I'm just a regular guy. My dad is the guy that's rich, not me. I have a full-time job, and it's my senior year of college. No way I'm affording a Maserati, but he can. I asked for a Hyundai, this is what he got me."

"I'm sorry I judged you so harshly."

I remove my hand from her face and smile, "It's ok. You don't know me that well. It was a valid assumption."

I lead her over to the passenger door and open it for her. She looks in the car and then back up at me.

"You have all the control here, Devin. I can get you a rideshare if you aren't comfortable with me yet."

She puts her hand on the door and slides into the seat. I nod my head at her and shut the door. I slide into the drivers side and set my phone and wallet in the cup holder.

She's already buckled herself in and has her hands in her lap, nervously wringing them slowly. I can smell her scent filling up the SUV. Her curly hair falls over her shoulders and I resist the urge to run my fingers through it.

After I buckle in, I start the SUV to 'Like You Mean It' by Steven Rodriguez playing. Interesting choice for the car to start playing from my Spotify app. I want to see if she squirms.

I put back the panoramic roof. I see her look up, and out, and smile. Ok, that's good, she's relaxing more around me. After what happened to her last night, I can't blame her for being nervous. I'm a complete stranger.

I look over at her, resting my arms on the steering wheel, I ask, "Do you want to put your address into the GPS?"

"Oh sure, but I'm sure you know how to get back to Clemetville. I live on Second Street, above the boutique."

"Ok, then that's not hard at all." I know exactly where she's talking about. "I live in Clemetville too."

"It's across from the Mexican restaurant. They have amazing food, by the way. Me and Clover sometimes go there for tacos and margaritas." I see her wipe her hands on her pants in a nervous gesture.

"Wait, how are you getting served alcohol?"

"They have never carded us. And we have never not left a great tip," she giggles.

"That's amazing." I laugh. "Want to go there tomorrow night with me?"

Her big beautiful green eyes look up me. I watch her bite her lip. "I have to work tomorrow night."

"Oh, alright then, what night are you off this week?" She answers with Wednesday.

"Wednesday then. Will you go with me for dinner?"

"Yeah, I would like that."

'Slow Down' by Chase Atlantic plays it's last notes as I put my hand out, palm up, on the center console. I want to see if she will let me hold her hand. Will she be brave enough?

She looks over at my hand. I feel her hesitation. I mean it when I said she's the one in control here. I won't make her do anything she doesn't want to do.

'PLEASE' by Omido and Ex Habit starts streaming through the speakers next. Slowly, I see her raise her left arm and she places her hand in mine, then looks out the window.

I give a grin of triumph. I curl my fingers around her small hand, content with this baby step. I turn up the music by the steering wheel and enjoy the ride sitting next to this beautiful creature I'm enraptured with.

Chapter 10: Devin

Was it a good idea to get into a stranger's car? No.

Even if he is a piece of eye candy.

No, it wasn't smart.

I've been telling my ovaries we have to think with our head. Good gravy, this man is temptation incarnate.

He hasn't made me feel uncomfortable at all today. He has been really sweet and caring about my feelings. I like how he asks me permissions. And he did save my life, so there's that too.

I have a boyfriend.

This guy's my boyfriend.

He has to be joking and just poking fun with me.

How the hell did that even happen? It happened so quickly! I was in a relationship in one blink.

I don't know if he's serious. He could be leading me on. Maybe he really is one of those jerks from school but he's only being nice to me to get in my pants. He will eventually lose interest.

Like I said, guys like him don't date girls like me.

But he does seem different. My gut says to believe him when he told me he wasn't like them. My gut has been all over the place while around him, but it's settled on he is who he says he is and I'm not in danger. He sets off butterflies in my vagina but it's not the ones from fear.

I've not had a lot of experience with sex if he wants that, I've only had it a few times, but it was nothing like what's in my books. That's all I really have to go from, that and porn.

Mmm damn. How I've fantasized about those men. I have no shame with my imagination. I've wished for one of those men so bad. Is Oakley my own book boyfriend coming to life? He's certainly playing the part well so far. I mean, he hasn't been an asshole to me once.

Maybe that's why I want to rub my boobs all over his face with my legs spread wide, beneath him.

Jesus fuck, Devin.

This mind is straight gutter trash.

Stranger Danger, bitch.

I chuckle to myself as I feel myself blush. I look back out the window and I shift in my seat and squeeze my thighs together a little harder.

Involuntary thigh clench.

Hoping he doesn't notice. He seems quite content with himself right now when I relented and put my hand in his.

It has to start somewhere, I suppose. I have to be into this too. I agreed to this, well I think I did. My gut wouldn't lead me wrong. It's gotten me out of plenty of situations by steering me clear of people.

I don't feel that with Oakley. I feel drawn to him. It's magnetic. As careful as I'm trying to be, he is lowering my walls. Faster than I thought.

I want to keep this secret right now, until I know if he's actually serious. I won't be calling my mom to gush over my new boyfriend anytime soon. I don't want him to hurt me and this is some cruel joke or senior prank, but a girl can never be too sure.

I look over at him, "Tell me about growing up. Did you play sports? Was it around here?"

He squeezes my hand, "I come from a small farming town about 2 hours east of here. I was raised by my dad. My mom died while giving birth to me."

I raise my hand to my mouth, "Oh, I'm so sorry."

He rubs my knuckle, "Thanks. It's ok. I had a fairly normal childhood despite her loss. I played baseball and football and wrestled. I also tried track but I sucked at it. It was short lived."

I giggle at that. "I can see you being an athlete though."

"Yeah? What about you?" He steals a glance at me again.

"Well, I played softball until I was 16, but the coach changed, and I didn't like him, I gave it up. He gave me the creeps." I look over at him and admire how handsome his profile is. I'm still not truly believing that this hunk of a guy wants to be in a relationship with me. I still have my suspicions. "My parents are divorced. Thankfully."

"Why thankfully?"

"I came home from school early one day and found him playing cowboy with this coworker in my parents' bed while he was balls deep in someone not my mom."

"Holy shit Devin! Oh my god."

"Yeah, I have PTSD from it." I give a small shiver. "Anyways, my mom divorced his sorry ass and moved 2 hours away to the south. I miss her terribly. She's my best friend." I look out the window before he can hear the emotions in my voice and I get choked up.

"I'm truly sorry that had to happen like that."

"Thank you." I look back over to him and watch as he pulls my hand up to his mouth and his soft lips kiss the back of my hand.

I am shocked. My breath catches in my throat. He is so gentle setting my hand back down. He turns his head to look at me and slowly grins at me, twinkle in his eye.

Involuntary thigh clench.

My thoughts are all over the place. This car ride wasn't what I expected. I have no choice but to go with what fate has planned for me. It sure would be nice to prepare or know what to expect. Is this what dating like an adult is like?

The only kind of relationship I know is high school drama filled romance. It didn't really excite me. Even then I knew it was a crock of shit and I'm better off without it.

I want a man so full of passion and love for me, he wants to combust. I want him to be so possessive and protective of me he will burn the universe to keep me from harm. He will kneel at my feet and worship me, so I can bow and love him back with that same fierce fire. I want to set my soul on fire and burn the world with him.

I pray every day I find one like that.

I never want to settle. I figure I will probably have to wait until I'm older and guys mature more. This era of dating and the men being offered up is cringe.

It's hard for men to live up to a woman's expectation if she's a romance reader. I get it. But men of the world, do better.

I understand not all men are assholes. Just the ones who float in and out of my small world.

Except for the one sitting beside me.

I could get used to being around him.

I already want to be wrapped up in his scent. It's down right seductive on it's own but mixed with who he is, it's irresistible. Woodsy, manly.

I'm a goner.

Smells are very important to me. I associate places and people in my memory with scents. His is making me press my thighs together harder. I'm going to need some of it to spray on my pillow so when I touch myself long after he's gone, I can remember how bad I wanted him in this moment.

"Why Clemet? Why not Clemson?" I ask him.

"There's a story there. My dad graduated from Clemson, after he went to Columbia for two years. I didn't want to be like him so I picked Clemet, and he didn't like it. I wanted away from home but not too far away. My dad lives like 2 and a half hours east of here. I can go see him on the weekends if I want to. I left home because I was lonely there. It's out in the middle of nowhere and kids in high school just wanted to be my friend because my dad had money. Coming here I could start over. Be me, because no one knew my family. I could be me without the rich boy stigma."

And that makes me feel even worse for judging him.

"I'm sorry I thought you were just another rich asshole."

That gets a smile out of him and a glance my way, "It's ok, Kitten, I deserved it. This is a pretty pretentious car," he laughs and it makes me laugh too.

We are flying down the freeway towards home and there's a

nice breeze coming in through the roof. It's a nice evening and I'm pretty relaxed now. It's a far cry from how I was when I first got in here. We are still about 30 minutes from my apartment.

"What kind of music do you like?" he shakes my hand lightly.

"I like all kinds of music actually. I mix genres pretty hard."

"You have Spotify?"

"Yes I do."

"Good, put your info into the search and play me one of your playlists."

My mouth wants to drop on the floor, but I play it cool. "You want to hear my music?"

"Yeah, I want to know what you get lost to. That's what music does for me. It makes me get lost in a good way. It makes me feel high and weightless, it washes over my soul and helps bring light to the dark parts of me."

"Oh my God, that's beautiful. I feel the same way." I place my hand he's not holding up by my heart. "It has helped heal some of my dark places too."

I start to pull my hand out of his and he instinctively squeezes. "I need this to put my info in," I can't help but giggle.

He nods at me but keeps his eyes on the road. I enter in all the info and my account with my playlists comes up. I find my favorite list named 'Devin's' and hit the first song, 'Way Down We Go' by KALEO comes playing through the car.

I sit back and place my hand back in his since he left it laying there. I was very aware of his hand that close to me. It made it hard to concentrate with his hand practically 2 inches from my left breast. One dip in the road and it would be forced into his hand. Would that be so bad?

Involuntary thigh clench.

Sigh. He makes me want to be a wanton slut in heat. Slut for him, always wanting him, always wanting to please. I've never really thought about being submissive to someone. He makes me feel a certain way though, I can't deny, kneeling on my knees with a collar on does sound appealing.

Another involuntary thigh clench.

It's getting hot in here even though the outside temp is in the 60's for a fall evening. The sky is starting to turn shades of pink and orange, waiting patiently to swallow the sun.

I catch myself stealing a glance of him through my hair as we drive along peacefully. Hoping he doesn't catch me staring, I fantasize about that face between my thighs.

Christ. I'm never going to survive this ride.

Involuntary thigh clench.

I see a smile come over his face.

He knows the thoughts going through my head. I feel the flush come over me. I swear I hate blushing. I can never hide my emotions.

'Not Enough' by Elvis Drew and Avivian plays softly between us while I continue to watch him through my side eye.

"Is there anything else you want to ask me?" He stares straight ahead, driving, with a smirk.

I clear my throat and turn towards him, "Umm...yeah...why don't you already have a girlfriend? I...I mean you're really good looking and it just seems like women would be all over you. Do you have one and you're just fucking with me to get in my pants?" I bite on my thumb nail, waiting for his answer and continuing to stare at him.

He clears his throat and shifts in his seat. "I had a girlfriend. For about a year. We broke up 10 months ago. That's when I found out about her cheating. I've not dated anyone since that. I've had girls, but I've not dated any of them." He looks over at me, "None of them mattered enough to be my girlfriend that's for sure." He squeezes my hand again. "And I'm not just trying to get into your pants. I genuinely want to get to know you."

My heart lurches in my throat.

What makes me the exception?

Please let this not be a joke.

"Why me? You don't even know me, but you're my boyfriend all of a sudden."

He chuckles at that, "Why not you? I like you. I'm drawn to you, and I want to get to know you." He brings my hand up to his lips and kisses the back of my hand again, with his eyes over to me, "Don't be mistaken, I want to fuck you too, but I really want to know you."

I'm suffocating in my seat as he turns back to the road.

I feel like I'm making a puddle in his fine leather seat and my ass feels like he turned on the seat warmer. I had to go and pick the fucking baby-making music playlist.

How fitting 'Do It For Me' by Rosenfeld starts playing. Jesus. As if that doesn't add to the already charged sexual energy in the air in this small space.

He has a big cheshire smile as the lyrics start playing. Yep, I can bet I know what he's thinking of. Probably some of the same things I am.

Please let this man be a fucking rockstar in bed.

I face forward and look at the road, thinking to myself. Oh God. I just realized, he's older than me and definitely has had more than 1 partner, unlike me. I don't even know half the shit done in my books. I've never had my pussy licked, no anal play, nothing besides missionary. I'm basically a virgin with no cherry. Will that turn him away?

What if he thinks I'm awful at it? What if he forces me and I'm not ready? What if he makes a fool of me?

I swallow against my dry throat. I am a breath away from a panic attack. Please don't let this happen right now.

"Hey.....look at me."

I peel my gaze from the road to his ocean blue eyes. "You are in control here. We go at your pace. You hold all the power." He drops my hand to place his hand on my jawbone, pulling me closer to him. He looks from me to the road and back. "I would never force you to do anything you don't want to do. I promise on my soul."

I let out the breath I was holding. I feel my lungs fill up quickly.

"Shhhh, breathe. I would never Devin. I'm not that kind of man. Please don't be afraid of me. You will get to know me. We can take it slow. I promise I am a good person."

I feel my watery eyes overflow.

He reaches up and wipes a tear away. Softly he says, "Oh no, Kitten, don't cry baby. ShShh. It's ok."

He continues to rub my cheek once again while still glancing at the road. Hoarsely, he quietly says, "I know you are afraid. After last night you have every right to be paranoid of men. I'm not like them, give me a chance, baby, let me prove I'm not like them."

I am so mad my fear is bubbling out of me.

But I feel my walls crumbling. I feel him working past my guard.

Please let me not be a fool.

I nod my head.

"Use your words, Kitten."

I softly reply, "Yes. Ok. I'll do it. I'll be your girlfriend if we go slow." I sound so breathy.

He smiles, dimples and all, happily he says, "That's my good girl."

I think I just came in his seat.

Chapter 11: Oakley

Right now, I don't understand my actions, or the goddamn reactions my body is having. My words are just as confusing. I have never acted like this before. She brings this out in me. I want her badly and it will be hell to not throw her down and fuck her, but I will be a patient man.

I think this as I'm pulling up to the curb in front of her apartment. *Who the fuck am I?*

The guy that swore off relationships months ago, just wiggled his way into capturing this beauty.

I can't explain my pressing need to make her mine. I am undeniably attracted to her. I want to know her inside and out. But I want her to only think of me. I want to be her whole world.

I will play this out with her as long as she will let me. I will never complain about going at her pace.

My gut tells me she's worth every moment I have to wait.

Getting out of the SUV I come around to open her door and wait for her to get out, then I go to the back and open the hatch. She stays back on the curb. I look over expectantly at her, I am not sure how she wants to handle this. Do I bring them up or, no?

I stand there with all her bags in my arms. She has about 5 or 6 large sized bags and I don't want to see her lug all these up the stairs. But I will respect her wishes.

She narrows her eyes at me and says, "You can come up, IF you promise to behave." She has her hand on her hip with her head cocked, and its adorable.

She turns and walks up to a door labeled 'B' and shoves a key in the lock. She opens the door and holds it open for me. It puts me in a closer proximity to her and I can smell the scent that is her. It's a drug I am quickly becoming addicted to.

I try hard not to look up, but with that glorious ass in front of me, sashaying up the stairs, I just want to reach out and bite it. Fuck.

I feel my dick growing hard again and I groan. That was the most uncomfortable ride home I've ever had. Being near her makes me feel high.

She's smart, quick witted, beautiful, humorous, she's the perfect package so far. Is there something bad hidden under the good girl persona? Is she a crazy bitch and that's why no one has claimed her?

She doesn't think I'm serious for her. This is my girlfriend now. She will come to like it. And accept it. She isn't going anywhere if I can help it.

We come to the next landing and she sticks another key into a locked door. She pushes it open and I get my first look of where she lives with Clover.

It is tastefully done in tans, beiges, sage green, dusky blues. There are plants everywhere. A comfy couch with blankets and pillows, and a coffee table in front of it with another plant and a few candles. Mushroom pictures on the wall, a painted canvas hanging on the far wall, and a few pieces of Anime art hanging up.

It's very homey. Looks like a calm and peaceful place to hang out.

"Umm...where do you want me to set these?" I hold up the bags.

"On the couch there is fine. Thank you for carrying them up here." She sets her purse on the counter as I finish laying the bags down and turn back to her. I'm not sure what to do now.

A fluffy, beige cat comes trotting in, screaming, right up to her. She bends over and pets the cat rubbing all over her legs. "Hey Luna, I missed you too, but I wasn't gone that long." She stands up and looks me in my eyes and says, "Luna, this is our new boyfriend, Oakley. You have to be nice to him."

I smile down at the cat and squat down. Luna comes right over to me and sniffs my hand. I must pass the cat test because she starts rubbing up against me. I look up at Devin and say, "I passed the test, you have to keep me now." I give Devin a wicked grin as I stand up, not taking my eyes off her.

We must bore Luna because she scurries back into a bedroom, which I will assume is Devin's.

I can tell she's nervous. As bad as I want to touch her, I know it will spook her. *Take it slow, Oak.*

Devin looks at me a few feet from her. She is leaning on one hip on the small island, one foot over the other and her arms crossed. I can see all kinds of emotions passing through her eyes.

I put my arms out and say, "I should probably go. I don't want to make you feel uncomfortable being alone with me just yet, unless you want me to stay."

She drops her arms, and I back up towards the door as she takes a few steps towards me. My heart is hammering so fast.

I want to kiss her, but I don't want to do anything she doesn't want.

Fuck it.

I take the few steps up to her and put my hands on the sides of her face, and sliding my fingers up the back of her neck. I tilt her face up to mine. Her beautiful green eyes are staring into mine.

Through extreme restraint, I softly say to her, "Can I kiss you, Devin?"

I watch her eyelids slowly blink while she licks her lips and whispers, "Yes."

I waste no time putting my lips to her pouty pink lips. She tastes like cherries from her frozen drink we stopped for on the way home. She feels like heaven.

I tilt my head so I can go deeper. I open my mouth more and I place my tongue on her lips, licking them open. She opens for me, and I meet her tongue. Shy at first but she opens for me.

I hang on to her face and invade her mouth as she leans into me and moans.

I have to stop but I don't want it to ever end.

Her hands come up to my stomach, and she splays her hands across my ribs.

I have never experienced this kissing anyone else. I'm drowning in a cherry river that smells like flowers and vanilla and it's driving me wild.

I hear her moan softly and I slow down. I pull away from her and lay my forehead on hers. Both of our breathing is erratic. I step back from her.

I have to or I will take it too far, too soon for her.

It takes everything I have to drop my hands away from her face as she releases me with pleading eyes.

Taking a deep calming breath, lowering my voice I say to her, "If I don't leave, this will turn into something too soon for you and I don't want to spook you away. Do you want me to continue?"

I watch her lick her lips and bring her hand up to touch them and she shakes her head No. She whispers, "Not yet."

You can tell she's been kissed. Her swollen lips show it, and her eyes tell me she would have allowed this to go further, but she would have regretted it. I must play by her rules. I don't want her to regret anything about us.

It has to be me to stop it right now.

I plan on keeping her as long as I can.

I take another step back towards the door and reach for the handle. I look at her and say, "You have my number now, call me, text me. Don't be afraid to. Please."

She nods at me, and softly says, "Yes. Same. I will answer unless I'm too busy at work or in class."

Smiling at her, "Take care, Devin. I'll see you tomorrow." She raises her hand and waves and sweetly says, "Bye, Oakley."

I close the door and let out a breath. I walk down the stairs and get in my SUV. I glance a look up through the sunroof, at her windows, and I see the cat in the window but no Devin.

Soon, Kitten. You will beg me to stay.

Because I am ready to beg you to let me stay.

Chapter 12: Devin

I watch him walk out and stand there holding my bruised lips.

That really just happened.

I've never been kissed like that. I've only read about them. I'm afraid my knees can't hold me up.

After I catch my breath, I go throw all the locks. Then I head for my bedroom and shut the door and lock it. I say, "Alexa, finish playing Devin's list." 'Glitter & Gold' by Barns Courtney plays throughout my room.

I hurry and strip my shoes and pants down, yanking off my shirt and black lace bra. I take off my matching black lace boy shorts.

Climbing on my bed, I lean over, and I get my vibrating bullet from my nightstand and pull a pillow down to straddle it, sitting back on my calves, spread my thighs wide. I grab the headboard and put the vibrator to my clit.

I imagine Oakley telling me to bend over the couch. He runs his hands up the back of my thighs over the swell of my ass.

He grabs my hips and says, "You are mine, and I'm going to

make you believe it. How do you like it, Kitten? Hmm, do you want me to go slow?" as he pushes a finger in to my wet center.

He puts his fingers in my hair with his other hand, and palms the back of my head, grabbing hair by my scalp. He pulls my head back until it slightly hurts, "Or do you want it rough and painful, Kitten? Which way will make my pussy purr for me? I know you want this as much as I do, baby."

I pick up my humping pace. My breathing picks up and I feel a sheen of sweat starting to gather on my body.

If he would have stayed I would be sitting here on his face. Fucking his mouth with my pussy.

Goddamn. I'm on fire.

I grab my tits and pinch my nipples, rolling them around between my fingers.

I whisper to the empty room, "Make it hurt, Oakley, make me cry to God and beg to die."

I bow my head as my body starts to shake. I feel the coil start releasing through my pussy walls and it travels up my lower belly until it explodes across my thighs. Biting my lip, I squeeze my eyes shut and sob through my orgasm. "Oakley."

I hang my head panting. Holy fuck. The thought comes again, *'Please let him be great in bed, he seems so perfect already."*

I have no idea how old he is, but I guarantee he has more experience than I do. I hop off the bed and bring my bullet with me on the way to clean myself up in my bathroom.

As I sit on the toilet, I see a shadow moving in my room in the darkening light. No one is here but me and I just left Luna out on the couch, shutting the door.

Suddenly, I am afraid, waves of fear falling off of me. I don't feel alone anymore. I know Oakley couldn't have gotten back into the apartment, the door is locked. I would have heard if someone came in.

I get done and wash my hands. I hesitantly peek out the door to my darker room. The only light is the soft glow of my salt lamp.

There is no one there. I know what I saw. Someone was in my room. I grab my robe and throw it on and open my bedroom door. Luna comes running up to my legs.

I quickly look around and see no one here and nothing out of place. I go over to the front door, the only entrance into our apartment, and see none of the locks have been moved. I turn around in time to catch a flash of movement through the doorway by my bed.

"EEEKK! What the fuck?!?!" Someone is fucking with me. I grab the bat we keep by the front door and tip toe around the couch back to my bedroom.

I still see nothing amiss. There is no one in there. I tip toe over the threshold like a cartoon robber, and peek around the door jamb at the bathroom again, but see nothing.

The hair on the back of my neck stands up as if someone is standing directly behind me, breathing down my neck. I scream and whirl around with the bat.

No one is there.

Am I getting creeped out for nothing?

Calm the fuck down.

The thought penetrates my fear that is strangling me. What if this is a ghost?

I call out into the room, "W-Who are you? What do you want?"

I hear a voice right beside me, "It took you long enough to notice me."

I scream and run. I bolt for my bedroom door and run out into the living room, bat and all. I turn around towards my bedroom door on shaky legs, expecting someone to walk out.

I hold the bat out in front of me, like it's going to protect me from a ghost.

But nothing comes out of the room.

My heart is pounding in my ears. I most definitely heard someone talking. I didn't see them beside me, but I heard them. It was a woman.

I take a couple deep breaths and call out, "Who are you?"

No one answers me after I wait a few minutes.

"Are you going to show yourself?"

Nothing happens.

I don't have that freaky feeling anymore and I feel like I'm alone. I don't have goosebumps any longer.

I think the spirit left. That had to be what it was.

Oh God, NO. That means I inherited my mom's gift.

Mother trucking shit balls hell!!

Not enough swear words for this kind of fuckery.

I'm going to start seeing ghosts and hearing them everywhere I go like my mom does.

That alone is enough to make me sob.

I never wanted her gift. It's always like she can never get a moment of peace. She used to say rooms are full even when you're alone.

My hands tremble and it's getting harder to hold the bat. I drop it to the floor and start crying.

What the fuck is happening to me?

I know one thing; this ghost is going to be back. That's the scary part. I don't know when, and it's not like I can make an appointment with it so it doesn't pop in and scare me.

Chapter 13: Devin

Classes this morning were a breeze. I already have my assignments done for all 3 classes I have today. That means I don't have school work for them until Thursday's class. I should have everything done so I can have a relaxing weekend.

I finish putting my mascara on and draw on my top lid winged eyeliner. I rub on my mauve lip stick and rub my lips together. Smacking them open, I look in the mirror and say, "Do good things and slay the day."

I look down at my phone. I haven't heard from Oakley since lunch time. He checked in with me last night before I went to sleep. I got a 'Hello Beautiful' text this morning when I woke up. He must have to get up early for work. Least I know he's thinking of me at 6:45 in the morning.

His text made me smile and gave me butterflies.

I check my messy bun and make sure this mess of heavy hair is up where it belongs. I have a pair of black leggings on that end right above my ankles, a white shirt that says Book Nook on the upper left chest, and my tennis shoes with ankle socks.

This is my normal work attire. I take the hair tie and gather my shirt in the back and loop the hair tie over the fabric, pulling it tight across my squishy but flat stomach.

My mom had to go and pass on her hourglass figure to me. I should be grateful, but this ass knocks small children into next week if I'm not paying attention.

I spritz my favorite perfume on and grab my apron off my bed, kissing Luna on the top of the head. "Bye, baby." I dash over to the counter and snag my purse from where I left it last night.

I could walk to work but since I'm closing tonight, I don't want to be walking 3 blocks in the dark to get home at a late hour. Not after the other night.

My shift is from 5-11pm almost every day. My last class ends at 3:30 pm and I have time to come home, eat and get ready for work.

We are always short staffed it seems. No one wants to work that late. Except me. It didn't bother me to be there alone.

Until the other night.

I now understand why the female student population is starting to run in packs or just not go out at all.

Those kinds of people sneak up on you in the dark when they see an opportunity. I never thought it would happen to me. But it did, and it's made me more vigilant.

I get in my car and turn my Spotify on and 'Lose My Breath' by Rhea Robertson floats around in the car. I pull my gray 2016 Toyota Corolla out into our street.

I worked hard through high school to buy this car. My mom promised to give me half if I saved up the other half. Knowing how much they cost, I set a goal and a few months before graduation, Mom took me to go get a car and I picked this one.

I am so proud of my car. To me it's the nicest thing I own.

I pull into the alley behind Book Nook and freeze for a minute. Do I want to park out back here? Am I going to let fear make me park in front?

But I'm supposed to park back here with all the other cars.

I look up at the back door and see there are cameras around the outside and a new spotlight and motion senor floodlight on where the cars park.

It makes me feel better, so I go ahead and I pull into a parking spot, then kill the engine. *I can do this.* I grip the steering wheel and let out a big breath.

I'm stronger than this.

I grab my purse and apron and force myself out of the car. *I will not let fear control me.*

Laying my purse inside Pam's desk, I put my apron on and walk up towards the front, behind the counter.

Pam sees me and runs up to hug me. I was taken off guard and didn't expect that. I awkwardly hug her back. She pulls away and says, "I'm so glad you're ok." There are unshed tears in her eyes.

I smile at her and say, "Thanks, Pam."

Pam clears her throat and says, "It's been a pretty busy day. But your man out there has been here for awhile now waiting on you."

I chance a look out front. As my eyes survey the sitting areas, I come across a round table in the corner, up by the front windows. The lighting is low due to the sun going down. There's an empty chair across the table from none other than my new boyfriend who sits in that corner, on the phone, with a laptop open in front of him, casually wearing a suit and tie.

I open my mouth to say something to Pam about him, but

she puts her hand over her mouth and whispers to me, "He's gorgeous, girl," and winks at me. She shoves me towards the opening in the counter. "Go on, we don't need you for a little bit. Go talk to him."

I can only nod my head as I walk back towards the office where the counter opening is.

I wipe my hands on my leggings as I take off through the café in search of one man. I come around the corner and hang a right towards the front sitting area. I stride up to his table and set my hands on the back of the chair across from him.

Here he sits looking all yummy in a baby blue dress shirt that looks so soft to the touch and rolled up to his elbows, and black dress pants, with black dress shoes so polished I can see the reflection of the windows on them. His dark blue tie is loosely hanging around his neck and I would be lying if I said I wasn't thinking of my hands tied over my head to the headboard.

Focus, bitch.

He looks up at me and immediately smiles, then says into his phone, "Gotta go, Luke," then hangs up and places his phone down, standing up. "Hey," he leans across the small table, that's just big enough for a laptop, and takes my hand and brings it up to his lips, "I missed you."

I didn't just dream him up. He's real, as real as the blush creeping up my chest.

His voice still makes my thighs clench.

"Hey," I manage to get out weakly.

He points his other hand to the chair my hands are gripping like a lifeline, and says, "Do you have time to sit with me? Just for a little bit. I know you are working, but I wanted to see you. Pam said it would be no problem."

I take the seat out and sit down, his eyes never leaving me

as I lower myself into the seat. They are undressing me from bottom to top.

When I'm fully seated, I look up into his face and his brilliant blue eyes sparkle, along with his wolfish smile that makes my heart rate speed up.

When are my nerves ever going to settle around him?

"Yes, Pam let me know I was fine, uhh...because my man is here." I give him a tight grin.

He brings his hands in front of him and starts rubbing them together, still smiling. "I told her I was your boyfriend. She looked confused at first, but I told her it was new. She got an all-knowing look, nodded, and told me I was good to wait on you and steal you for a little bit when you got here." He holds his hand out to me, "And here you are, beautiful as ever."

I slowly slip my hand in his. He closes his other hand around ours. "What's your favorite flower?"

The question takes me off guard. Because this is totally the perfect time for my mind to go blank, and ping pong balls bounce around in the emptiness.

I just blink at him a few times. "I'm boring, I mean ordinary, I like roses. Pink ones. Any shade." I hold his gaze and ask him, "What's yours?"

He peers at me so intently; it makes me want to squirm. He half smiles and says, "Me too, roses. I don't care what color."

I clear my throat because I'm picturing him looking at me like that while between my legs. *Vagina STAHP!* I look away from him to the table next to us.

He squeezes my hand, and I look up at him through my lashes. "Why are you here? Don't you work in an office?"

His gaze devours me, and I feel like I'm drowning. Oakley looks at me like I am the only human in the room. "I can work wherever I want, whenever I want. I chose to work right here, right now. The view is much better here than at the office."

Oakley pulls my hand, pulling me closer to him across the small table, he whispers for me to hear, "I've thought of nothing else except seeing you again."

He reaches across to me with his right hand and slides a piece of escaped hair behind my ear. "Pretend I'm not even here." I feel his strawberry scented breath on my hand that he has by his mouth. Pulling me close enough that his forehead is within an inch from my face, I can feel his breath on my cheek now, "I will just be here thinking of all the good things I want to do with you while we date."

Something that sounds so innocent is immediately made dirty by my naughty little mind. I fight the urge to lay myself across his lap so he can spank me. My mind is trash garbage. I have no shame.

I'm supposed to be going slow. Tell that to my clitoris, and the guy giving me baby-making eyes.

I make a small whimper as I try to even out my breathing.

He leans back slightly, his finger trails down my cheek and down the left side of my neck, "Can I kiss you again?"

I nod eagerly before I have time to think the request through, and softly say, "Yes."

He makes me feel like I'm under a spell when he looks into my soul like that. The world falls off around us. The only sound I register is our mingled breathing.

He angles his head and lightly pulls my neck to bring me closer. I melt into him as our lips touch. I open my mouth wanting him to come explore. I love the feeling of his tongue rubbing against mine.

His tongue meets mine and they slide around each other, tasting and dancing. I taste his strawberry smoothie he's been drinking. I savor this feeling, of butterflies erupting in my core. I want to curl my toes and I moan into his mouth. I suddenly remember we are at my work, in public. With my boss surely watching us.

I pull back from him while I lick my lips and commit to memory the way his lips feel on mine.

Now I understand book kisses.

I clear my throat and say, "I have to get back to work." I turn my head and flick my eyes up to the counter, at the same time I see two heads try to quickly duck and hear giggles. I shake my head with a smile, "We have an audience." I knew Pam and my co-worker Emily were going to be nosy.

Oakley sits back with a big grin and lets go of my hand. "I will kiss you in front of everyone if you allow it. I don't care who sees it."

I stand up and push the chair in, "If you need anything, you know, like to drink or eat, let me know."

There's that wolfish grin again. His eyes tell all kinds of dirty thoughts in his head, and I feel my face getting warm.

"If you need food, that's what I mean."

"I'm good. I'll just be over here." He winks at me.

I turn to walk to the counter, and I feel him smack my right ass cheek. I whirl around and deadpan stare him, trying so hard not to crack a grin.

He nods his head and puts his hands up in surrender, giving me the most amused smile with eyebrows raised.

I point at him and try not to crack up. I will give it to him, he's bold.

I continue on and get behind the counter and both of them are grinning at me. Pam says, "He seems like a very nice man and clearly, he is interested in you. He has my vote."

I put my hand on my hip and look at her. "He could be a serial killer, and we don't know."

Pam laughs off my comment, "Honey, serial killers don't save you from other serial killers. You can tell, he's crushing hard on you. Why else would he be here working instead of in a quiet office with no distractions?" She raises a brow and goes back to the front of the counter.

From my angle back here, I can't see Oakley at his table in the far, right front corner of the cafe, but if I move up closer to the front, he can see me. This new level of stalking from him is endearing, and somewhat alarming.

I don't know how to react to any of this. I make a reminder to myself to call Nicole tonight. I don't want to bring this up to my mom or Aunt Jilly yet. Both of them will show up unannounced and track him down to pester him with questions. It's best to keep him nameless and faceless to them. Nicole won't run her mouth, and she will not tell my family.

I have no idea where I'm going to fit a boyfriend in with my schedule. Or find the energy to deal with him.

I reckon him showing up to my work is killing two birds with one stone. It's actually quite convenient.

I watch him from the corner of my eye. He is typing something on his laptop while his shoulder balances his phone to his left ear. I can tell he's busy, but he looks up at me every so often. His eyes have tracked me all over this café.

It's like a predator watching prey.

It makes my tummy do a summersault when I catch him watching me. I try to play it off like I don't notice, but sometimes I will look him in the eye and stare right back with my own grin. That makes his dimples come out.

"He's really cute, Devin. You are so lucky," Emily, my co-worker, tells me as she's wiping the counter close to me so she can lower her voice. "He keeps watching you," she says as she giggles and moves away.

I'm making sandwiches to wrap in cellophane for the lunch rush tomorrow and I have to agree. "He is definitely easy on the eyes, that's for sure."

Pam leaves about 5:30pm and Emily soon follows her at 6 pm. It's just me in the store....and my so-called boyfriend in the corner.

I walk from behind the counter over to his table with his now closed laptop. He has been sitting back watching me like a hawk while I did prep for tomorrow.

It's Monday night and we usually aren't that busy. I don't expect anyone to come in to the rest of the night except a few stragglers. I'm all alone with this man.

I sit down at his table across from him and cock my head, "How long are you planning on staying here?"

He leans forward putting his arms on the table, "Until I get tired of being here, I suppose."

"Will that be any time soon?"

"Are you trying to get rid of me, Kitten?"

"Not at all, it's just we close early on Mondays at 8, it's 7:45 right now and I'm just wondering how much longer you are going to watch me." I lean forward and put my arms on his small table too, making our faces inches apart. "I feel like I'm constantly being undressed with your eyes, and it's unnerving at times."

He chuckles, "Am I making you uncomfortable?"

I shake my head.

"Use your words, Devin." He picks up a piece of my hair that's escaped again.

I want to do all the things with him but I'm afraid of him. He's practically a stranger.

I've never been one for one-night stands. I mostly identify as Demisexual, meaning I need to form some kind of bond with people before sex, but this guy is breaking all my preconceived thoughts on my own behaviors. I am most certainly attracted to him from the first time he burst into my life.

It's scary how strongly attracted to him I am.

I sit back and rub my hands on my thighs to wipe off my sweaty palms. "I have more questions, if you don't mind just talking to me."

Oakley continues to give me a mischievous look and says, "Yes, let's get to know each other better. Ask me anything."

"I don't even know your last name. Mine is Bennet."

"My last name is Grayson."

"How old are you?"

"I am 23."

I put my head down and shake it slowly. I bring my eyes back up to him and say, "See, I am too young for you. I'm just out of high school and you probably think of me as just a kid."

He leans forward more, "That's where you are wrong, I absolutely do not think of you as a kid. I recognize you as a woman, you may be young, but you have an old soul and don't seem like most people our age. So no, I don't think you are a kid, and you are not too young for me. I am not that much older than you."

"Ok, I just didn't want you to regret this or treat me like a kid."

"Devin, I do not plan on treating you like a kid. Far from it." There's that look again.

I puff out a breath, "Alright. Where do you work?"

"Grayson Enterprises."

My eyes go big. "You already have your own company?"

"No, technically it's my dad's company, but one day I will inherit it. He asked me to learn some of the ropes at the business, so that's what I do. I am a junior CFO."

Holy fuck. No wonder he can do whatever he wants.

Why is this man dealing with me? He could have anyone. He should be dating models or beautiful women in high heels with perfect makeup. Instead, he sits across from me, the plain, ordinary girl with wild red hair and freckles.

I look out the window to my left and see how many people are walking by. There are none. It's a chilly October night and most people don't venture out this early in the week.

"Do you have any siblings?"

He shakes his head, "Nope, I'm an only child."

I nod. "I have an older brother, David. He goes to college here too. It's his senior year."

"I imagine it would have been nice to have a sibling, even if we didn't get along. It would have given me something to do other than be alone."

"Siblings aren't all they are cracked up to be. He tortured me more than anything."

"I see." He sits back and crosses his arms over his delicious chest, I mean his regular man-like chest.

A chest I can lick honey off of....it's over behind the counter....

Fucking hell.

I look down at my hands in my lap, so he won't see what's written on my face.

"Why don't you have a boyfriend? A girl as good looking as you, I would have thought you were taken and had a line waiting for that guy to fuck up."

I snort at that and wheeze out a laugh. "Not quite. There is no line. Never has been."

"But there wasn't a boyfriend, or you wouldn't have said yes to me."

"Fair point. No, there is no boyfriend." I shrug my shoulders.

"Why not?"

I look up at him. I don't want him to feel sorry for me or think I'm a stupid twit.

"I've only ever had one boyfriend. I used to have another best friend, until they decided to sleep together, then try to bully me into a threesome with them. When I refused, they both turned on me and made my last two months of high school living hell. There has been no one since." I hold my empty hands out in front of me, then cross them over my chest.

"That is unfortunate. I'm sorry that happened to you. That must have been heartbreaking to lose both your boyfriend and best friend."

"It was. To be fair, neither of them were good people. My whole family hated Aaron, and my mother mildly tolerated Talya. No real loss."

I shove some of my hair back into the messy bun while I continue to talk, "I feel like an idiot for not seeing it, and letting him take advantage of me." I finish fidgeting with my hair and slump my shoulders.

"Do you think I want to take advantage of you?"

I bite my thumb nail and mull over what he's asking. Do I think this? Do I think he's just out to get in my pants?

"I am uncertain what your motives are for jumping headfirst into a relationship with me, without even knowing me yet. Some would say that's a huge red flag. Others would say it's romantic. I have no idea what to think and the overanalyzing is giving me a migraine. There. That's where I am."

"I appreciate your honesty, and I can assure you I am not just pestering you for a quick fuck and then be on my way. I really don't know why I'm so strongly drawn to you, but I am, and I want to see where it leads. I want to be part of your life. You're cool, intelligent, fun to be around, so far from what I've seen, and I want more of it."

Oakley sits up and leans his elbows back on the table, "I'm all in. I will stick around as long as you will let me. I am following my gut, and it tells me not to let you go. If you don't want to do this anymore, let me know. If the time comes, we have to part ways, I will not cause you any drama. I ask that in return."

Why does he have to say all the right things? I feel my innards melting more and more with every word he says.

I nod my head at him and take a deep breath, sliding my gaze over to the front windows. The street is dark now except for the streetlamps. There is one car out front, his SUV. I am completely alone with him.

"Words, Devin. Tell me how you are feeling."

I let out a sigh, "I'm scared."

"Why are you scared?"

"I'm afraid you are going to hurt me, and I will look like a fool again." I feel my eyes starting to tear up and my face getting hot. Goddammit. Why does my body always default to tears when I'm mad or afraid?

He gets up and comes over beside me, holding his hand out for me. I put my hand in his and stand up. He is so very close to me, up in my personal space.

I can smell his amazing cologne.

I can see the headline now 'Woman dies from being lured to her killer by cologne.' Even in my head that sounds stupid.

"Devin, I'm going to hug you now because you need one. Is that alright?"

I bite my lip and nod, then remember to use words, "Yes," I quietly reply.

Oakley wraps his arms around me, down by my waist, as he slightly bends to pull me to him. I am surrounded by his masculine energy, his scent, his warmth. This feels so right.

Being in his arms makes me feel safe.

I take a deep breath of the essence that is him and close my eyes as I bring my arms up around his neck. I feel him relax more as he holds me tighter to him. I let my ridged back muscles lose some of the tension always stored there, and lay my head down on his shoulder.

He's right. I did need a hug.

Chapter 14: Oakley

Devin feels amazing in my arms. I don't want to let her go. My favorite part was when she put her arms around me and hugged me back.

We are getting there.

My gut is screaming she is worth it, keep trying. Something in me just won't let it rest. From the minute she popped into my life, I cannot stop thinking about her.

I hope she's not a psycho.

If she will just let her guard down enough, she will see I'm not a bad guy. I've already learned I have to be patient with her. I understand her fear and I don't want to add more to it.

I pull away and stand up, but still keep my arms around her. She looks up at me and I put my forehead on hers. I breathe her in for a moment and savor everything about her.

I tentatively kiss her lips. She relents and opens her mouth to me, kissing me back. I run my hands up her ribs to her hair. I angle my head to go deeper as she moans into my mouth.

Devin runs her fingers through my hair and tries to pull me

harder to her. I use my other hand and lay it on her ass, pulling her into my erection.

The dinging of the bell over the door brings us out of our stupor. She jerks and pulls her arms from me and steps back.

"DEVIN EMILIA!! Who's this? And why are you sucking face with him?"

A shorter girl with tanned skin and blond hair walks around chairs and tables to come stand in front of Devin with her hands on her hips. She looks like your stereotypical cheerleader.

"I...uhh....this....umm...well, this is my boyfriend, Oakley." Devin gestures to me with her hand and I grab her hand and hold on to it.

"No way! Why haven't you told me?"

"I was going to call you tonight."

"Is this why you texted me to come see you at work tonight? So I could meet him?"

I can see how uncomfortable Devin is.

"No, I sent that before I knew he was going to be here." Devin looks at me and says, "This is my best friend, Nicole."

I put my hand out to Nicole, and she takes it and we do a small shake. "It's nice to meet you."

"Likewise. How long have you been dating my best friend and keeping it from me?"

I look down at Devin and smile, "I think it's been like 24 hours, maybe 26."

Nicole's mouth drops open, "So like this is brand new. Wow. No wonder I don't know. But why haven't you mentioned you were talking to someone? Someone serious enough to be mouth raping when I come into the café?" Nicole now has her 'admonishing mom' look going on her face.

"Look, he's the one who saved me the other night. I have not had time to talk to you about it, stop giving me a hard time. I was going to talk to you tonight. Damn. That's that."

I can feel Devin getting frustrated with Nicole. It's been a whirlwind 24 hours.

"Why don't I sit here with my new friend Nicole, and let you get back to work. I can fill her in." I offer.

"I'm not sure that's a great idea," Devin says.

"Why not? I won't ask for all your dark and dirty secrets. Unless Nicole," I gesture to her with my hand, "wants to supply me with them, then I won't turn it down." I wink at Nicole, and she smiles.

"Yes, Devy, let me interrogate your Loverboy here."

Devin looks up at me and laughs, "Yes, my Loverboy." She looks at Nicole and says, "Do your worst, I suppose. If anyone can scare him off it's you."

She looks back up at me and has a saccharine grin, "If you survive her, you'll work out." Devin goes to move away from me, but she must have forgotten I have a hold of her hand.

I didn't forget.

I pull her back to me and lightly kiss her lips. I murmur, "Be good, Kitten." And then I release her.

She stands there for a moment, looks between Nicole and I, and walks to the back of the café to the counter opening.

Nicole levels me with a look and says, "Soo, where did you come from?"

I look at her standing there and say, "I came out of the darkness from the bar to save your best friend, and now I don't want to give her up." I gesture to the open chair Devin vacated, "Care to sit down with me?"

"Are you truly wanting to date her?"

"Yes, truly. Something about her. I want to know all about Devin and what makes her tick. I want to be the man she deserves to have." I look towards the counter and see her restocking chips.

Nicole says, "She lost her faith in humanity when Aaron and Tayla did that to her. She was so vibrant, happy, and outspoken. Devy has retreated into herself as a defense mechanism."

"I want to prove to her I'm not like them. I know I have to give her time, and I'm willing."

"She's worth it. That fucker never deserved her." Nicole stands up and looks down at me, "I have to run, but I think you will bring her back, if she allows you in, I feel like you can bring our hurt girl back to us. Trust me, her mom will go crazy over you. But I guarantee Devin is keeping you a secret from her overprotective momma for as long as she can," Nicole laughs.

"Why's that?"

"Her mom is her best friend but also a hardcore momma bear and tries very hard to be all up in Devin's business. I know she cares, but that lady is a little much sometimes. She's gonna eat you up though, because you're perfect for Dev. This lucky bitch."

"Well, when the time comes, I hope I pass that test. It's all up to Devin."

She walks towards the front counter and peeks around, she turns back to me and whispers loudly so I can hear, "Be gentle with her and don't make her cry, or I'll stab your pretty face."

And with that Nicole walks around the counter to say goodbye to Devin.

I guess I passed the best friend test.

I observe Nicole walking to the front door, I hold up a hand and she waves. I watch her walk down the sidewalk and out of view.

Gathering my empty cups, I go to the front counter. Devin is back there doing dishes. She has everything ready for closing. I head further down the counter and walk through the entrance by the office.

As I'm walking up to Devin, I ask, "Is there anything I can help you with?"

She turns to me and once again I am struck by how gorgeous her eyes are. I momentarily forget why I'm even standing here.

She does strange things to my heart. It's feels like a million butterflies just unleashed from my chest down to my dick.

I want to burn down the universe to keep her safe. I would do it over and over if it meant she stays happy.

She smiles up at me, seemingly more relaxed than before, "Yeah, just put those in this water and if you want, you can take the trash out for me. I have it gathered by the back door."

"Sure, no problem. Be right back."

If it means she doesn't have to go out there in the dark again or face that awful memory, I will do it, no questions asked.

I step out the back door and immediately I see there is a new light. There is also a motion sensor spotlight on the dumpster. I spend a moment looking around to see if there are any out of the ordinary cars with people sitting in them. Nothing out here.

We don't know if she was targeted or whether it was random.

That is truly why I'm here today. Plus, I wanted to make sure her first day back to the scene went smoothly.

And it's a great excuse to be around her.

The bar isn't too busy right now so there's no one on the back patio. I shudder to think what would have happened if she hadn't gotten out that one half scream. Or if I hadn't of heard it. Would anyone else have heard it and intervened?

Coming back inside, "What else, Kitten?"

She smiles and shakes her head, "All done."

She walks around humming and putting away dishes here and there. When the last one is in its place, she hangs the towel up to dry, then walks into the office. She bends over the desk and retrieves her purse from the bottom drawer.

I didn't mind this show one bit.

She turns around and I have my arms crossed with my right hand on my chin. I can't keep the grin off my face.

Devin walks up to me and slaps my arm and says, "You're horrible, you know?"

"What? I didn't do anything." I back away with hands up in surrender.

"MmmHmm, sure. Now I need you to get your shit and get out," she says while laughing.

I pick up my laptop bag and slip my phone in my pocket, "All ready, Kitten."

She unlocks the front door, and I shake my head at that. "Not tonight, Kitten. I'll be going out the back door with you and making sure you're safely in your car before I walk around this building back to my vehicle."

She looks like she's about to protest, "Don't fight me on this,

Devin. Please. Let me do this for you, but for me also."

She locks the door again and says, "Ok, come on."

I follow her out the back door and wait for her to lock the door. She walks over to a gray car, and I mentally approve. It's a safe car.

"I know you just got off work, and it's 8 pm, but would you like to hang out with me some more?"

She looks over at me and I see the openness of her thoughts.

"Where do you want to go? You want to just go home alone? Do you want me to come with you, or I can go home now, if that's what you want."

I move towards her and hold out my hand.

Devin looks at my hand and puts her small hand in mine. I love how she naturally does it now. I will take this small victory.

Baby steps.

I pull her to me slowly, feeling her give in and move closer. I put my right hand up on her temple and smooth some of her hair back. I look into her eyes, "I don't want to give you up just yet. I just want to be around you."

She puts her other hand lightly on my arm, "If you come home with me, are you going to remember the boundaries?"

"Yes, Kitten. I promise I won't do anything you don't want me to." I give her a half smile.

She's too smart for loopholes because she says, "That's the problem, I want a lot of things."

Color me shocked! Devin just admitted she wants me.

"I'm sure we can find something to do."

"Alright then. Do you remember where it is?"

"Yes."

Devin steps back away from me and I drop her hand. "After you, m'lady."

She gets in her car and starts it up and the doors automatically lock. I watch her pull out of the newly lit parking lot.

I jog around the building and get in my SUV. The excitement is killing me. Devin is allowing me to come to her apartment again!

Fuck yes.

Dick, behave.

I fully plan to respect her boundaries, but if I can push them just a little, I'll make the first moves and see what she will allow. It's extremely hard to keep my hands off her.

I see her standing on the curb and she waves at me. I park beside her and leave my laptop in the SUV. It's not like this is a high crime area. I can get away with just locking the doors.

Devin unlocks the first door, and we walk up the dimly lit stairs to the second landing. She unlocks this door, and I see there are a few glowing lights on from her salt lamps displayed throughout the place.

Suddenly, there is a furball loudly yelling for us.

"Luna! Aww babygirl, you are just fine," Devin says as she picks up Luna and buries her face in her neck fur. It's an endearing moment.

I'm jealous of the cat.

One day that will be me, too.

She sets Luna back on the floor and looks at me. "I usually come home and shower to get the coffee and food smell off of me."

"You can trust me, Devin. I won't bother your shower. Lock the door if it makes you feel better. I'm not here to hurt you, baby."

She nods, "Ok. I trust you. For some reason, I do. I don't think you are going to hurt me." She moves towards a door across the living room on the left side.

"I promise I'll be quick."

"Wait! I've never read one of your smutty books. But I want to, for you. Which one do you suggest? And do you have it here for me to read while I wait?"

Devin looks at me with her head cocked to the side. She walks into a room I can only presume is her bedroom. She comes out holding a book out to me.

I look at the cover. It's a silhouette of a woman on her knees, hands in front handcuffed together, facing a man standing forward with his hand on her head while he holds a whip.

I raise my eyebrows and grin at her.

She rolls her eyes, "This is one of my favorites and if you get far enough you will discover one of my kinks."

"Ohhhoho girl, you know I'm reading the whole thing now, as fast as I can."

Devin laughs out loud and says, "Well, if you don't, you owe that back to me. I'll be quick, promise," she says as she enters her bedroom. She closes the door, but I don't hear it lock.

We are getting better.

I take my tie off and set it on the island. I untuck my dress shirt and unbutton it down to my chest where you can see my undershirt. There is a smidgen of dark hair peeking out of the V in my t-shirt. I look down and see the tattoo on my arm.

Hope she likes men with tattoos. We haven't discussed that yet.

I grab the book back off the island and come around to the

couch and sit down.

I've watched videos about how important sex books are to some women. They love reading them, fantasizing, and discussing them online.

I see a Kindle sitting on the coffee table. Good lord, she's that much of a bookworm?

I have my work cut out for me if I'm going to start reading them too, so I can be what the horny ladies on social media call a book boyfriend. Maybe it was fate the algorithm showed those videos to me last week. Now it all makes sense. I'm supposed to be getting to know her and Nicole says this is what Devin spends all her free time doing.

I crack open my first smut book and settle into the cushions.

Chapter 15: Oakley

I'm a little into the third chapter, on an extra spicy scene, and her bedroom door opens. She's in a fluffy robe, house shoes and glasses. She comes to stand by the couch while I put my book down and she says, "Well, this is me 99% of the time, not like you saw me yesterday, with my hair done and my makeup on. I actually tried to look somewhat pretty yesterday. But anyways, yeah, this is me." She holds her arms out and gestures up and down herself.

Don't mind me just sitting here like an idiot staring at this beautiful creature. She is just as beautiful with no makeup on and in pajamas. Her glasses are so cute on her.

I shut my mouth and stand up. "Devin, you are gorgeous." I hold my left hand out to her, "Come here."

She holds her hand out to me and wraps her fingers around my hand. I pull her gently to me. I lick my lips and try to form words.

"I wish you could see what I see." Pushing her hair off her shoulder, I put my right hand on the side of her neck. I step into her space and smell her body soap.

That's where the peaches scent comes from.

A few inches from her face, I whisper, "Every time I look at you, I want to drop to my knees and do what ever you want. I want to drown in your green eyes and starve myself from kissing you so much. I want all the things with you."

I slide my nose and cheek down her hair, over her temple to her cheek, careful not to disturb her glasses. I tell her softly in her ear, "You are beautiful to me. Every bit of you. Every way. Soon, you will beg me to worship you, and I will be here for it, I'm ready now, but I'm a patient man when you need me to be. Make no mistake, you are already mine, but when I claim your body, I want no reservations, no regrets. You're going to cum all over me willingly."

I hear her erratic breathing and can see her chest rising and falling as I nuzzle into her neck. She whimpers and I drop her hand and bring my left arm up to her waist and wrap my arm around her, bringing her closer to me as she grips my bicep.

I inhale her scent and groan. I lay my head on her shoulder for a second while I get control of myself, then I drop my arms and back away.

Gruffly I tell her, "I have to stop. I only have so much control." I clear my throat and look at her.

She steps into me and puts her hand on my chest. Her touch sets off fireworks under my skin. I take a deep breath and set my jaw.

"I want you, Oakley, but I also want to protect myself."

I look at the ceiling and close my eyes, holding the fingers of my right hand over my eyelids.

I groan again, "Devin, I'm just waiting on you."

I bring my face back to hers and put my hands on her shoulders, "If you want me to take you right now, I can do that. If you want me to wait, I will do that then. But you're playing with fire right now, Kitten. I need a moment."

Devin has the audacity to giggle. "Ok, Loverboy."

"Cute. I see that stuck."

"I kinda like it. I'm keeping it." She's got a big smile on. I love the way her face lights up. It makes me even more mad her ex did that to her and stole her smile.

My new life goal is to make her smile as much as possible.

"Do you want to sit with me on the couch?" I ask her.

"Yeah, let's do that."

She comes around and moves some pillows and sits down. She sits facing me with one leg folded under her. I get a peek at the pink satin sleeping shorts with hearts on them that she is wearing. They only go to her high thigh area.

God, this torture keeps getting worse.

Fuck.

Chapter 16: Devin

The tug of war inside me is draining. I want to hop in bed with him, but I don't want to. I'm ready to throw caution to the wind.

My pussy aches for him, it aches for something I know he can give me.

I want to hang out with him more, see who he is, but if he keeps kissing me like that, I will give it up in a heartbeat. Be damned logic, lust will prevail.

Tonight, may be the night I give in. I feel so comfortable around him now and I admit, I'm highly attracted to him. Let's just see where this night leads.

He didn't run when I came out in my swamp hag outfit.

Besides, his tattoos alone are about to make me cum just thinking about him.

I have a feeling sex with him will be like something I've never experienced. He appears to know what he's doing, unlike me. I wish I had the confidence in the bedroom that I have for sticking up for myself in public.

I wish I could dominate and use my words to demand what I want. I've never uttered dirty words while having sex. There wasn't enough time for one. It was over as quickly as it started.

I hope Oakley knows all the dirty things to whisper in my ear while he's inside me. I hope he knows how to be rough but gentle at the same time.

I've put on my satin pj cami and shorts set, but I made sure my robe was over it. I put it on to feel sexy and confident around him.

I guess I'm also terrified this man will rip my clothes off and rape me.

I said it. That's my biggest fear. He's older and stronger. If anything, the incident a few nights ago proved I am no match for a man hellbent on getting what he wants.

I have to learn to trust people again after what Aaron and Talya did to me. It's been hard to let anyone in.

Oakley seems genuine. He has not given me one reason to doubt him.

Then what's your problem?

JUST FUCK HIM ALREADY!

Fear of being inadequate. Fear of being rejected. Fear of being made a fool of. Fear of falling too fast, too hard.

Sigh. I am letting fear hold me back from something that could be the greatest thing for me.

NOW OR NEVER, HEIFER!

I stand up and let my robe drop to the floor.

Oakley's mouth drops open.

I smile at him and tell him, "I'm too hot in my robe and I figure you like looking at me."

I see his fists ball at his sides.

The raw lust and desire in his eyes sends thrills to my already pulsating clit. I want this man. A LOT.

Fear be damned. I'm taking what I want.

I walk the 2 steps over to him, lift my left leg, and straddle him, my knees on either side of his body. I look down at him and smile, showing him my tongue between my teeth. I lick my lips and huskily say, "Tell me to stop if it too much, but I want to feel you under me."

And I sit down across his lap.

My satin shorts are already damp and it's noticeable.

I feel the air leave his lungs and his chest caves, and he tries to take in another strangled breath. I know I'm not that heavy, he's just fighting control.

I put my hands on both sides of his head, leaning on the back of the couch. I use one hand to momentarily run my fingers through my downed hair to get it out of my face. I toss it over my shoulder and look down at him.

My breasts with noticable rock hard nipples are inches from his face, and he is stone still with a clenched jaw. His eyes travel up my body and meet mine.

The eyes of an ocean, waves crashing over rocks, raw and untamed, are looking back at me. Yeah, his control is immaculate.

Oakley whispers. "I don't know what to do here, Devin."

I sit up, leaning back on his legs. His eyes rake over every inch of my body. I let him look as much as he wants. I feel my hard nipples pressing on the satin. I know he can see them.

His breathing is labored, and he still hasn't moved except for his jaw working to clench.

"Kiss me. Take me in your arms and kiss me. However you want."

His movements are quick as lightning.

He reaches up and encircles his arms around me. His right hand goes up to the base of my head with his fingers in my hair, slightly pulling. His left arm that's around my waist has a vice grip low on my hips, laying across my ass crack.

Oakley pulls me down to meet his lips. This kiss is frantic, wild and unruly. He isn't holding back. I am fully into this kiss like the others, but this kiss between us seems more natural, yet uncontrolled.

This is how I want to be kissed every day.

His tongue parts my lips and he unleashes like fury on my mouth. Oakley's tongue is everywhere all at once. His tongue dances over mine and he softly bites my tongue, nipping it just enough to hurt but still feel good.

Oakley moans into my mouth and pulls me down to him harder as he tries to cut off my airway with his tongue. Hot. As. Fuck. I feel the hardness of his dick growing under me, pushing up into my burning heat, and I subconsciously gyrate down on to him, making him moan more.

I wrap my arms around his neck as he moves his right hand to my ass cheek. His left hand now cups the other cheek. His fingers dig into my flesh, so hard I think I'm going to bruise. He uses his hands to push me back and forth over his hard dick.

He's going to have wet streaks on his black pants from my pussy leaking. I feel how wet and slick it is against the satin. I know it has to be overflowing onto him.

Oakley's breathing me in like it's his last breath.

He breaks the kiss and immediately bites my neck and kisses down my chest, where he stops to catch his breath.

I throw my head back and gasp for air myself, pushing my chest harder into his face. Chest heaving, pussy tingling, I am burning up with need.

"Fuck, Devin, I'm about to cum in my pants, baby."

I giggle and move my hips in a little circle.

"God. You're going to kill me." He nips the top of my boob.

I take my hands and run my fingers through his hair from his neck up to the top. I use his hair and pull his head back so I can kiss him again.

"Soon, Kitten." He painfully tells me.

"How about now, Loverboy?"

"Are you asking me to fuck you right now?"

I nod my head and breathlessly tell him, "Yeah, I am."

He kisses up my neck and pauses at my words, "Oh my fucking God, Devin. How do you want it, baby? You want me to be gentle or rough?"

"I'm not sure, but you can give me both and I won't complain. Let's start with rough."

Oakly grabs my face, both hands running into my hair to bring my face to his while he pushes his hard dick up to me, "Show me to the bedroom, Kitten."

Chapter 17: Oakley

She stands up quickly and grabs my hand, leading me to her room and shutting the door behind her.

I reach for her and bring her close to me. "Strip for me, Devin."

She has wild desire written all over her face, but a moment of panic laces through.

I run my hand down her face, "What's wrong? What are you panicking over?"

Barely loud enough, Devin says, "I don't know how to be sexy, or even how to have sex. I don't want to disappoint you." She has tears in her eyes.

Holy fuck, is she a virgin?

"Oh, baby, shhh. You being you is sexy as fuck. Devin, are you a virgin?"

"No." She shakes her head and tries to look away but I hold her face to mine. "I've only had sex a few times, on my back, and it lasted for like 3 minutes every time. I don't really know how to have sex, you are going to have to teach me."

I kiss her. I wrap my arms around her holding her close. I pull away and learn my forehead on hers, "I can teach you whatever you want to learn, and if I don't know it, we will try it and learn together. That sound good?"

Devin nods her head against mine, "Yes, thank you."

"Now, what do you want me to do, since that's out of the way?"

"I want you to fuck me and make me cum. I want that. I want to feel it all."

"Oh, Kitten, baby I can totally do that." I nuzzle her neck and start tickling her, "Watch me get undressed."

I step back watching her arms drop. She looks so glorious in this outfit. I can't wait to see it on the floor.

I unbutton my shirt as she says, "Alexa, finish playing Devin's Playlist."

I nod my head to her and smile as 'Play With Fire' by Sam Tinnesz and Yacht Money flows through her room.

"Turn on the light by the bed."

She hesitates, I say "It's ok, you're a goddess and I'm for fuck sure going to look every bit my fill at you." I drop my shirt on the floor, and reached behind me to pull my white T-shirt off. I dop it on the floor as Devin turns on the bedside lamp.

I nod to her, "Your turn, baby."

She gives me a half smile and crosses her arms in front of her and grabs for her shirt hem. She pulls the shirt over her head and drops it on the floor beside her.

I lick my lips and nod my appreciation with a grin.

I unbuckle my belt and undo my pants and start dropping them. They fall around my ankles with a whoosh. I take a foot out and take off the sock. I lift my other foot out of my pants and take off the other sock, all while watching her.

I stand up fully again and grab the waistband of my boxer

briefs. I pull them down and my cock springs free. I am hard as a rock for her right now.

I pull my underwear off and drop them on the floor with my eyebrows raised and her mouth drops open. I know I'm not the best showwer, but you would think I have a monster cock with how big her eyes are.

"Your turn, Kitten."

She has a moment of panic and then I see her internal battle. Devin is having a 'FUCK IT' moment and I am loving it.

I put my hands in prayer pose and rub them together, watching her every move, "I'm dying to see you spread wide on that pretty little blanket you have over there, I'm going to eat your pussy until your legs shake."

She's got her thumbs hooked into her shorts. She starts lowering them and I about lose my mind. I'm impressing myself with the restraint and patience I'm displaying to her because this is absolute torture.

Fuck it, whatever makes my girl feel safe and comfortable.

She steps out of the pink satin shorts and stands up to her height....then drops the shorts on the floor.

I get my first full look at her and she is fucking amazing. She is so goddamn gorgeous it stops my heart.

"Jesus fuck, Devin, you are stunning. Lay down on the bed for me like a good little girl, Kitten."

I watch her come over to her bed and crawl across it. I'm going to cum standing here looking at that ass. She lays back on her pillows and draws her legs up, hiding from me.

I come to the bottom of her platform bed. This works out perfectly.

I reach up and grab her ankle and I grip the other one and pull her down to the end of the bed. I reach up and grab the pillows and put them behind her. When she can properly see me I drop to my knees

Devin has her legs drawn up again. I spread her legs and slowly run my hands down the inside of her thighs. I kiss the inside of her right thigh as her soft, orange pussy hair tickles my cheek. I am so happy to see some hair here.

"I can smell your arousal, Kitten, and it's driving me wild." I hook my arms around her thick thighs and keep her spread open.

"My favorite thing to do is eat pussy. Tell me Kitten, have you ever had it done?'

Devin whimpers and quietly says, "No."

"Oh, Kitten, lay back and watch me make you scream my name. Watch me eat your pussy, Devin."

I look at her through my lashes before I lick my way up from her ass to her clit and lay a kiss on it.

Her whole body shivers and her breath gets stuck in her throat.

I swirl my tongue around her throbbing clit and suck gently, causing her hips to buck. I continue the barrage of swirling my flattened tongue and lightly sucking. She's panting.

I look up at her. She has her head thrown back and her hands are grabbing her nipples. Fucking hell, she's glorious.

"Kitten, lean up here and watch me, baby. You taste divine. Look how beautiful you are," I tell her as 'FEEL' by Beneld and Bury plays nicely in the background.

Hell yeah, Devin has a playlist of fuck songs.

She leans up on her elbows and her eyes are glazed over when they clash with mine. Her lips are separated, and she's breathing heavy.

"There's my Kitten. I want you to cum all over my face. Make your pussy purr for me, baby. Let go, Devin. Just let go." I pull one hand from around her thigh and shove my finger in my mouth, getting it wet. I watch her eyes as I push my finger inside her.

Devin whimpers and moans. "Now, cum for me Kitten." And I slide my tongue over her clit. I flatten my tongue and press it harder against her clit and close my lips around it.

I bend my finger and find her inner wall and massage her g-spot. I pick up my pace on her clit while watching her. She's still watching me and moaning so loud.

Taking my finger out for a moment, I run my tongue down her slit and push my tongue into her opening making her wiggle on the bed.

It's just fuel to my fire.

I fucking love her pussy.

I hum and shove her pussy in my face harder. My tongue is really working her clit when her legs start shaking.

"Oakley, please," she's practically sobbing. Devin is leaning on one elbow and working her tit with the other.

I slam my finger into her past the knuckle, and she drops back onto the pillows and screams as her thighs hug my head and her hips rock.

My Kitten is screaming my name.

It's about fucking time.

I've been dying to hear her cum with my name on her lips. Most beautiful sound in the world.

I pull my finger out and lick it clean. I untangle my arm from her slackened leg.

"Devin, slide up the bed, baby. I have to be inside you."

She scoots up the bed and throws a bunch of pillows off the bed.

I crawl onto the bed, staring into her eyes, I lean down and kiss her left calf. "Devin, I want to fuck you so bad, but I don't have a condom, I don't carry them on me."

She licks her lips, "I have an IUD, and I was just tested at graduation. There's been no one."

I continue crawling to her and perch between her legs, throwing her legs around my hips. "I was just tested too, about 3 weeks ago, and there's been no one since. I'm clean. If you're ok with it."

Devin reaches out her arms and says, "I'm ok with it Oakley, come fuck me now."

I can't resist that.

I rub my hand down and back on my cock a few times and line up with her slit. I send up thanks to all the angels and demons as I sink into her perfect pink pussy. She's so tight, and so, very very warm. This right here is what's been missing in my life.

Her.

I throw my head back and hiss. I pick up my pace while I pull her leg up to my shoulder, bending her knee and push my cock in harder.

I hear her moans get louder.

I stare into her eyes getting lost. I look down and see my cock glistening with her cum. "Kitten, watch me, look baby, watch me go in and out of you, watch my dick fuck you. Isn't it beautiful?'

My Kitten's pussy is perfect for me.

Devin' sits up more to get a better look and her eyes trail down to where my dick and her pussy meet. "See that baby, that's me and you." I rub my thumb over her clit, "My beautiful, sexy as fuck Kitten. Devin your pussy is magical, baby."

Devin lays back and reaches for me, and I slip her leg from my shoulder and lay down on top of her like she wants. Balancing on my hands, I move inside her and rotate my hips to hit her clit. She makes the sexiest noises.

Devin's arms are shaking around me, and she cries out and digs her nails in when I go deeper. Leaning on one arm, I run my splayed hand from her ribcage, over the swell over her breast, up to her neck where I stop, gently putting my fingers around her neck.

I keep her in place and make her look at me as I lean down by her face while I fuck her harder, rubbing her clit with my bone, "That's my Kitten...my beautiful baby, Devin..give it to me baby....cum on my dick.....make your pussy purr...be my cumslut."

Devin's back arches as she starts to cum. She throws her head back and closes her eyes, "No Devin, watch me, look in my eyes, baby." She opens her eyes and looks up at me with her head tilted. Her eye lids flutter and her mouth is open as she's yelling my name.

I really hope there are neighbors so they can hear her.

"Yes, baby, that's it, that's my good girl, baby you're gonna make me cum." I ram into her pussy one last time and I hoarsely yell, "Devin!" I moan with her, "Fuck, baby."

Best experience of my life.

I lean down and kiss the side of her neck, laying my head on her shoulder. Our breathing is erratic. She leans her head onto mine and runs her fingers through my hair while I lay on her chest.

My voice is muffled when I say, "Oh man, I didn't even get to taste these delicious tits."

That makes her giggle. "Next time, Loverboy."

I chuckle and lean up on my arms. I kiss her nose, "Are you ok?"

"Yeah. I'm great actually."

"Good. That makes me happy."

I feel myself slide out of her and I push to a sitting position on my calves between her legs. I watch cum ooze from her opening. "Devin, I love watching my cum drip out of your pussy while your legs are spread wide for me."

I back off the end of the bed and stand up, "Stay there."

I go into her bathroom and grab a towel hanging up. I come back to the bed and I wipe her off gently, as best I can. I put my hand out to help her up. She puts her hand in mine and she sits up and stands directly next to me, touching me, I wrap an arm around her and pull her to me, "That was amazing Devin. Thank you."

She reaches up her arms around my neck and kisses me.

I've already fallen so hard for this girl.

It's so scary how fast.

She's the one. I feel it in my bones.

I don't normally believe in destiny, but this can't be a coincidence.

Chapter 18: Devin

After showering and ordering food, we laid in bed talking, until we fell asleep last night. He convinced me, by waking me up with round 2, to skip classes today and just sleep. He said I was going to need all my energy for later.

Before he leaves this morning, Oakley comes over and runs his warm hand down my cheek, "Behave, Kitten. Think of me when you touch yourself later." He winks at me and grabs his phone off the island, pocketing it, and putting the book I gave him under his arm.

"I have been."

His surprised look makes me smile so much that I wrinkle my nose.

"Mmm naughty Kitten, I like it." I love his smile.

His body gives me chills when it's pressed up against me, but that smile, whew.

"You behave yourself too, Loverboy."

He laughs and takes a step back, "Yeah, Loverboy behaves around everyone but you." He kisses my nose and reaches for the doorknob. "I'll text you later, Kitten." I walk up to kiss him good bye. I shut the door, lock it, and yawn, excited to crawl into my bed.

I go to the kitchen and fill a cup with water and take a drink. I grab a banana and turn to head to my bedroom when a girl my age comes walking out of my room like this is an everyday occurrence.

I silently scream, drop the banana, and put my hand up over my mouth and try not to heave while my eyes track this spirit.

This is a full-bodied ghost walking around my apartment. Holy fucking shit. I can see right through her!!

"I thought you two would never stop."

All the times I doubted my mom. All the times I listened to my friends' parents call her a weirdo and say she had mental issues. All the times she had to see people who weren't there and couldn't say anything to anyone.

I'm so sorry Mom.

My skin is goose bumping and my legs start shaking. This can't be happening. I take a gulp of air, trying to get my body to breathe again.

She is blond and shorter than me. She looks really pale with sunken eyes. Her lips have no coloring, and her sad blue eyes have silver lacing through them, no life in them. She is dressed in leggings and a sweatshirt that says Clemet U.

I notice she is barefoot as she comes around the end table towards the island where I am.

"S-Stop right there!" I put my hand out, palm facing her, backing up against the counter, "Don't come any closer please."

She halts her progress and just stares at me.

"W-Who are y-you?"

"Britney Lyons."

"I don't know you," I still keep my hand out as I back my way to the apartment door, ready to run. I get into a defensive position by the front door with the bat we keep there. I don't know how I'm supposed to defend myself against something I can swing through, this just makes me feel better.

"I was a student here. I was told to come to you."

"By who?" I am so scared and now I am confused.

"My Guardian. They told me you could help me, that you could see and hear me."

I look frantically around and see if there is another ghost lurking around. I don't see anything else. I zip my eyes back to her. She stays put and doesn't try to come closer.

An unrestrained snort escapes me, "Whoever they are is wrong. I didn't even know I could do this until you showed up. This has never happened to me. How would they know?"

"I don't know, I didn't question them. I finally found you a week ago and I've been trying to get you to notice me. I've been standing beside you screaming, I've knocked things over, I've watched you sleep."

"Eww, no, just no." I am icked out now. Watching me sleep?

I get a full shiver while she's talking as my body adjusts to her presence. And all the creepy things she says.

This is so unnerving. Is this what my mom went through? Why hasn't this happened before? Why now?

And who in the spirit world knows I can do this when I didn't even know yet?

I feel my chest rising and falling. I don't dare take my eyes off her. She holds her hands out, "I didn't mean to scare you, I swear it."

I lick my lips and say, "This is scary as hell." I lower the bat some. "I mean my mom can do this, but it's never happened to me." I lower the bat all the way, "I don't know how to react."

"I've never found anyone that could see me."

"What do you want?"

"I need to find out who killed me. I can't remember how it happened or who did it. I don't even know where my body is. I just appeared somewhere and had to figure all this out. But there are others. They need help."

"I don't know how you expect me to help. I'm just a college student."

"You can follow me."

Appalled at the idea, I retort, "I'm not going anywhere with you."

"You have to. They need our help." She holds her hand out to me.

"Nope, not doing it. Find someone else." This ghost is crazy if she thinks I'm going to go find killers with her.

Britney looks over her shoulder and says, "I have to go." Then disappears as quickly as she came.

What in the fuck?

Guess who's not sleeping now.

There's fucking ghosts in my apartment.

Go the fuck away. I don't want this so-called gift.

Chapter 19: Devin

The ghost has not appeared since yesterday morning after Oakley left. I have been trying to ignore anything that may happen that's spooky. Because ignoring things is fine.

Yesterday I showed up to work for my shift and there was a giant bouquet of pink roses on the counter, all different colors. The card said, 'To my perfect Kitten. I can't wait to see you again. XOXO Oakley.'

He came by the café last night to walk me to my car. He didn't come over because he had an early meeting, and it was almost 10:30.

Right now, I'm waiting for him down on the sidewalk for our Wednesday Mexican night in a pair of skinny jeans and a hoodie. Clover ditched me. We were hoping to make it a double date with her and X.

She has been away a lot more spending time with him. I can't complain, my free time is being occupied by his best friend.

I will hand it to Oakley, he is persistent.

He texted me every morning since we met a few days ago, he stays in contact with me all day long, whether it be silly memes or videos. It seems like he is always thinking of me.

He calls me before my shift at the café to tell me to have a good night and he will see me later. He video chatted me last night before bed. Tried to get me to prop the phone up and have me strip down, or finger myself for him.

I told him he should have came over if he wanted to see it so bad.

He showed up about 11:15 pm. As soon as I opened the door he grabbed me, bit my neck, kicked the door shut and quickly locked it, picked me up and hauled me to the bedroom. Where he then fucked me senseless until I passed out.

He left this morning at 6 am to get ready for his 7:30 am meeting. We are both really tired and dragging ass, but it was so worth it.

Pam decided to give me tonight off because Oakley asked her nicely for one night this week for a date night. The audacity of this man to charm my boss. It worked. He must have forgotten I have the weekend off.

I watch him pull forward into the parking spot by the curb. The front of his SUV comes up right by my legs. I walk over to step off the curb and see him open his door.

He steps out of his expensive SUV wearing blue jeans and a black long-sleeved shirt. Of course, his hair looks perfectly unruly. I notice he has a 5 o'clock shadow that I would like to run my thighs over.

Oakley walks up to me and puts his arm around my waist, pulling me to him, taking in a deep breath of me, and kisses my lips, then trails his mouth down the side of my neck. It makes me hum out my appreciation.

"Hello, Kitten."

I dip my chin to rub my face on his scrub, "Hey, Loverboy."

He growls into the crook of my neck and replies, "I missed you."

I chuckle and say, "You just saw me this morning."

"It wasn't enough."

He nuzzles into my neck, tickling me and making me belly laugh. "God, I love your laugh."

I sigh in contentment as he stops tickling me.

I pull my arms from around his neck and say, "Come on, I'm hungry."

I take his hand and lead him into the restaurant on an official date.

Dinner was fun. We talked about all kinds of stuff. We've gotten to know each other more over the past few days.

He's just a regular guy. I almost feel stupid for being so afraid of him.

It's scary how fast I'm falling for him though. What would my mother say? Or Aunt Jilly? 'Devy, don't give your heart away so quick, make him earn it.'

I'm doing swimmingly well fucking that up.

Oakley has managed to work his way in and break down most of my walls in such a short time.

We are getting ready to leave and I timidly ask him, "Can I see where you live?"

He looks up surprised, "Absolutely. What ever my lady wants." He puts his wallet back in his back pocket.

"Thanks for dinner."

"You're welcome, Kitten," he takes my hand and leads me

through the restaurant to his SUV.

"Do we need to make sure the baby is good?"

I give him a perplexed look. "Baby?"

"Yeah, Luna. Is she going to be ok?"

I laugh, "Yeah, she'll be fine." He shuts my door for me and circles the SUV, climbing in. "Are you cold?" he asks me, while he starts up the car.

"I'm a bit chilly." I rub my biceps. We are having a cold snap come through. Fall is here.

"Where do you live?" I look over at him.

"I live in an apartment complex about 10 minutes from you."

"Oh. Do you live by yourself?"

"Yeah, I didn't want a roommate. I like walking around naked too much," he gives me his devilish grin.

"I can only do that in my room. I'm not sure Clover would appreciate me walking around in the buff. Then again, she makes some of the most lesbian comments to me. I'm never sure if she's serious or not."

"She's serious. I've seen her making out with other girls. Better watch yourself, I'll have to fight a woman off my girl."

"I think you are fine. I'm not sure I swing that way honestly. I've never had the opportunity to test it out."

"It can be arranged. I don't like sharing but if it's something you want to try, I'm open to you learning about yourself."

"Most men would jump at the chance to see their girlfriend with another woman."

"I'm not like most men. I think you are learning that. I don't mind sharing you to experiment, but there will be no relationship there, and I have boundaries. I meant it when I said you are mine. Other than learning your likes, we are not sharing each other with people."

"Possessive, I like."

Oakley reaches for my hand and kisses my knuckles, "I'm dead serious when I say I'm not letting you go."

Involuntary thigh clench.

"Oh, I finished your book. I need the next one in the series. It gives me some great ideas. I liked reading it, it gave me a glance into what you like and some of what you would want done to you."

"Seriously? You would read the next one?"

"Yeah, I would. Just to get to know you better and see if I can pull off some of those things."

"If you wear that mask again, I can't be held responsible for my wanton actions."

"Ohh, really? That can be arranged too, ya know."

"I didn't think I had a masked man kink until I saw you in one."

"Oh Kitten, we will have so much fun, you and I. I can't wait."

We arrive at his complex and he parks the SUV. He takes my hand and leads me up the stairs and to the left. We come to a door marked 3162B, and he unlocks it and stands aside so I can walk through.

It's a total bachelor pad. He has a leather couch up against one wall, and a coffee table with a rug under it, a TV on a gray wooden stand, and a small table with 2 chairs in the dining area. The kitchen is small but clean.

It's very impersonal with its stark white walls and lack of adornments on the walls. I see there are a few pairs of shoes by the front door, so I take mine off too. Oakley follows suit and takes his off also.

He holds his arm out and says, "Welcome to the Devil's playground." And he puts his arms behind him and grins at me through his lashes.

He walks me over to a door, "This is my bedroom, it has its own full bath, and the other bathroom is right over there by the kitchen. That hallway goes back to the other bedroom which I use as an office when I work here."

"It's so bare. It's nice but there's nothing that says someone lives here."

"When you move in with me you can decorate it how you want."

I snort and shake my head, crossing my arms over my chest, "Mighty bold of you to assume I will move in with you."

"You won't be able to resist. I'm telling you," he circles my waist with his arms and pulls me close, "I will have to beat you off of me with a stick when you fall madly, deeply, passionately, irrevocably in love with me and can't stay away. Mark my words Devin, you WILL be addicted to me." He wags his eyebrows up and down while giving me his dimpled smile.

I really do laugh out loud. "Oh yeah? We'll see."

"Oh shit, she pulled out the 'we'll see' card. We all know that's means no. But I'm telling you, it's going to happen."

"Can your ego get any bigger?"

"Yes, my ego can. My dick can't so you're stuck with it, but I'm pretty sure you can handle it."

"Show me."

"You want me to strip right here."

"Yes, I do."

"Ok, Kitten, but don't faint at the awesomeness."

"Just get on with it."

He steps back and reaches behind his neck to pull off his shirt. It really does take my breath away.

His arm tattoo goes all the way up his arm, around his shoulder, on to his chest. It's angels flying in the sky, fighting demons, with swords and shields. His chest has a giant shield over his heart.

He unbuckles his belt and unbuttons his pants. "Underwear on or off?"

I can't form words. "Umm, on."

Oakley drops his pants on his living room floor and steps out of them, kicking them away. He looks up at me and grins. "What's next, Kitten?"

I take a step towards him, and he stays still. I close the gap and reach out a hand to his chest. I run my fingertips across his pecs, his tattoo, and trailing my fingers as I go, I walk around his backside, making sure to notice his ass in these boxer briefs. I see the tattoo comes around to the back where a devil is tattooed on his shoulder blade. The only colors in his tattoo are black, white, gray and red.

It's sexy as hell.

He shivers as my fingertips breeze across his skin lightly. I continue walking around him, trailing my fingertips, but applying a little pressure with my nails. I come back around to the front of him and put my palm in the middle of his chest, twirling my finger in his chest hair. I rub my palm up his chest, onto his neck, and on his scruffy cheek.

He leans into my hands and groans. He leans his head back and closes his eyes. Hoarsely he asks, "What do you want me to do, Kitten?" He brings his face back down to mine.

I back up from him and see the uncertainty and raw lust in his eyes.

I put my hands on the hem of my sweatshirt and pull it up and over my head. The next thing I take off is my tank top that was underneath it.

I unbutton my jeans and watch him as I start to slide my pants over my thighs and ass. I take them down to the floor and step out of them.

I'm standing in front of him with a see-through bra and matching thong.

I take the clip out of my hair and let it fall over my shoulders. I shake it out, letting the waves fall into place.

When I look at Oakley, he looks like he's in pain. Eyes glazed over with want. The front of his boxer briefs has started to grow again and his mouth is open.

I love how he responds to me.

I walk up to him and put my arms around his neck, "I want you to fuck me, Oakley."

Goddamn he moves fast. Before I know it he has me picked up off the ground and legs wrapped around him, carrying me to his bedroom.

He tosses me onto his bed where I bounce a few times. He takes off his boxer briefs and I watch his hard dick stand out in front of him. It makes my mouth water just seeing it.

He reaches over to me and says, "As delightful as this ensemble is, I want it off, now." He reaches for my hips and hooks my thong around his thumbs and yanks them down off of me. He comes back up and throws my legs apart, smiling, "Yeah, there's my pretty pussy."

He holds a hand out to me, and I take it to sit up. He reaches around and unclasps my bra and tosses it on the floor, "Those looks really nice on my floor."

Oakly climbs on the bed and I lay back with my hair fanning his pillows. He positions himself over top of me and says, "I want to give you the world. I want you to have all the things you deserve and more. We are going to have a long talk about what you want." He kisses down my neck and trails his tongue across my collar bone causing shivers.

He moves down to my left breast and cups it in his hand. His mouth is so hot when he covers my nipple with his lips and swirls his tongue around it. It instantly beads up for him.

"I love how your body reacts to me, Devin. It craves me." He moves to my right breast and does the same, sucking gently on it.

The jolt into my clit makes me whimper for him. "Oh God."

I have my fingers in his hair and tell him, "I never knew it could be like this."

Oakley leans up to my face and replies, "Baby, we are just getting started." Then his lips collide with mine and I moan into his mouth as I melt under him.

Chapter 20: Oakley

I move across her body laying kisses and small nips until she is panting beneath me.

"Kitten, you're going for a ride," I roll over and take her with me and pull her on top of me.

Her eyes get big as she looks down to me. She bites her lip, uncertain.

I reach up and caress her boobs until she moves her hips on her own accord, and she holds on to my wrists, moaning.

"I feel your wetness on my cock. Sit up and put me inside you, Devin."

"I don't know what I'm doing, Oakley."

"I'm going to show you, then just go with what feels natural. You're going to ride my cock and cum all over me, baby, I'm going to help you."

I pull her up with one arm and take her hand to grasp my dick. I guide her hand in the motions to rub the head of my dick in her dripping wet slit. "Like that Devin, get it nice and wet."

I find her center and lower her down on my cock. I push up into her and hear her breath hitch. "Yeah baby."

She groans out, "Oakley."

"That's my good girl. Now move your hips, grind on my dick, however you want, but I'll help." I put my hands on her ample ass cheeks and dig in, moving her back and forth.

Her hands drop to my chest and she moans out, "That feels so good."

Leaving my right hand on her ass, I reach up with my left hand on her neck and bring her down to kiss me.

I'm surrounded by a curtain of fire and her perfume lays a spell over me. In this moment, I am lost for her.

I kiss her deeply and move her hips on mine. She finds a rhythm and takes me inside her deeper, lifting and sliding back down, rotating her hips.

I smack her on her ass cheek and feel it jiggle on my thigh. I fucking love it. I smack her 2 more times and cause her to gasp into my mouth.

I sit her up slightly and take her nipple into my mouth. It draws a long, wanton moan from her throat.

With her nipple still between my lips, I rub my hand up her chest to wrap my fingers around her neck and push her head back.

I buck up into her harder and she moves faster. Putting my hands back on her ass, I pull her hips back and forth and feel her body start to shake. "That's it baby, ride this cock and cum for me....you're so close."

She is almost sobbing as she rides my cock. I quickly reach up and put my hand on her throat and tighten my grip until she cries out her release, yelling my name.

Letting her come down from her orgasm, she sags against me. I pull her hair away from her face and whisper, "You aren't done yet, Kitten. Get on your hands and knees for me."

She looks at me surprised as she tries to keep her wild hair from falling into her face. I tap her leg and tell her, "Let's go, that's an order. On your knees."

She scrambles to get off of me on her wobbly legs. She stands there as I peel myself off the bed. I get behind her and tell her, "Hands and knees, ass in the air, in my direction."

She looks back at me over her shoulder.

"Do you trust me?"

She nods and says, "Yeah."

So I smack her ass and tell her, "Do what I tell you to do then."

She crawls onto the bed and sticks her ass in the air. "Devin this is one of the most beautiful sights I've ever seen." I rub my hand over her plump ass cheek and smack it, watching the jiggle clear into her thighs. "It's fucking gorgeous."

I grab her ass cheeks and spread them, then dip my head to lick her asshole.

She jerks and rasps, "Oh my God."

I continue my assault on her asshole and run my tongue over her puckered hole. I stick my tongue in a little and move it around the rim.

Devin's squirming all over the bed moaning, hands fisting the duvet. She is quickly losing her inhibitions.

I lean back and huskily say, "I've always been a pussy man, but this ass has me in a grip, too." I smack it again for good measure.

I ache to be inside her. I climb up onto the bed and rub my cock up and down her opening a few times. I circle my cock around her asshole a few times and it makes her moan in a higher pitch, "Not yet baby, you aren't ready, but soon Kitten, I'm going to be in that ass and you will lose your mind."

I find her opening, line up and put my head in. She hums with pleasure. My pretty kitty is purring for me. I grab her hips, pulling her back as I slam into her pussy from behind. It makes her yell out and clamp down on me.

I do not stop. I reach up and gather her hair in my hands and fist it, "Who's pussy is this, Devin?"

"Yours," she says in her throaty tone.

"I can't hear you, Kitten," I give a tug back on her hair making her cry out as I continue pounding her pussy. "Louder."

"Yours. It's yours Oakley, all yours," she says sobbing.

"That's right baby, all mine."

I take my hand off her hip and reach around to her clit, taking it between my fingers and rolling it around.

"Oh, God. Do it again," she tells me, out of breath.

I rub her clit in circles with my fingertips. I pull her hair back and tell her, "Come here, lean back here."

She pushes off the bed in front of her and lays her body up against mine. I take my hand out of her hair and run it up the front column of her throat, griping her there. "I control the air you breathe, I control your body, whose Kitten are you?"

Breathless, she answers, "Yours."

Keeping my fingers working magic on her clit and my pace fucking her pussy, I gruffly say in her ear that's close to my mouth, "Purr for me, baby, be my good little Kitten and cum again."

Devin's head is dropped back on my shoulder slowly shaking it back and forth, moaning my name.

"Give it to me, beautiful. Cum all over my dick and fingers. I demand it, do as I say and be a good girl."

I rub my 3 fingers over her clit in a circular motion and apply more pressure. Those words are what releases the dam for her.

Devin's whole body jerks as she calls out my name and her body quakes. I release the hold on her neck and and move it to her hips, digging into her flesh, pulling her back into me while I pump a few more times and unload into her with a groan.

"Devin, fuck, baby." I put my head on hers. "Yes baby." I slowly stop moving. She is still leaning up against me, chest heaving, and her hand over my hand on her clit.

I wrap my arms around her torso and hold her tight. I bury my face in her neck, "Are you ok? Did I hurt you?"

She snorts and giggles at the same time saying, "It only hurt in the best ways."

She bends her elbows and holds my forearms to her chest. I feel myself slowly slide out of her. "Bend over so I can watch my cum drip out of you. One day I'm going to be shoving it back up into you so you can give me a dozen kids."

"Umm, maybe 3, possibly 4."

"I'll take that as a win, you didn't say no."

She falls forward on the bed and leaves her ass in the air. She listens so well. She pushes her arms straight out over top of her head and turns her head off to the side as her breathing regulates. She is stretching out just like a cat. My Kitten.

I watch as my cum leaks from her pussy. I put my finger up to catch it and smear it around. "You truly are fucking beautiful, Devin. Don't ever feel that you aren't."

I hear her let out a sigh contentment.

Chapter 21: Devin

After taking a shower at Oakley's I asked him to drop me back off at my apartment so I can get some studying crammed in for my test tomorrow.

I am really struggling with Geometry and the professor is an asshole. He is nice to only certain people. It's like he hates his job.

I have done all the extra credit I can to raise my grade. I am hoping it's enough and I can ace this test.

My other problem class is American Government. Perhaps, the wrong question to ask an instructor was, 'Why do we need to understand this system, clearly it doesn't work.'

Now that earned me extra course work. I hate that class. I don't understand why we have to take classes like this to earn a Nursing degree. I'm not going to be reciting American government facts to people I'm running an IV in.

I learned all about this broken system in high school.

I'm not failing the course; I just have to do double the work.

Grabbing my books I lay on my bed with my textbook and

workbook. Luna comes to lie next to me.

Everything is fine...until it's not.

Luna starts hissing and I look down at her and she's getting fluffier. "Luna, are you ok baby? What's wrong?"

"Nothing is wrong, she just doesn't like when I'm around." The ghost girl comes waltzing into my room from the living room.

"What the fuck? God damn!"

I scramble to sit up and back off the bed. She stops right inside the doorway and crosses her arms.

"Are you going to help me or not?"

I feel like I'm about to have a heart attack at the rate my heart is beating out of my chest. My hands turn clammy, and I feel like I have to pee all of a sudden. *Please don't let me piss myself.*

"I don't know what you expect me to do."

"You can help me find them," Britney says.

"Find who?" I can only stare at her whispy figure, just floating there.

"The girls who've been taken," she pleads with me.

"Do you know where they are?" I stand up straighter.

"I know there is another girl that was with me when they took me, but I don't know what happened to her. They took more girls, and they are holding them in a house somewhere. You have to go there and save them."

"I am not about to go get myself killed! No, I can't just go there. Are you nuts?"

"Someone has to save them." Her ghosty eyes form tears. "If someone would have come for me, I wouldn't be here talking to you like this."

This girl knows how to guilt trip. Fuuck.

"Why don't you tell me where they are? I can call the police and send them." I offer the compromise.

Lightly she says, "I don't know the address. I only know how to get there."

"No, I'm not driving somewhere at night, in the dark, that I don't know where, or the people staying there. It's dangerous."

Britney puts her hands over her face and sobs while disappearing.

"Britney?"

I wait for her to appear.

When she doesn't appear after a few minutes, "Britney?"

I don't think she's coming back.

"You don't understand. It's scary. I'm just a girl. I could get killed." I say out into the apartment.

No one answers.

Great. Now I've pissed a ghost off.

Getting in my car the next day to go to school, I look over and shriek, almost dumping my coffee on me.

"What are you doing here?" I say staring at Britney in the passenger seat.

"I'm going to be by your side all the time until you go to the house."

"Why did you ghost me last night?"

Britney levels a look at me, "Is that supposed to be a bad joke?"

"What?" Suddenly getting the pun. "No, bad choice of words. Why did you disappear and not come back?"

"I needed to get away."

I pull out onto Main Street, "I'm sorry I can't go to that house. I'm scared."

She puts her hands over her chest and pouts. "That's why I'm here. I'm going to be extra annoying until you do." She gives me a ghostly smug smile.

Just fucking great.

Pulling into the school parking lot, "Look, I don't need you to do this. I can ignore you. Go get an address for the house and we can talk more."

I sling my bookbag over my shoulder and walk into the building. I notice in the hallway, she's following me. I turn around and she stands there. She smiles sweetly and gives a little wave, wiggling her fingers.

This creepy bitch.

I go through my two morning classes, and she sits beside me, humming and singing loudly, making faces, jumping up and down in front of me, through each motherfucking lecture. I couldn't say anything to her and risk looking like a freak.

She knew it, too.

I make a mental note to eventually ask my mom if there is a way to make ghosts shut up. A supernatural gag order of sorts. Ghosty duct tape. Anything to make her off key humming and half ass singing stop.

I stop in the hallway and look around and see no one nearby, I turn to her and say, "Please, I'm begging you, leave me alone in this class. I'm almost failing, and the instructor hates me already. We can talk afterwards. I promise."

I go into the geometry classroom, my last class of the day, and take my seat in the middle of the room. I see her out in the hallway, just staring at me.. Thank God she listened! I would be lying if I said that wasn't intimidating. There's a ghost just staring me down.

It gives me shivers.

I try to focus on the instructor and this lesson but keep an eye out for Britney.

Finally, class is over, and I gather my things, bringing out the extra credit I did, intending to hand it in, but Mr. Beasley calls out to me, "Miss Bennet, a moment please."

I glance to the hallway through the door and Britney is still there. Being creepy.

I walk up to Mr. Beasley's desk with the papers out, offering a small smile, "Hi, I have the extra credit to hand in."

He takes his glasses off and looks up at me, "Let's hope it helps." He sticks his hand out and takes the papers. "I heard you had an altercation at the Fall…"

Before I know it, Britney is beside me; I can't spare her a look, but I feel her fear. She whispers to me, "Oh my God, Devin, it's him, he's from the house."

I have a split second to school my shocked reaction on my face, so Mr. Beasley doesn't think I know as I continue to listen to him.

"..Festival. I am sorry that happened to you. Next time I hope you have another knight in shining armor at your disposal. As a certified self-defense instructor, I urge you to take some lessons for yourself. That's all."

This is why I've hated this man since the first day I stepped into this classroom. He is vile. Evil.

I swallow the lump in my throat and frantically reach for my voice, acutely aware I am alone in this room with him, it comes out croaky, "Yes, great idea. Thank you, sir."

I have to get away from him. Immediately.

I spin around and march my ass right out of that room. I need space between us.

What the fuck is my geometry instructor doing at a house that keeps girls prisoner?

Chapter 22: Devin

I hurry home, and once I'm in the apartment my heart stops racing. I walk over to the island and set my bag down. I take a few deep breaths while resting on my arms. My hands are still shaking.

I look up and see Britney. "I need you to work extra hard on getting an address for that place. Like ASAP. Please do that for me." I start rubbing my temples.

"Ok, Devin." Then she vanishes.

Trying to keep my composure, I go through the motions of making me tea. I can't stop shaking. My mind is racing with so many possibilities.

What is Mr. Beasley doing with missing girls? Is he in on it? Does that mean he's involved in my almost abduction?

If he is one of the men at that house, maybe I can follow him there. See for myself where it is, and I wouldn't need an address.

I pull up the school's class schedules. I see he doesn't leave his last class of the day until 7 pm.

This is doable. I just have to call off work. Or trade shifts with Emily. I send her a quick text and ask if she would like to close tonight for me. I will go in her normal time and work 3 to 6, which is Emily's Thursday shift.

I hear a ding, and my phone vibrates on the counter. I pick it up to see a text from Emily confirming she will happily take my closing shift with a few smiley face emojis.

I knew she would jump at it. She's trying to buy a prom dress and just told me on Monday she needed another job or more hours, and she was going to speak to Pam about it.

If I do this, I'm going to have to tell Oakley about this new gift. This is not something I can keep hidden. However, I'm not ready to say anything yet.

Maybe I'm stupid, but I'm just not ready.

But I also don't want to go to this house by myself. I don't know what I'm walking into. I couldn't fend off my attacker, what happens if they are there and there are guards?

What happens if there is more than one kidnapper there?

I don't stand a chance. As sad as that makes me, I have to admit I am just not strong enough.

Maybe Mr. Beasley is right, I do need to take some self-defense classes. After all this, I will look into them. I mean it can't hurt to learn some basics. I need to be able to kick ass and not have someone save me all the time.

Sigh. I'm dreading this, but it's time to call my mom.

Before I can do that, my Aunt Jilly is calling. I pick up the phone, "Hi Aunt Jilly!"

"Hey Pumpkin! How's it going?"

"That's a loaded question."

"Oh boy, what's happening? Do you need to talk about it?"

"As much as I want to talk to you about it, I feel like I should tell my mom first."

"Devin Emilia, are you pregnant?"

I scoff and reply, "No. Not hardly."

"Ok, alright, well when you get done talking to your mom, if you want to talk to your poor ole Aunt, holler at me. Or I can just hear it second hand from your mom," she laughs.

"Oh yeah, I know she's going to call you immediately afterwards. It's a given," I chide.

"Alright. I look forward to hearing from you then. I love you kiddo! Don't forget to call me."

"Love you too Aunt Jilly! Bye"

The moment of hesitation. The held breath, clammy hands, and butterflies in my stomach.

Stop being a fool. This is Mom. She's the coolest person you know.

Give her some credit.

I hit the green button and hear the ringing. Two rings later, "Hey baby! How's everything?"

"Hey Mom. I'm alright. How are you?" I try to sound normal.

"Oh me? I'm fabulous. Now tell me some more about why my little fire ant sounds miserable. I've got all night." This woman misses nothing.

I try not to sob, "Mom...."

"Devin, what's wrong baby?"

"I-I can see ghosts now." I say quietly.

"Oh, honey! How do you feel about this?"

"I'm scared."

"Yes, I can see how it's scary. When my gift came to me as a little girl, it was so scary for me. Is there anything I can do for you? How can I help?"

"How did you ever get over the fear? I feel like there are going to be ghosts everywhere now. I've only spoken to one."

"Oh yeah? Who was it?" My mother is so nosy.

"It's a girl my age. Her name is Britney. She says she's one of the missing girls from campus."

"Wow," my mom gushes out. "Did you know her?"

"No, but she says she knows where the other girls are being held and can take me there."

"Devin, honey no, you can't. Oh baby, call the police." I hear the panic rising in her voice.

"That's what I'm going to do, Mom. Britney says she doesn't know the address, so I sent her to the house earlier, and told her don't come back until she knows it."

"Good. This is so dangerous."

"Mom, I wanted to know, how would you handle this spirit? She followed me all over today, humming and singing, making a damn fool of herself, until I agreed to go to that house with her. I feel awful there are girls being held somewhere," my voice cracks, any minute now I'm going to explode into tears. "But I'm so afraid to go there. The police aren't going to believe me."

"Oh Devin, honey. That spirit's heart is probably hurting so badly. They don't normally follow around and try to aggravate. I've only ran into a handful of spirits that would do something like that. I'm sorry your first spirit is like this."

"I'm not sure how to handle this. I just know I've told her three times now I'm not going to that house. I'm too afraid to go. I want to call the police but I'm not sure how to explain a ghost told me."

"Honestly, the police are more understanding of this stuff than we give them credit for. There has been a change of minds on taboo subjects such as using psychics and mediums."

"True." I sit back on my bed. "I just don't want to feel guilty for not going."

"I can see that. I've had that guilt numerous times, it truly is a shitty feeling. But you can't hold it against yourself. Self-preservation is a strong trait for a human, the dead don't have a need of it anymore. Always trust your gut to lead you to self-preservation,

"Pay close attention to how your body responds to a spirit. Keep a journal if you have to. Write down each ghost like it's a diary. You will see a pattern of how your body responds, then sends you response signs to discern what are truths or lies from a spirit."

I chuckle, "Is that how you always knew if David or I were lying?"

"Yes, it is actually. You develop a really trusty gut instinct. It's part of the gift. Those reactions could save your life, Devin. Learn them fast."

"I noticed today, Luna does not like it when Britney comes near. Luna actually hissed a few moments before Britney appeared." I pet Luna who's sitting beside me, curled up, purring. I think it's because she hears my mother. Luna misses mom too.

"Promise me you won't go out to the house alone. Devin, please."

"I promise Mom." I opt not to tell her about Mr. Beasley just yet.

I'm not sure if that's true.

"It creeps me out to think there are dead people out there everywhere and they will now gravitate to me because I'm a beacon in their darkness."

"Well, yes, it is creepy. But it's the shine of the Lightworkers. Your light will get brighter the more you use it. You know we nurture this gift to help others with their nice ghosts, but there will be less than savory ghosts who are attracted to your light also. They will try to trick you. Never make a deal with a spirit, Devin, and always carry pennies."

"Pennies?"

"Yes, you can trap a spirit on a penny. It's only used in extreme cases, but you never know when you will need it."

"Mom! Is that why you always had pennies encased in plastic as a charm for our book bags and then car keys? Ohh! There's literally one on my keychain right now."

My mom has the audacity to giggle.

"Yes, it was my emergency stash. Hidden in plain sight." She is belly laughing now. "Y'all just thought it was a good luck charm."

"What else of my childhood is a joke?" I roll my eyes.

"Whew, we don't have time for all that."

"MOM! Damn, woman."

"Seriously Devin, be guarded. Lay your salt boundary down to keep them out of your apartment. Just make sure there are no spirits in the apartment at the time, or you'll trap them in there with you."

"How did you ever cope with this? I am so afraid to go out anywhere now, Mom." I can barely get it out as the first tear falls.

"I was terrified at first. For years, even. It wasn't easy to adjust to that's for fucking sure. Just one day I told myself, this is ridiculous, they are going to be there either way. I just went about with my life because I was tired of living in fear. I learned how to ward myself and keep up a shield. Oh, do you remember how to do that still?"

"Yes Mom, I do, I've been doing it regularly as you advised."

"Good, it will keep them from touching you. You never want them to touch you, it's the worst feeling ever. You can definitely tell they are part of death if they touch you." I can hear the shudder in her voice.

"Britney has not tried to touch me, thankfully. Although the first time she appeared I was going to hit her with a baseball bat," I laugh out loud, "Well, try to anyways. Probably wouldn't have done much good."

Mom giggles and says, "I can't blame you at all. However, the good thing is you knew what she was. You knew how to handle it due to being around it your whole life."

"True, I didn't think of that." I put one of my throw pillows over my lap and lean my elbows on it. "I do have something else I want to tell you about."

"Ohh, what a fortunate call!"

"I have a boyfriend."

I hear mom squeak and say, "DEVIN! That's so awesome honey. Who is it? Do I get to meet him soon? Oh my God, how long you been dating and not tell me?"

Sighing, "Mom...Mom...we just started dating this past Sunday. It's been like 4 days. Chill. I am not telling you or Aunt Jilly who he is so you can cyber stalk him. Nope, not telling."

"Ohh it's that new new. So, are you just dating aka 'fucking' as the kids call it, or in a serious relationship since you already call him your boyfriend?"

"Mother!" Moms miss nothing. She would never talk this way to someone else, except Aunt Jilly. Them's some raunchy old birds when they get together.

Omitting his name, I explain how we met up at the mall on Sunday, and then he decided I was his girlfriend.

"Ha! That is so romantic, Devy. My little fire ant got herself a man. I'm happy for you baby."

"Mom, he is amazing. We have spent so much time talking and getting to know each other. He is perfect and I keep thinking this is all a dream or a sick joke."

"Devy, don't think that way. You are so worthy and so deserving of love, too. You are worthy of a happily ever after." I can hear the sadness in her voice.

"He's too pretty for me, Mom. He's everything I've dreamed about," I say softly. "He's gorgeous. And so kind. He truly cares about me in such a short time." I lay back on my bed and stare at the ceiling.

Luna gets up and repositions herself on my head. She's in protective mode, I see. I reach up and run my fingers through her fur.

They say petting an animal can take off heaps of stress. I just want to lay Luna across my face to take it all away.

"So, when do I get to meet him?" I hear the excitement in her voice again. She is not going to drop this.

"How about I bring him home for Christmas. He is going to stay with his Dad for break and he thinks y'all live 2 hours apart and he's willing to drive me all over the state so we can all meet each other. That is the soonest. I want to make sure this will last, even to Christmas. I have a feeling it will, but I just want to be sure, ya know?"

"I understand. I'm just excited. Has he seen you mad yet?"

I can't stop the bark of laughter, "No, he hasn't."

"There's a reason you are called Fire Ant. Maybe I should prepare him. Let me have his number and I'll call and do it."

If I was sitting there with her I guarantee you she is batting her lashes to get her way.

"Ha. Nice try, Mom. Nope, you are going to have to wait until Christmas."

"Fine, fun sucker. I guess I will just wait. If you want to bring him before Christmas, I won't be upset."

"Yeah, yeah Mom. Still not happening." Giggling, I sit up and look at the time. Shit. "Hey, Mom, I have to leave for work in like 10 minutes. I will have to talk to you later."

"Ok, baby. I love you lots. Stay safe."

"Love you too, Mom, thank you."

"Anytime, Devy. Bye, baby."

I hang up with my mom and go change my clothes, getting ready for work. I put on my mascara and eye liner and spritz my perfume on.

I shoot a text to Aunt Jilly and tell her I just got off the phone with Mom, and I will have to call her tomorrow now.

I take one last look at myself in the mirror and approve. I stop to snuggle Luna for a bit, then moving over to the island for my purse, I breeze out the door.

Please be a good night.

Chapter 23: Devin

My car starts and 'Half Of Forever' by Henrik is playing. I pull out humming and think about my wonderful boyfriend and how I can tell him 'By the way, I see ghosts now'. Nope, not crazy at all..

Oakley is the sweetest man. I can't believe I was so scared of him in the beginning. The way he cares about me is something every woman wants, so plain facts, I'm scared to lose that.

I know my mom will love Oakley. That's the problem, she will be all up in his business. She will google him and try to find all his social medias. The overprotective momma bear.

I think this is why my brother stays single. He knows what our mom will do.

It doesn't help that she is super duper nosy. She tries to be all nonchalant with it, but she isn't as slick as she thinks she is.

Put her and Aunt Jilly together and you will have a whole family tree and pictures back to kindergarten by the next day.

I share everything with my mom, but I want to keep this to myself. I want to grow as a woman with Oakley and discover who I am on my own. I can give her highlights. Besides, it hasn't even been a week.

This could all go to shit by Christmas. Especially when he learns of my nifty new trick.

Hope you believe in ghosts.

I park in the back of the café and as I'm getting out I look over to the bar. It's not so busy at 3 in the afternoon, but it's gotten to be habit to be so alert out here.

Is it bad that I'm secretly thankful I was attacked so Oakley could save me and be mine?

How fucked up is that thinking?

No one wants to be attacked.

Ehhh, well, maybe. Controlled environment. Role playing.

I guess in a round about way, Clover was semi responsible for getting us together. She will never let me live it down.

I have to mentally prepare for the smug 'I Told You So' she will send my way, blowing a kiss.

After I park, I pull out my phone and text Clover real quick, checking in with her. I feel like she hasn't been to the apartment in like 24 hours. I think she's just with X now constantly. Good for them. I'm happy they get along so well.

While I have my phone out, I snap a selfie with the bar behind me and I send it to Oakley with heart emojis.

He replies with drooling emojis.

I smile to myself as my tummy does a summersault. This man thinks I'm the most beautiful person in the world. He's delusional or truthful. Maybe both. I'm just happy he likes me.

I really think I'm quickly falling in love with him.

I have no idea how this happened so fast. Like this man makes me want to think about marriage and babies. The way he looks at me sometimes. I swear I could get pregnant just from one of his smoldering gazes, or his playboy smiles when he bestows one on me, making me feel like the only woman in the world.

He makes me think of a house in the country, picket fence, flowers everywhere, kids swinging on tire swings, dog in the yard.

I swear to all that's holy, I must be ovulating. Who the hell wants to settle down at 19?

Girl, don't fall for the ovary's trick.

I have been extra clingy and horny today. Up until Britney dropped that bomb on me about my instructor. Up to that point I was daydreaming of Oakley nonstop instead of studying.

I pull open the door then put my apron on, walking in.

Pam greets me at the back door, "I can't wait for you to see." She claps her hands together. Clearly, she's excited about something.

I walk behind the counter, and she leads me up front. There on the counter stands a giant bouquet of blood red roses with a big black lace ribbon.

Oakley.

This is because I told him last night if we were to ever have a sex dungeon, I would want it to be red and black, leather and lace.

He asked me, 'what about blue?' I said it depends on the shade of blue. Then he told me he had something to show me at his dad's house in the future. Not cryptic at all.

"Aren't they gorgeous? Devin, you caught the heart of a good man." Pam rubs my bicep and smiles, looking longingly at the flowers.

"Would you like to keep them here on display?" I slip the card out of its holder and open it,

To my beautiful Kitten,

These make me think of you. Long & Hard.

Love, your Loverboy

I smile to myself and feel myself melting more. Oakley says all the good things. Everything I ever wished for. It's perfect.

"I need tables wiped down after lunch and the dining room area straightened up, please." Pam let me know my duties, and I grab a spray bottle and cloth, and head out to wipe tables and be in my head.

This is not a recipe for an overanalyzing meltdown, sure it's not. Ya know, creating 20 more questions and scenarios to obsess over.

Yes, it is.

I question my very existence most the time so focusing on someone else every once in a while is a treat.

I really ask myself is Oakley too perfect? I have nothing to base what too perfect is except some high school crush. I've never had an adult relationship. Am I even doing this right? What if he gets sick of me?

I'm not complaining about his sweetness. No, I'm leery because all I've ever dealt with is an angsty teenager that hardly paid attention to me unless he wanted to fuck me or grope me.

My mom once told me there are guys that come into your life to teach you how to be a better woman. Then there are guys who teach you your standards to measure the rest after him. Then, there are the guys who stay but don't want to commit. They are waiting on their forever but passing time with you.

Then there are the guys who commit and stay, and love you

with so much passion and fire that the world stands still when you are near them. You are his everything, his anam cara, and he will stop at nothing to keep you his.

She always said to make sure to keep that feeling alive. Make sure to give and take, and work hard at it and learn compromise.

Mom said learn each other's boundaries and be compassionate enough not to push too hard. Communication is key. I feel like we have been doing a lot of communicating lately. Mom said your partner should be your best friend and to keep that friendship thriving.

Then told me not to listen to her since she couldn't keep a marriage working and it ended in divorce.

We had this in-depth conversation when she broke the news to me that she had filed for the divorce. She said she felt like a failure for trusting he was loyal, safe, and loved her.

No one that loves you would ever do what he did.

She said she felt like a fool for believing him and trying so hard to keep him. That he was selfish for not letting her go when he was so glaringly stepping out on his own.

I learned from my parents what I didn't want in a committed relationship. I learn that it must be 50/50 but somedays it might be 10/90, or 75/25. People need grace. Couples pick up where the other can't for that day, either due to illness, depression, or exhaustion. I understand that. But Mom said try to balance everything between you.

My dad never lifted a finger in our house. My mom did everything. Plus worked a full-time job. My whole childhood and through my teen years she seemed happy. There were down days too, but she always hid any serious depression.

She recently came out to me that she has had depression for

years and has been on medication for it. I had no idea. Guess that means her medication is working or she's really good at hiding things from us. I'm going to say both.

I knew my parents had a rocky marriage when I learned from the cookie cutter TV shows that parents are supposed to be lovey dovey towards each other. Now, as I'm older, I realize those were fake situations, but it makes me question, can it actually be like that though?

It's everywhere; in my books, movies, TV shows. There has to be some truth to it. Right? Does happily ever after really exist?

It's the things I pray I get in my life. I'm sure everyone does. Every day, I hope I will one day meet my forever person who will love me the way I need and is worthy of my love back to them.

Granted, it's only been a few days, but I am loving how Oakley treats me. I'm trying to absorb it all in, and learn how I should be treated and never settle for a shitastic marriage like my mother was handed.

As I wipe down tables, take trash out, sweep the floors, I silently ask the Universe 'Is there like a time limit on how long before you know you love someone.' If I had to admit it, I love Oakley. It's really soon but I just know. I feel it in my soul.

As crazy as it sounds, if the man asked me to run away and get married, I would just get into his SUV with the clothes on my back and buckle in, then wait on him to start the engine. I will put my hand in his and I will go wherever he goes.

As long as he wants me.

I would fight the world to keep him, too.

Why can't I want to burn the world for him? Why does it always have to be this alpha male type guy in all my books? Why can't someone like me tear through space and time to keep my man safe?

I will shank a bitch over him.

He's mine.

I've never been one to be jealous. I mean, maybe if I was more jealous my best friend wouldn't have been fucking my boyfriend. I didn't even get mad enough to want to beat her ass. I just cried.

But with Oakley, I get a fire in my gut whenever I think of another woman even touching him. Don't talk to him. Don't breathe near him.

Who knew I was an alpha female over a man?

I chuckle to myself until I hear a voice behind me, "What's so funny?"

I whip around to see a man, much larger than me, standing a little too close for my liking. I size him up and take a step back. He advances.

My mouth goes dry, and my palms start to sweat.

This motherfucker thinks he's going to intimidate me. *Stand your ground, Devin, you are out in public, there are people around.*

I stand up a little straighter and say, "Can I help you?"

Oh, he positively looks like a mean asshole with his smirk and air of defiance. You can tell this guy is used to pushing people around and getting his way. His momma didn't tell him No enough.

He licks his lips while looking me up and down, "I certainly hope so. Can you tell me who Devin is?"

What does this asshole want?

"Depends on what you want."

"That's business between me and her."

He has the audacity to wink at me.

"Well, she isn't here. Care to leave a message for her?"

"Yeah, sure, let her know next time she won't get away."

With that he turns and walks out the door. I just stand there, shocked. What did this cocksucker just say to me?

I run to the door and fly through it. There is no one on the sidewalk, very few cars driving by. It's like he disappeared into thin air.

I quickly walk through the café to the back door and open it and look out. The dying sunlight makes the shades darker and harder to make out shapes and dimension. Dusk is like looking through fog for me but I try to spot anything moving out there.

I don't see any movement. Not even over at the bar.

Pam comes out of her office and takes one look at me, "Devin?"

I look over at her in panic.

"Honey, what's wrong? Come in here and sit down, talk to me."

"There was a man. Young guy. He walked in and asked for me. He just oozed evil. I pretended I wasn't me, I told him I wasn't here. He said to let Devin know she won't get away next time." I feel the panic attack coming on.

"We have to call the police. This is a threat, Devin."

"I don't want to call the police to come here. I don't really know what to think about his words. I can just call the detective who handled the original call. He gave me his number. Can I call him from here?"

"Sure, honey, I will step out. Just let me know how it goes."

Pam pats me on the shoulder as she exits the office. I dig into my purse in the desk drawer and come up with the detective's card with his information. I pull my cell phone from my apron and place the call.

The call went better than I expected. I gave a description of the guy and was told it was pretty smart of me to say I wasn't here.

He also said he feels this was not a random attack based on this visit. I was targeted. They know my name and what I look like. The guy knew I was lying to him.

The detective asked if I knew of anyone who would want to play a cruel joke on me who knew of the attempted abduction. I let him know there is no one that I can think of.

Sure, a whole patio full of drunk people saw it, but I've told no one it was me except for those close to me. Unless, Oakley told a bunch of people, not a lot would know of this. Word could have gotten out, I mean Mr. Beasley knew somehow, but after thinking too hard on it, I still came up with no names of possible people wanting to play a joke on me.

Is it even safe for me to leave my apartment anymore? I sure as shit can't come to work and be safe. That's been proven twice.

I don't know if I should be terrified or pissed off? Because right now I'm both.

"Is everything ok?" Pam comes up to me and lays her hand on my arm, "If you need to go home, I understand. I can stay until 6 to cover."

"I would appreciate that. I would like to go home and call Oakley. I'm having feelings about not being safe."

"I completely understand. If there's anything I can do, please don't hesitate to call me."

"Thank you, Pam, you are always so sweet to me, and I appreciate it." I give her a genuine hug. She hugs me back with one of her tight mom hugs.

"Go get some rest, honey."

I grab my purse from the office and ask Pam, "Do you think you could watch me go to my car, please?"

"Yes I can, absolutely."

"Thanks." I open the back door and see the flood lights come on from my movement. I walk to my car and unlock it. I slide in and start it up.

I curse the season change for the dying sunlight so early now.

Chapter 24: Devin

I want to sit and cry in my car but I cannot sit out here in the dark behind the shop. I can cry like a big girl when I get home. For now, get the fuck out of here.

I put the car in drive, and head home. I keep checking my rearview mirror to see if anyone is following me but I don't see anyone.

My plan is to call Oakley after I get home. I'm at the stoplight and 'Freak Like Me' by NoMBe has been playing. How very fitting. So fitting I snort and roll my eyes. The Universe has jokes.

I'm going to have to tell Oakley about Britney soon. That's all there is to it. Hopefully Britney has an address I can call the police with.

If not, I'm following Mr. Beasley to wherever he's going tonight.

Is that the best plan? Probably not.

Is it the safest plan? Hell no.

Will Oakley be mad? Most definitely.

I still have to google Mr. Beasley to see if I can get an address or any dirt. He's not leaving for another couple of hours. I have some time to kill.

Setting out a pair of black leggings and a plain black t-shirt, I get ready for my recon mission. I pull out a sheer mesh black bra and matching panties set. Because if I die I want to have pretty underwear on. I get on my knees and look under my bed for my tennis shoes.

This is when Britney decides to reappear in the doorway and scare the shit out of me. Again. Making me almost piss myself. I see that's the reaction my body is going to have when a ghost pops up to scare me. Perfect.

"DEVIN!"

"Jesus, fuck Britney!" I sit up and grab my chest. "We have to work on how you get my attention!" I damn near yell at her.

"Oh my God Devin, it's so bad." She starts sobbing again. My mind drifts to old castles and the crying ghost ladies of the lakes or lighthouses. I swear to all the holy fucks, I better not get stuck with this crying ass ghost. I'm trying to be as sympathetic as possible here.

I stand up, and put my shoes on my bed, walking over to a set of double doors that's my closet and ask, "What? What happened?" I'm in my closet grabbing a black hoodie and trying to pick between two different ones.

"Please," she begs, "They have my sister," she sobs.

My head snaps over to her. "I'm so sorry, Britney."

"I keep going back to the house to check on her. She's still there with the others, but one of the men said they are going to be moved Saturday night. I have to get her out of there before then." Her hands are over her eyes as she cries.

I walk over to the spirit, "Hey, hey, it's ok. We'll think of something. Don't cry." It's not like I can hug her, or even touch her to give comfort.

I get an idea.

It's now or never.

"I think I have a solution for at least one thing." I pick up my phone and call Oakley. As soon as I hit call my stomach drops out of my ass from nerves.

This could potentially ruin everything we have built so far. It could be a deal breaker. It's going to rip my heart out if that happens. I'm so invested in him already.

He answers on the first ring, "Hello, Kitten."

I try not to word vomit as I rush out, "Hi babe!" God, I sound so nervous. "Can you do me a favor? Can you come over here so I can show you something, and if you think I'm crazy I will accept that. Just know I had the time of my life with you."

"Devin. What? Say that again."

"I just need to talk to you, but you have to be here for me to do it, please. I promise I will explain."

"Uhh, you're scaring me baby, what's wrong?"

I feel like I'm totally butchering this. I let out a sigh.

"I'm getting my shoes on now, Devin."

"Oakley, I'm safe, I'm ok, I just need some assistance right now. Don't drive breakneck speed getting over here. Be cool. That's about as cryptic as I can get," and then I giggle, of all things.

Oakley says, "I'm headed to my car, give me 10 minutes, I'll be there."

"Thank you, babe. See ya when you get here."

I hang up the phone and look at Britney. She is idly picking at her sweatshirt. "Hey, I will try this. I will explain and hope he doesn't think I'm crazy. But I'm not going to that house without him or the police. Final."

Britney looks at the floor and nods her head slowly, "I understand. I'm sorry I couldn't get an address today. The house nor the street are marked with anything."

I nod my head and say, "Can I leave my room now? I'd love to go make me some tea. Can you stick around though? I'm going to need you to try like hell to get him to believe me. Start throwing things if you can."

"Why? You didn't notice."

"Fair enough, but I also wasn't aware or knew to look for it. Now can you please move so I can slide by."

She disappears like poof and I walk out of my room. It always amazes me she can just poof and reappear somewhere else. I'd like that gift, without the being dead and all. Maybe then I wouldn't be late to things.

I start fixing my tea, then use the restroom. After I finish I change into my black 'robber' ensemble. As I put my shoes on there is a buzz from the bottom door.

I look at Britney and say, "Stay here."

I go down the stairs and unlock the bottom door and let Oakley in. He has this very protective vibe rolling off him as he takes up the entire door frame. He immediately rushes to me and puts his hand on my face, turning my head this way and that, looking me over with worried eyes.

Putting my hand on his, I smile at me, "I'm ok, I promise." I lean up on tippy toes and kiss him. "Come on."

Once we are back in the apartment, my tea has finished steeping, I look at him and say, "Ok, I'm sorry to make you worry. Let's sit on the couch."

Oakley comes over to the couch, never taking his eyes off me. He sits down and faces me with his back straight.

Taking the seat next to him, I look over with trepidation, and start with, "What I'm about to say may make you think I'm crazy. It's not something I talk to people about. So, here goes." I spread my hands wide over my lap, "My mom, she can talk to ghosts. She can hear them and see them. I've been with her while she goes to people's houses and speaks to their ghosts. I was skeptical at first, but it's real. I swear to you on my life, it's real."

I nervously finger the fringe on the throw pillow while I look at him. This is the moment I dread.

Looking him in the eye, "I just learned 2 days ago I can do it too when a girl named Britney Lyons showed herself to me and spoke to me."

Please don't run.

Oakley is staring at me with his mouth partially open, absorbing every word I say.

I wait for him to say anything and when he doesn't, I continue, "She was one of the girls that have disappeared from the schools. There are others being held. One is her sister. She wants me to go to the house where..."

Oakley finally speaks, interrupting me, "No. No, Devin, you are not going to that house."

He stands up and runs his fingers through his hair. He puts his fingers to the bridge of his nose for a second. Oakley looks over at me, "You absolutely cannot go there by yourself. I will take you. On one condition, we bring my gun and X."

I stand up, facing him, across the length of the couch. I'm so nervous. "That's why I called you, to ask you to take me. I told Britney I was not doing this without you, or the police."

"For the record, I vote for calling the police and giving them the address. Let them do their job, Devin."

Taking a few hesitant steps to him, I say, "That's the problem, Britney doesn't know the address. There are no street signs and no house numbers. She only knows the way to the house by sight." My eyes tear up, "The police aren't going to believe me anyways, they'll laugh at me."

He's been pacing from the kitchen to the living room. He finally stops and looks at me, "Wow. This is a lot to take in, Devin." And continues into the kitchen with his arms up over his head, with his hands on his neck, hissing out a breath. "I mean I've never really thought about believing in ghosts. I've had no reason to."

My tears overflow. He thinks I'm a freak. Or I'm crazy. Or I'm just making shit up for attention.

I barely speak loud enough in a thick voice full of emotion, "You don't have to take me, I will go to the police and hope they believe me. I know this all sounds crazy, I understand if you want to leave," I half sob, "me."

He jerks around and looks horrified to see me crying. Oakley takes the few steps to me. He reaches up to cup my face, and wipe my tears away, "Hey, baby....heyy...I believe you Devin, I believe every word you said. I don't think you're crazy."

He holds my face in his hands and kisses my lips, then my nose, and my cheeks. Oakley leans back then kisses them again, "Devin..baby...have a little bit more faith in me, baby. I'm not going anywhere, ok." He keeps wiping the fresh tears away.

I sob and my body jerks. He pulls me into his chest and holds me tight. He kisses the top of my head while my arms come up around him and I cry.

I cry because I am so scared of this new gift. I'm terrified he will leave me. I'm scared of what this ghost wants to show me and is asking me to do.

Oakley is rubbing my back and petting my hair, softly murmuring in my ear, "It's ok....I'm here for you...not going anywhere without you...you're my baby...I'm not letting you go....shhhh baby."

My crying subsides to a hiccup. He steps back and holds me out in front of him, "Are you ok now?"

I slowly nod.

"Use words Devin. I need to know how you feel." He runs his fingers through my hair to brush it from my face.

My voice cracks when I say, "I'm scared."

"I'm scared too, but we will get through this together. We'll see what we can do."

"I called my mom; she made me promise not to go there alone." Technically, I won't be alone.

"You won't be alone. If I had it my way you wouldn't go at all, period, but we need someone to tell us what your ghost says. I'm here with you every step of the way."

I look up at him through my wet lashes, "How did I get so lucky?"

Oakley lovingly wipes my cheeks off with his hands, "No Devin, I'm the lucky one. This is just another speedbump to test us." He tilts my chin up, "This is one more thing to love about you."

I smile at him, and sniffle.

"Come on, you have tea getting cold."

He gently pulls me to him and leads me into the kitchen. I immediately grab for tissues, turning to me, he says, "I'm going downstairs to call X real quick. I'll be back up in a few minutes."

He kisses my forehead and goes to the door, and then I hear his footfalls as he goes downstairs.

"That went better than I thought it would." Britney says brightly as she walks into the living room from my bedroom.

Motherfuck! "Look, we are going to have to establish some boundaries here. You can be with us here right now, and when we go to this place you want, but when it's me and him time, I need you not around. I can't constantly be thinking I'm being watched. And for fuck's sake, knock or something to announce your arrival."

Britney floats off back into my bedroom. I probably hurt her feelings, but it's important I set this boundary.

How did my mom ever put up with this shit?

I have a new respect for her. This shit is bananas to get used to! Britney popping up wherever and whenever she wants is going to make me too paranoid to function properly on a day-to-day basis.

I'm already paranoid enough.

One crisis at a time, Dev. The most pressing thing is helping the spirit to save these girls.

I finish my tea and rinse out my cup as Oakley comes back into the apartment.

"X is down to go." He faces me and puts his thumb on his lips, "Have you talked to Clover today?"

I shrug, "No, I don't think so."

"When was the last time you heard from her?"

"I-I don't know. Let me look. Why? What's happening?" I grab my phone and go to my message thread with Clover.

"X has not heard from her since yesterday evening. She was

supposed to text him when she got home from work. He thought she was ghosting him today. He is at Kitty's right now to see her and Clover hasn't shown up for her shift. She's almost two hours late."

"Oh God, I last talked to her yesterday about 3 when she canceled on Wednesday night Mexican. I texted her this morning, but she didn't answer me. I thought she had stayed with X."

I set my phone down and yell, "Britney!!! Britney come here!"

She comes from my bedroom, doing her float walking. It looks bizarre but I don't say anything about it.

I rush up to her, "When was the last time you were at that house?"

"It was earlier today."

I run over to the fridge, I snatch the picture off the front and quickly walk over to Britney, "Is the girl in this photo there?" My hands are shaking as I show her the picture.

Britney looks at the playful photo of me and Clover, her arm around me and us laughing. It was from the day I moved in.

"Yes, I heard the girls talking, she got there last night."

The sob catches in my throat, "Oh God, oh God. Nooo."

"What is she saying?" Oakley asks me, placing a hand on my shoulder.

"Britney says Clover got there last night." I put my hands over my eyes to hold in the tears.

I start crying again holding our picture to my chest. Oakley reaches over and holds me up. He puts his arm around my shoulders and another arm under my knees and picks me up. He carries me to the couch and holds me tight against his chest. Oakley slowly starts rocking me and petting the side of my head, holding me to his shoulder.

A knock at the door and Oakley is calling, "It's open" knowing it had to be X.

X walks through the door and he appears justifiably upset. Oakley says, "Devin just talked to the spirit, and she confirmed they have Clover at that house."

X pales and says, "No, no, fuck!" He pulls his Glock 21 out from behind him, out of his waistline. "When are we leaving? I brought my piece you asked for."

I look up at Britney by Clover's bedroom door. "Can you find it in the dark?"

Britney starts sobbing, "No, I don't think I can, I can't really see in the dark, that's why I go during the day."

I relay to the guys and X says, "Fuck that. We have to try. Tell her we have to try, Devin. Please, we have to." X brings his pleading eyes to mine.

"Britney can you please try it tonight? We still have some daylight."

"I'll try." She looks hesitant but with enough pushing I think we can manage. We are losing daylight though.

"Thank you. We can leave as soon as I grab my phone and purse."

I hurry into my bedroom to grab my purse, phone off the charger, and grab the hoodie.

"We are stopping by my apartment first," Oakley says as he nods to X.

Chapter 25: Devin

"Britney, how long are you able to stay with us tonight?" I ask as I walk from my room to the kitchen.

"I don't know. I will stay as long as I can. I promise, Devin." She gives me a small smile and crosses her fingers in front of her for luck. "If I feel wonky, I will let you know, if I can. Let's hope for the best."

Suddenly I stop walking in the middle of the living room, "W-Wait, there was something else I needed to tell you!" I proceeded to explain the strange guy's visit and what he said to me.

I have never seen Oakley angry. I watch rage spill over and fill him up.

"Why didn't you call me from the café to come get you?" His hands are fisting by his sides.

"I didn't think of it. I was handling it. Until I wasn't." I say softly.

Oakley stares at the floor with his eyes closed for a few seconds. "Thank you for telling me. Let's go." He holds his hand out to me.

I know this has got to be overwhelming for him. He's handling this like a rockstar.

He doesn't look as mad, but he still looks like he wants to murder someone. I guess I didn't expect him to go alpha male on me.

"There's one other thing." I watch his eyebrows shoot up as he looks me. I tell him and X about Mr. Beasley and his involvement, and my plan to follow him.

Ok, now he looks enraged.

Maybe I shouldn't have said that.

I expect him to yell. I know it's coming. He simply nods, presses his lips together, and holds out his hand again.

Not even a second of hesitation, I slip my hand in his and say, "Come on, Britney."

As we drive towards the city limits, Oakley watches me in the rearview mirror. I'm sitting in the back seat with Britney. They didn't want to take a chance on anyone seeing me since I was a target. Plus, X didn't want to sit in the back with a ghost.

I totally agree. I'm still trying to get used to being around her and not be creeped out.

We stopped by Oakley's apartment. Oakley changed his clothes, and he and X are now locked and loaded. I've never been around so many guns. I didn't even know Oakley owned any.

Apparently, he told me while he changed, him and his dad are avid hunters and enjoy going to the shooting range. X used to tag along with them when he could. X advised me while Oakley was using the bathroom that Oakley did competition shooting and is an excellent marksman.

Well, alrighty then. That's a hell of a lot better than me who's never had to fire a gun. Never once crossed my mind to take the bat with me either. I really am out here trying to get myself killed.

Britney has done amazingly well directing us so far. Being from around here, I know the area better than X and Oakley but once we are further out of town, those are roads less travelled for me. We are traveling east out of town and it's starting to be more country, rolling hills and open fields. The houses are much further apart and some of the side roads are gravel and red dirt.

Unfortunately, the sun is setting very quickly this time of year. Oakley is flying over the speed limits as Clemetville gets further behind us. We need the light until we get there so Britney can keep giving directions. I don't know what the plan is if we can't find it tonight.

Personally, I feel sick to my stomach. Really though, what if we can't find it?

I have already made up my mind, if we can't find it tonight, I am going to the police in the morning. I will beg them to believe me and then I will have Britney lead us out to the house, even if it takes all day.

So far, we are trusting a ghost to lead us to the right house. I pray she knows what she's doing. This is my first circus, so I don't know shit.

I just know this is fucked up shit.

Britney looks over and says, "There is a road to the right, by a barn, take it." I relay the directions to Oakley.

We are roughly about 40 minutes outside of town in bum fuck. Darkness is coming quicker now.

"Turn left at the stop sign. Then there's a gravel road to the right, take that road. There is a house down there on the right side. They are kept there."

I let Oakley know we are close and give him the rest of the directions. I look around and see there is absolutely nothing in this area. This is the perfect spot to hold kidnapped girls. No one can hear them scream. There is no one around to pay attention to the comings and goings of the captors.

"Ask her if it's the only house on the road."

Britney nods. "She says yes."

Oakley looks over at X, "This is a complication."

"What's wrong?" I scoot closer to the front seats to hear better.

"They are going to see us coming," X says. "If there is one house then why would someone else be coming down that road."

"Good point." I can't put those details together right now, thankfully he did.

We slowly ease our way onto the road and kill the lights. There is a hill in front of us and you can't see the house from here. Which means as long as the lights are off, they can't see us either.

"We are going to park below this hill and walk up."

"NO! No, please! Don't Oakley. No, l-let me send Britney in." I look over to Britney, "I need you to go get the layout of the house, tell me how many girls and what room, and how many captors are there, and where they are. Look for guns too and any booby traps."

"Ok, got it." And poof.

Oakley turns around in his seat. "If she's there, we are going in. You are going to stay here. I need you to use your location on your phone to see where we are and call 911. You're going to sit in the driver's seat, and I will call you when I need you to bring the car. That is your only involvement."

"But I can…"

Oakley cuts me off, "No. You're staying in this car. It's not up for negotiation."

I don't know what to do but sit back there in the silence and pout. I am out of my element here. I feel like I could be of use rescuing Clover and the other girls. But I also know I could potentially be in the way and fuck this whole thing up.

Trust me, I know he wants to protect me, but I want to be helpful.

Communication is key.

"I want to be more helpful somehow." I honestly admit.

Oakley reaches out his hand to me in the dark. Naturally, my hand slips into it. I would follow him into Hell. Which is quite possibly what I'm doing now.

"Baby, we wouldn't know Clover was there, or where the house was if it wasn't for you and your gift. None of this rescue is possible without you. Let me and X deal with the rest, ok? I can't be worried about you right beside me while I'm going up to that house. Do this for me." I hear the pleading in his voice.

I hate when men use logic on us.

"Ok, I'll stay in the car and be the getaway driver."

"That's my good girl." He kisses the inside of my wrist, which sends off a flight of butterflies in my core.

I see Britney appear beside the SUV staring at me, effectively scaring me shitless. AGAIN.

This is really getting on my damn nerves. She could have just walked to the damn car so I could have seen her approaching so as not to scare me. I will never be like this when I'm a ghost haunting someone like me. I'll be a cool ghost. And I won't manipulate living people to do what I want.

She floats into the car. "There are four girls, in a back bedroom, far left corner of the house. Clover is one of them. There is one window, very back wall, boarded up."

I relay all the instructions to Oakley and Britney continues, "There are two guys, your guys' sizes and ages, they're in the front room. They do have guns on the coffee table in front of them. They are drinking beer and watching TV. I think they are the babysitters."

Oakley asks X if he's ready and they nod to each other, getting out of the vehicle. I get out too and try to keep from jumping up and down. I'm so scared and nervous I'm shaking.

I come around to the driver's side and hop into the seat. Oakley is right there to buckle me in. He reaches in and grabs my face with one hand, squeezing my cheeks, and pulls my face to his, kissing me hard on my puckered lips.

"I mean it Dev, stay here and call the police." I see the intensity in his eyes. I know this is a direct order and I should obey, but part of me just wants to tell him No and go anyways. That's the part I have to tell to shut the fuck up and go sit down.

Oakley goes to the back hatch and opens it, reaching in for his balaclava and hands a looping of rope to X and takes one for himself. They both have Glocks strapped to their sides in their holsters. X insisted on rope. I'm surprised they don't have a grenade tossed in a pocket somewhere. Maybe they do in their arsenal I have yet to see.

Before he closes the back door, he looks at me where I'm turned around, "Start finding out where we are, baby." He throws one last air kiss at me and softly shuts the back hatch, then jogs around the SUV to stand by the hill X is looking over. They speak briefly and start walking towards the house.

I pull up my phone and ask, "Where am I?"

I watch the circle goes round and round, trying to find me with barely any service.

Under my breath I urge the circle to spin faster, "Come on, please, find me, hurry."

Britney is sitting in the front passenger seat chewing on her ghostly nails. Do they even grow back?

Finally, an address pops up. I punch in 911 and hit the green icon.

As soon as the operator answers I rattle off who I am and then I'm giving the address and telling them it's near this address as I am parked down the road, that it's the only house on the road, and that the missing girls from Clemetville and Clemson are held captive inside. The operator says they know of the road I'm talking about and has someone on the way. I stay on the phone and give more details.

I give them my name again, spell it out, and I verify the call back number.

I see headlights pulling onto the road behind the SUV, and tell the 911 operator, "Wow, that was fast, there's already a car pulling up." I roll down the window as the car is approaching and see it is indeed not a police vehicle. But it's too late.

I vaguely hear the operator say, "That's not us, we aren't there yet ma'am."

I watch as a man gets out of the car and looks through the window at me. I'm doe in headlights, stunned.

The 911 operator is asking me what's happening. I can only whisper as the horrified realization sinks in, "Mr. Beasley is here and he's one of the captors. He's my geometry teacher."

I hurry to roll the window back up. Why the fuck does it take so long for automatic windows to come up? Britney is freaking out and screaming, what for I don't know, she's already dead. We need to worry about me.

Mr. Beasley reaches into his car and pulls out a tire iron. He busts the passenger side window open in one hit. I do start screaming then as he reaches in and tries to open the door.

I drop the phone trying to fend him off, slapping at his hands and trying to punch his face. Of course, I do nothing to him with my weak hits compared to his strength.

Suddenly, his hand reaches around his back and pulls out a gun from his waistband and aims it directly at my head through the window.

I immediately stop all movement.

Jesus. Tap dancing. Christ.

He gets the door open and says, "What do we have here?" as he gives me an evil smile.

I have never in my life stared down the barrel of a gun, but this is my current situation right now. My whole body has been shaking hard and fear has wrapped around my body, holding it hostage. I'd rather deal with another ghost than this madman.

Speaking of ghosts, Britney is trying her damndest to beat the shit out of him, but her tiny fists are going right through him.

In all my insanity, I try hard not to giggle at her puny attack. I'm a maniac, too , apparently.

Focus. Gun. Madman.

Mr. Beasley gets into the passenger side with the gun still aimed at me and says, "Drive up to the next house, Devin, we are going for a visit."

I start the car as he shuts the door. I put the car in drive and crest the hill, seeing the old farmhouse on the right side of the road, with lights on. Just as Britney said it was.

I can only pray X and Oakley are seeing this. They have to know I'm not going against the plan willingly. Please don't let them shoot me.

"This is seriously fucked up. Why are you doing this?" I ask, trying to keep my composure. On the inside I am freaking the fuck out. I'm also pissed that he has a gun on me. I want to rip his face off. But stay away and cower because he has a fucking gun.

"There is a lot of money to be had in human trafficking," he sneers at me. "You're too thick to fetch a really high price like your tiny friend will, but I still need a number to fulfill the bargain."

"You're disgusting." I said with as much venom as I can muster in this terrified state.

"And you're going to be sold to the highest bidder. I hope they like chunky girls," and then he starts laughing.

I've never wanted to kill some before, but this cocksucker, I would gladly take out. No remorse had. No fucks given.

We arrive at the farmhouse, and he says, "Stop the car over there, park in the front yard. Yeah, over there." He points to a clear spot in the yard. I pull up parallel with the house, and park down in the front yard.

Once I park the car, he says, "Put your hands on the steering wheel where I can see them. Don't even think about doing anything stupid because I will have this gun trained on you. They want you alive but that doesn't mean I can't hurt you first."

I hold my hands up and watch him quickly walk around to the driver's side and yank open the door. He reaches in and tries to pull me out, repeatedly. He keeps tugging on me until I finally scream, "I'm buckled in, you asshole."

I undo the buckle and as soon as I do, he pulls me from Oakley's SUV and I land on the ground, hard, face planting into a concrete sidewalk. I'm screaming for him to leave me alone. I roll onto my back as the wind is knocked out of me from him kicking my ribs.

I look up and he still has the gun pointed at me, "Get up, Devin."

You know how they say your life flashes before your eyes, what they really mean is everything you hold dear, and that love starts flashing. The love of everything you find joy in and all the happiness. The good ooey gooey, squishy parts of life. It's like pictures flashing quickly through an album. My mom, Oakley, Luna, Clover, Aunt Jilly, David. Enough for me to sob.

I don't want to die here, but I refuse to let him take me. There has to be a way out of this.

I hear the 911 operator yelling from the phone on the floorboard. I scream, "HELP ME!" Hoping Oakley and X have also been alerted.

I hope they shoot this motherfucker.

I usually don't condone violence but this time I'm totally on board.

Please don't get any brain matter on me, boys.

Mr. Beasley fires the gun into the ground right next to my legs where I'm lying when I don't move and it makes me scream louder.

Jesus, fuck. OK! I scramble to stand up.

I feel like I'm going to be sick or pass out. I can't stop. I have to think of a plan. I feel it in my bones, Oakley and X are waiting to shoot this fat fuck and I have to be out of the way. Wherever the boys are, they can't get to Mr. Beasley because I'm in the way. *Find a way to get them a clear shot, Devin.*

"Get moving into the house, Devin, or I will be forced to shoot you for real next time." I can't walk into that house. Fuck him.

My eyes narrow on him as I say, "The cops are on the way, you aren't getting away with this."

Behind him, I see Britney in my peripheral vision, standing there pointing to the side of the house frantically. I don't dare look over, so he doesn't see my eye movement.

I have to just hope it's Oakley lined up to shoot this psychotic son of a bitch.

I start walking to the house while he is behind me, pointing the gun at my head, pushing my head forward with it. I have 5 seconds to pull this plan off.

I've had the time of my life with you.

Suddenly, I pretend to fall, and quickly drop to the ground. It was enough.

A shot rings out as I'm sitting on my scuffed up knees with my hands over my head, screaming again.

In the echo of the gunfire I hear Oakley yelling, "DEVIN!" It sounds like a roar, and before I can scream anymore, I hear his boots coming closer very quickly.

I don't even have time to look up as Oakley pulls me up off the ground and crushes me close to his chest. "Oh my God Devin, are you ok?"

His scent that I have grown to love, wraps around me like a cozy blanket and makes me feel safe again. "Yeah," it sounds weak coming from me. I can't get my heart rate down and I feel like I'm going to pass out.

I hear and feel his chest rumble, "Devin..Devin."

He pats me down to find any injuries, and then holds me away from him to assess anything else. He doesn't find anything serious; I just have scratches and bruises, my face and ribs hurt really bad though. "Baby, oh my God, are you sure you're ok?" Oakley looks terrified, pissed, enraged, concerned; all of those combined and then he turns my head this way and that way, looking at my face in the light from the SUV headlights. I imagine my face looks rough. I feel the road rash on it stinging and burning already.

"Yeah, yeah, I am, I swear." I try nodding my head, but he has my face tightly between his hands, and then kisses my forehead as he wraps me in his arms again.

"Jesus, fuck. What happened? Where did this fucker come from?" X demands, standing by Oakley.

I pull back to look at Mr. Beasley. He's laying prone on the ground with X over him and a gun trained on his back. There's blood staining the side of his shirt.

"Is he dead?" I ask. I've never seen a dead body.

"No, I shot him in the side, he's just passed out." Oakley kicks him in the leg and Mr. Beasley just wobbles back and forth but doesn't wake up. "Are the cops on their way?"

"Yes, they are. I did get to call them, and I thought the car pulling onto the road was them but it was Mr. Beasley. Weird as fuck. Oh God Oakley, he busted out your window to get to me. He pointed a gun at me, and I had no choice but to let him into the car. I'm so sorry, I didn't have a choice."

"Devin, it's ok baby, you did the right thing."

In the distance you can hear the sirens coming closer. Out here in the country you can hear them approaching from over a mile away.

I've read enough books to know to say this, I look between

Oakley and I, and over to X, "They are going to separate us and ask questions, I'm going to tell them the truth. Their laughing at me be damned. They are going to want to know how we knew to come here. I'm going to tell them about Britney and then tell them I called police while you went to see if this was the right place and see if Clover was here."

I look over at X and back to Oakley, "Is Clover here? Are there others? What's happening inside?" My mind finally remembers why we came here. Shock has addled my brain.

"We've already tied up the other two guys that are here and took their guns. We only had time to get them tied up and then you pulled in. The girls are still locked in the house."

I break free of Oakley's hold, and I take off running towards the house, yelling for Clover, as the police are cresting the first hill almost a mile away. I reach the front door and hear screaming and crying from a bedroom in the back. They are banging on the door.

I don't even pay attention to the two guys hog tied on the floor, yelling. I follow the screams, and I run up to a closed bedroom door, and there's a deadbolt on the door and the handle is turned inside out. I bang on the door wailing, "CLOVER!"

I hear her yelling from inside, "DEVIN! OH MY GOD! DEVIN!"

I unlock the door handle and get fucking lucky as hell that the key is inserted into the deadbolt. I turn the key and throw open the door. As soon as I have the door open, Clover tackles me in a hug, knocking me against the wall behind me, and dragging us to the floor. We sit there sobbing and holding each other.

I pet her hair, and she grips my hoodie while she shakes in sobs. I hold her while looking over her head into the room. It's dark but there's a small light on in a corner, and I see 3 other girls. They are unsure of me and that's completely understandable.

I pat Clover on the back while rubbing intermittently, as the sirens' wails draw closer. The sirens are loud as fuck and you can see the blue and red lights flashing throughout the house as they come up the final yards to the house.

I let out a deep sigh and tell the girls, "We are not the bad guys, they are tied up out there and another one is on the ground shot. The police were called."

"How did you find us?" a short girl with dirty blond hair asks from the doorway.

"Britney."

"No, impossible, Britney Lyons is dead. I watched him break her neck from his fist. Don't lie." She puts her hands on her hips.

"My sister Britney?" asks a girl about 14 years old. When the light hits her face, you can tell this is Britney's sister as they look almost identical.

"I can see ghosts; I can see and hear them. Britney came to me, and she showed us the way here. Britney is the hero."

I look over my right shoulder, down the hallway, and Britney is standing there wiping her ghost tears away in flashing red and blue police lights.

"DEVIN!" Oakley is making his way into the house. I hear his boots thudding through the house on his way back here. He sees me on the floor and immediately drops to one knee, "Are you ok?"

"Yeah, Clover tackled me." I offer a half smile of gratitude.

"We quickly told the cops what went down and ran in here. They are starting to swarm the place, let's get you girls up and out of here."

Clover hears Oakley and turns around and hugs him too.

We briefly hear men's voices calling to the tied up guys on the floor of the living room. Oakley yells back to the officers that we are all back here in the hallway.

I hear X yelling over them, running through the house towards us, "CLOVER!!"

"X, oh X, I'm right here." Clover starts rising off the floor by Oakley picking her up and pulling her past him in the hallway, just as X rounds the corner. X runs up to Clover and wraps his arms around her, and Clover jumps into his arms, wrapping her legs around his waist, sobbing into his neck.

You can softly hear him talking to her, not loud enough to make it out. Whatever it is makes her cry more and hold him tighter, if possible.

He puts her against the wall and kisses her, and she hangs on to him for dear life.

Oakley puts his outstretched hand out to help me up. Once I stand up, he pulls me to his chest and lovingly holds me.

I love this man.

There is no doubt in my mind.

Chapter 26: Oakley

I can't let go of her standing in the hallway.. I know I have a vice grip on her. Fuck. This has scared the shit out of me.

Devin slowly pulls out of my arms and looks into the bedroom, "Do y'all want to come out here with us? The police are here, and they're going to want to talk to you immediately and check you out."

"Oakley?" an officer calls out.

"Back here." I yell.

Clover drops out of X's arms as the officer rounds the hallway with a flashlight. His light lands on each of our faces, and then he shines it into the open doorway, onto the missing girls' faces.

He speaks into a radio on his shoulder, letting them know the girls are here in a back room.

"You guys can all go wait outside and give reports please." He stands back as we all file past him. I'm sure he is going to search the room for any more scared girls. I hear him start talking to the girls in the room, assuring them they are safe now and can come out.

There are officers in the living room waiting on us, some are waiting at the end of the hall for us to move out of the house. I lead Devin outside, right behind Clover and X. An officer walks up to us and asks us to follow him over to an ambulance. As we are following, another officer joins us.

Walking over, I finally notice there are three ambulances parked out front and 4 police cruisers. Lights are flashing everywhere. There are uniformed officers walking all over the place. There are two more cars with lights coming up the dirt road.

EMTs get Devin into the ambulance, and she starts telling the two officers who escorted us, in detail, how she ended up here, and then I heard firsthand how she ended up arriving here at this house before the planned call.

It took everything in me to not take that motherfucker's life when I had him lined up. One shot. He is very lucky.

My split second of hesitation bought me time. Time to spend with her, not in a prison cell.

As soon as I saw that SUV's headlights crest the hill, I knew something was very wrong. Devin knew how serious this was, she wouldn't come without being told to.

And when I heard her screaming while I was in the house.

Her screams of fear kicked a primal feeling of rage within me, white heat thrummed through my veins, and I wanted to watch the life drained from this asshole's eyes. No regrets.

I hesitated and decided shooting him in the side would do for now, and still cause pain to him while saving her. I hope it gets infected, and he dies a slow painful death.

He got one shot off from his gun when the bullet hit his side, but Devin was already falling to the ground out of the path of his gun when it rang out. I couldn't take my shot until she was out of the way. No way was I jeopardizing her life like that.

After we all gave statements, and both girls were checked out by EMTs, we were allowed to leave. It made for a chilly ride back to Clemetville, because the window was busted, and the temperature has dropped into a chilly autumn night.

Devin sat up front with me, holding my hand. Every once in a while, I'll pull her hand up to my lips and kiss the back of her hand. It sends jolts to my dick every time it makes her sigh in contentment.

X has not let go of Clover since he first saw her. She is asleep in his lap while he pets her hair. She had said she hadn't slept and didn't eat, so we stopped at the closest fast-food place and fed her. After she ate the last fry, she promptly passed out.

She said she was walking to her car after her shift at the bar and someone came up behind her and grabbed her, effectively putting a gloved hand over her mouth to silence her. They then got her into the back of a van and took off. The only other person besides the attacker was a driver, who also had on a black balaclava.

Clover said she kicked and tried to hit them every chance she got but it was no use. They quickly overpowered her.

She told us about being thrown into that room with the other stolen girls, and when she sat up, scratched and bruised, she seen how many were there with her, and it broke her heart. Clover said she got to know some of the girls over the course of today. They had nothing to do locked in the room, so they talked, they plotted, and they cried.

X plans on staying at the girls' apartment with Clover tonight. I expect nothing less.

Devin said she could grab a to-go bag and stay with me to give them some privacy, if it was alright with me. Of fucking course it's alright.

219

I will never pass up an opportunity to hold her all night. Fuck, hold her, period. Any part of her. Maybe she will do that wiggle back into me move she likes so well.

When I thought I was never going to kiss her again, hold her, hear her laughter, the pang in my chest took my breath away. I thought I would die right then if that motherfucker shot her.

My dad has always told me, "Son, you will know when 'The One' walks into your life. You will feel it at a spiritual level and your body will recognize them as yours. You will know. She will consume your life."

I am confident I've found my 'One' and already know it, I don't know how, but my body just knows deep inside me, she is the one. I've already talked myself out of proposing to her so soon.

One thing is crystal clear, Devin is mine.

And I will shoot a man over her.

No fucks given about that man.

Do not come for my woman.

Far as I'm concerned, all three of them pieces of shit would be dead in a perfect world. It was hard to let them live.

That kind of restraint is god like.

Once X and I scouted the area and seen the two idiots in the living room, we just kicked in the wooden front door, moved fast as lightning, and knocked them the fuck out before they could even reach for their guns.

We scarcely got them tied up, before we heard the Maserati's car door open. He was already on the driver's side by the time we got out there and Devin was screaming. We had gone out the side door and hid in the overgrown bushes on the side of the house. The vantage point wasn't the greatest, but we were limited on time and options.

Then I see this motherfucker aiming a gun at MY girl. And she's screaming. And he fucking shot the ground where she laid.

I'm not sure what level of fear and rage that put me on but it was murderous.

He would have died then if he hadn't been holding a gun on her. I was not taking a chance on him firing when I hit him.

Even right now, driving down the road, I have to mentally calm myself down. Take a deep breath, it's over. I am probably never going to get the sound of Devin screaming out of my head.

I have to remind myself she's right here, she's ok, she's safe.

It makes me grip her hand a little tighter.

I thought my whole world was collapsing when I seen him jerk her in front of him. I just needed a split second. I prayed under my breath, 'Devin, give me an opening, baby.'

She was an absolute genius in fake falling. Brave as fuck, too. It gave me the kill strike moment. Then I hesitated from the fear of going to prison. I almost missed it by having a moral dilemma. So he got a superficial shot. He won't die from it. Unfortunately.

She's here now, that's what matters to me most. I'm proud of her for how she handled herself.

I park in front of the girls' apartment, by the curb. I watch X gently wake up Clover and she immediately grabs on to him when she wakes up. I think my best friend might have found his 'one' also.

Walking into the apartment behind Devin, we are greeted by Luna who launches herself at me, much to my surprise. I didn't even make it four steps into the living area before the cat was all over me and jumping into my arms.

"What the hell, Luna?" Devin scoffs while standing there with her hands out in front of her.

Clover comes in behind us and sees Luna and buries her face in her fur and sobs a few times. I continue to stroke Luna's head so Clover can lean on us. Luna knows Clover needs comfort and starts purring loudly.

Devin walks up behind Clover and lovingly puts her arms around her, laying her head on top of Clover's. We all stand here and let Clover have her meltdown in a controlled, safe environment. She needed this. She needed to come home and release her emotions.

When Clover finishes crying, it's calmed to minor hiccups, she runs to X and he pulls her over to her room. He opens the door and ushers Clover in, waving at me as he shuts the door.

Devin lets out a long awaited, deep sigh.

"Yeah, baby. I feel that. Do you want me to wait out here while you pack?"

She holds her hand out to me, and it's an unconscious action for me too, now, as my hand finds hers and I intertwine our fingers. "Come on, you're fine. Besides, I want to be by you."

I can't help it, I pull her back to me and groan, I lower my voice by her ear, "Hurry, Kitten. I want to be buried so deep within you soon. I have a mighty need." I push her forward and smack her left ass cheek.

She flirtatiously looks back at me with her own sly smile.

This feels like the longest night ever. And it's still going. But I am fucking my girl tonight.

Chapter 27: Oakley

As soon as I unlock my apartment door and set Devin's bag down, she flies into my arms, knocking me back a step or two. I instinctively wrap my arms around her.

I hold her until her body stops shaking. My baby tried to be strong for everyone else, but she's ready to fall apart.

I hold her for a bit, then ask, "You want to take a bubble bath, or you want me to take you in there and fuck you senseless? Which one will help the most?" I nuzzle into her hair.

She chuckles into my neck and sniffles, "They both sound amazing actually." I feel her relax and slide her body back down the front of me. "I would like a bubble bath first. I feel dirty."

After we take our shoes off by the front door, I guide her into the master bathroom that has an oversized tub and shower combo. This is an instance where I feel a jacuzzi tub would be worthwhile. I mentally put that in my growing list of things I want for a house.

I bend down on my knees and start running the hot water. I reach over to the shelf on the wall, and put some fancy bath salts into the hot water, with a bath bomb I picked up at a boutique uptown. It looked like something she would like. The lavender aroma starts drifting throughout the bathroom while the water fizzes.

"How did you know these are my favorite?" Devin asks surprised, as she holds the container, looking down at me.

"I may, or may not, have seen them in your bathroom." I open the curtain more and show her the shampoos and soaps on the new shelves I installed. They are all the hygiene products I saw in her shower.

"You bought all of my soaps and hair stuff?" she asks, bewildered as her mouth hangs open looking over all the bottles. I may have over bought. I don't know why girls have so much damn soap. Like you have one body, right?

"Yeah. I figured you were going to need to have something over here for the nights you stay." Was I not supposed to do this? I thought I was being observant and caring.

"This is incredibly sweet, Oakley." She smiles at me. Whew. I made this beautiful, strong woman happy and it makes my heart soar.

Right here is me, on my knees in front of her, praying to whoever, *please don't let me fuck this up, ever.*

She starts undressing and I'm struck by how a week ago she wasn't in my life but here she is, being so familiar with me she's undressing in front of me. This sign of valuable trust is not lost on me.

Devin holds the wall while I pull her pants down her legs and over her feet. I toss them to the side and pull her black lace thong down slowly, because why not torture me some more.

Devin may think she's plain and ordinary, and she portrays that well to the outside world. But underneath them clothes, whew, is a lace and satin wearing sex kitten. She wears some of the sexiest lingerie I ever did see.

She's told me before that lingerie is a weakness of hers. I was ready to take her wherever she wanted and clean out the store. Take my money already.

Mental note, buy a lingerie store.

Maybe that's what we can do this weekend when she's off work. Not buy a store, but go shopping. Even if I have to order the stuff online, we can sit and pick them out together. Goddamn it makes me groan out loud thinking of her in red lace.

Devin pats me on the head and says, "You can wait until I soak," then she leans over naked, and kisses my lips lightly. With her fiery red hair draping around us, she softly says, "If you're a good boy, I'll make you feel good." Devin pats my cheek and stands up to her full height, while I sit on my knees on the bath rug, drooling over her.

Jesus fuck. I'm a goner.

As she's putting her hair up in a clip, I ask her, "Do you want me to go get your Kindle?"

"That's really thoughtful, but I don't feel like reading. Thank you, though."

"Do you want me to sit here and read to you?" I hold her hand as she steps into the tub and sits down in the water.

"As enticing as that sound, not right now. I kinda just want to relax and process." She sinks deeper into the tub with a soft moan.

I rub the back of my hand over her unblemished cheek. "I'll at least get you some ice for your face, it will help with the swelling. I'll be right back."

I grab a bag of sweet corn and bring it back to the bathroom, handing it to her. "I'll be out here, holler if you need anything, beautiful." I put her a towel within reach and hand her a washcloth. One last lingering look and I head out to the living room where we dropped our stuff.

I bring her bag into the bedroom and set it on the bed. I hear her softly humming and water trickling. What I would give to watch the water run across those nipples.

I take off my clothes, underwear included and throw on a pair of red and black basketball shorts. I plan to take a shower after she's done. I grab the candle off the dining room table and light it. I light two more and set one on the coffee table and the other on the kitchen counter. It's giving off a good, relaxing glow and if it keeps her calm, then so be it.

"Alexa, finish playing Oak's List." 'Easy To Love' by Bryce Savage plays throughout the apartment's surround sound I had installed, especially for my love of music. This is a perfect song for the moment.

I go into the kitchen and get a mug from the cabinet. I take a glass measuring cup and get a bottle of water and fill up the cup. I have no idea how long to heat this water in the microwave; I just know I watched her do it a couple of times. Sure, 2 minutes sounds good. I physically shrug while talking to myself.

I did manage to buy her favorite tea. I wanted her to be as comfortable as possible in my apartment. I even bought a new fluffy blanket and pillows to put on the couch. I tried to pick comfort items she would love. The blanket is a sage green, the pillows are light blue and pale yellow. The candles are vanilla, cinnamon and almond.

I will do anything to make her comfortable. Even if it is ask a sales associate what do girls like right now. I bought everything that woman Devin's age put in the cart.

I also picked up a few of her favorite snacks.

I meant it what I said about her moving in. I would love to be around her all the time. It's like my soul gravitates to her. I want her perfume and laughter to wrap around me everywhere I go.

I want to see how she would decorate this place, how she would mark her space with her interests. Devin had said her apartment was already decorated when she moved in because Clover had been there for a year prior to Devin moving in. She said she can't wait to get her own place and decorate it how she wants.

I pour the water over her teabags and set it off to the side by the monkfruit and honey I've seen her using before. *I gotta take care of my baby.*

My baby. If I'm this lost over her so quickly, what's it going to feel like when this deepens? I look forward to that. I'm excited to be her boyfriend. I want to know everything about her and show her off.

I can almost hear my dad in my head telling me to take it slow, use the top head not the bottom one. He seems to have found someone really special in a fast space of time. From my understanding, they are moving just as rapidly.

He can't knock me for falling head over heels in love just as quickly as he did.

He told me she is 'beautiful, kind and a little firecracker.' He told me he wanted her to be a surprise for me and she is very excited and nervous about meeting me. He said he is madly in love with her.

Good. Someone needs to bring him back to life. He's been drifting alone for so many years. Someone needs to love him for the amazing man he is. I have always hated seeing my dad lonely. I could tell how it affected him, especially my teen years when I started staying away from the house more with my friends.

We were both lonely. We connected with each other, but it always felt like something was missing and I knew for him it was my mom, his wife, his love. For me, it was the missing piece of the nuclear family, a mother.

I really need to apologize to Dad for not being as receptive and happy for him as I should have been. I need to let him know some of my distance has been a depressive episode. He's going to recommend I get some help. I don't know if its to that point yet.

I'm truly happy for him. I am not in the least bit upset about him having a serious girlfriend. I know he can never replace my mother, but he can have just as serious and loving relationship with another woman as he did with Mom. I have to admit, I am excited to meet the woman who stole my dad's heart. I didn't think anything could make him give up his lifestyle.

I always found it hilarious how he tried to hide his lifestyle from me. He managed to do a great job of it until I was about 17 and found the room in the house he accidently left unlocked called The Den.

It's my dad's very own custom made sex room.

It's pretty bad ass honestly. It's definitely goals.

Maybe when Devin and I buy or build our house we can make our own room.

Holy fuck, dude!

Wow. *You are worse than a stage 5 clinger, already got the wedding planned, too?*

Go check on your girlfriend, ya lovesick fucker.

Softly knocking on the bedroom door, I slowly open it. Devin is standing by the bed with the towel wrapped around her.

Still breathtaking. I don't think there's a way that she can look and it not be beautiful.

I drown every time she looks at me.

Chapter 28: Devin

Oakley slowly opens his bedroom door as I'm standing there in nothing but a towel. All he can do is stand there and stare for a few minutes. It makes me smile.

Strange to me to have so much attention and see so much want, lust and need on someone's face when they look at me.

"Hey." I watch him snap back into reality at the sound of my voice.

He clears his throat, slips through the doorway to stand in front of me and says, "I was just checking on you. I've made you some tea."

The only thing I could think of while in the bath was being consumed by him and getting lost in how he makes me feel. I need him to chase away the fear that still lingers inside me.

I drop my towel and hear it swish and land on the floor around me. Stepping up to him, I stand on the balls of my feet and press my body to his, putting my arms up over his neck. I can hear him audibly swallow. I have to hand it to this man; he has incredible self-control.

"Devin," Oakley groans as he puts his forehead to mine.

I angle my face to whisper to him, "I'm ok, Oakley. What I really want right now is for you to fuck me, rough and hard, and hurt me. Test my boundaries. Make me forget tonight, even if for a while."

"I don't want to hurt you, Devin," he whispers right back to me.

My voice a tad firmer from need, "That's an order, Loverboy. I need you."

Oakley takes a deep breath and growls so deep I can feel it vibrate through my nipples. As fast as lightning, he bites my neck, leaving a mark. My head falls back as he pulls my head back by my hair causing me to sigh. He continues to bite and kiss my neck from one side to the other, as if he's giving me a necklace. It feels amazing and I can hear my breathing pick up. I know he can too.

Suddenly, he bends and grabs me by the back of my thighs and picks me up. *Holy fuck!*

I tighten my grip around his neck, and he carries me backwards, slamming me down on his platform bed. The air thuds from my lungs and my pussy clenches with want.

"Mmm, Devin. I will never get enough of you," I hear him say in that sexy, husky southern drawl of his.

His voice makes flutters in my stomach and the buzzing in my chest travels down through my clit at the moment he gives me kisses down my hip. He makes me feel beautiful every chance he gets.

My body is fired up with anticipation for him to be inside me. This time feels different, a tad more serious than the other times we have had sex, more possessive and dominating. The air is charged with wild, almost desperate energy.

He pulls my ass to the edge of the bed; it almost feels like my ass is hanging off the side of the bed. He drops to his knees and spreads my legs wide. He kneads the fleshy parts of my inner thighs. I know it's going to bruise from the force he uses, but I'm perfectly happy to wear them like badges.

The first touch of his tongue has me jumping. Oakley never lets that detour him from getting his fill and digging in. No matter how many times he does this to me or sticks his hands down my pants between my lips for a quick taste; I will never complain because this feels amazing.

Oakley is making my legs shake from the overwhelming pleasure he is enticing my clit with. I love how his tongue swirls around my tight bud. He puts one finger inside of me and begins to slowly move it in and out of me, caressing my inner walls.

I reach down and run my fingers through his hair, on my second swipe through his waves, I grab his hair and pull him tighter to me while my other hand pinches my nipple. The apartment is filled with my strained moaning.

Oakley puts two fingers in and curls them, hitting my g-spot. It sends fireworks off inside of my body. My skin starts burning and comes alive with electricity.

The burning spiral rushes up through me as I cum all over his face. I feel my cum squirting out of me while he milks my g-spot. My rapid breathing echoes off the walls as he slows down.

I lean up on my elbow and pull his face from my pussy. His face glistening, soaking wet. "Now fuck me, Oakley, I want you inside me so bad. I have to have you right now." I watch his eyes darken and he stands up while my hand falls away.

Watching him drop his shorts off his hips heightens the high from my orgasm. Goddamn he is gorgeous. His chest is entirely covered in my cum, chest hair glistening in the lamp light and his face is gleaming.

He isn't the only one who can't get enough. I don't think I'll ever get enough of him. He is glorious to look at. My fingers itch to run my fingers through his chest hair and hear him moan.

I can make him moan. I make him call out my name, drive him crazy. That's powerful.

Oakley runs his hand up my pussy and rubs the wetness all over his dick. He steps closer to me, and I feel his heat on my inner thighs. He looks me in the eyes and says, "You wanted this." He roughly kneads the inside of my thighs in both hands.

"Break me, Oakley."

Oakley rubs the tip of his dick all over my outer lips, then plunges into me powerfully, making me throw my head back and catching my breath in my chest.

I momentarily die from pleasure.

Oakley wasting no time, hooks his hands around the top of my thighs and pulls me down onto his cock, hard, until he bottoms out, making me cry out and fist the blankets. He pumps into me and it's so painful from his hardness and the angle, but I can't get over how glorious it feels. I never want him to stop. This is the best kind of pain.

Yes, damn skippy I asked for this.

I watch his muscles cord in his arms as he holds me. His veins pop out from the pressure he has on my hips.

I am walking away from this fucking battered and bruised in all the good ways.

Oakley lifts my legs higher, and uses his body to push up both my thighs towards my chest. Making me take his cock at a different angle, he puts my calves on his shoulders, leans into me. Just when I thought there was no way he could go deeper, he found a way.

I can only cry out and moan, lost on the ride of his dick.

This is much harder than anything we have ever done. His cock is so hard right now. He is so focused on me, his gaze intense. He won't take his eyes off me. There's unspoken words between us as our bodies speak to each other.

We were made for each other.

In and out of me, my slickness smearing all over his cock, he pounds away at my pussy, making my body on fire. He leans over and licks up the inside of my calf then bites it.

I have never been this frenzied with my need of him. I feel like my body will burst into flames.

"Oakley, please," I plead with him. I have to cum. I rip and paw at my chest because my body is so overstimulated. I'm out of my mind with want and need, and love for him.

"Yes, Kitten, use your words with me baby, tell me what you want," he breathlessly tells me as he slaps one of my breasts, making me lose my breath.

"Oakley, please baby, let me cum, I have to. Please, my body is on fire."

His smile is absolutely feral, and he smacks my tit again.

He drops my legs to the side and they automatically go around him. Oakley leans over me, placing his right hand on my throat. "Oh Kitten," he hisses through his teeth as he finds a hard, swift rhythm. "You're so warm and tight. I want to stay inside of you forever." His thumb rubs circles around my clit, driving me closer to the ledge. I will gladly jump off this ledge for him.

He is so deep in me, driving with such force it's pushing me up onto the bed, but he holds me in place with his hand on my neck. My one hand is on his wrist and the other reaches up to cup his face.

I sob in pleasure as his hand slowly decreases my air. I give over to the feelings and emotions racing through me, relishing in his actions to try and dominate me, but I am me, and I tell him, "Fuck me like you mean it, Oakley, harder, break me."

My words spur him into a pounding, painful frenzy. I grab at my nipples and shout, "Yes, more. Oakley I want it all."

I feel like I'm going to pass out, and Oakley's hand is on my clit with just the right pressure and direction, I'm racing towards another orgasm. I feel it on the cusp of washing over me. His grunts mingle in the room with my loud moans and sobbing.

He leans over me to look into my eyes as he pistons in and out of me, "Devin….nothing will keep me from you….when I thought I'd lost you…..my heart stopped baby…" he slams into me harder. "I already know Devin…I'm so madly in love with you…I love you Kitten…I would stop at nothing to make you mine forever and keep you safe.." he breathlessly tells me between gulps of air.

His words hit directly into my core and vibrates out through every nerve in my body. I throw my head into the mattress and howl my pleasure as I cum all over his dick. I pant, calling out his name while my nails dig into his wrist as I feel my walls pulsating around his cock. I arch my back at the power of my orgasm rocking through my body.

This is a claiming. Oakley has ruined me for anyone else. It can't get better than this.

Oakley pumps into me a few more times and I feel him get harder and hit deeper, if possible, then feel his cock erupting inside of me as I cum, filling me with his cum while he yells my name in that sexy hoarse voice of his while staring into my eyes.

I crave to hear him cum and moan. It's so sexy sounding. It sends shivers into my soul every time.

He brings his arms to either side of me, balancing on his hands. "Devin…baby.." he takes a deep breath in and brings his hand to the side of my face, rubbing away the tears that leaked out. He says, "Devin…" then runs his thumb over my lips.

I put my hands up to his face, "I don't know what I'm supposed to do but I know I love you too and I want to spend every day showing you how much."

He drops down to me and scoops his arms around me. As he cradles me, I softly tell him, "I think I've found who my soul will burn for and it's consuming me."

He groans into my neck, "Dev, I want you for forever. My soul wants tied to yours." He sits up on his hands again, "One day you will be my wife, count on it, and until I ask for your hand: I'm going to love being your boyfriend and show you every day the depth of my love."

I love the sound of being Mrs. Oakley Grayson.

He pulls out of me and stands up, pushing my thighs up and spreading me wide. He loves seeing his cum inside of me.

"I'm going to put a baby in there Devin, plenty of babies, I can't wait to see you swollen with our child."

He tries to shove his cum back inside me.

He takes his wet finger and puts it to my mouth. Instinctively I open and wrap my lips around it, tasting us both on him.

"Mmm, my beautiful Kitten. Has anyone ever told you that you vibrate like you're purring when you cum?"

"No, because I've never came with anyone else. No one except you."

Oakley looks at me confused. "But you said you weren't a virgin."

I sit up on the side of the bed and I put my hand in his, "You never asked if I ever came, you just asked if I had had sex, which I had, but in no way fucking near this level. This is every bit of my twisted smutty dreams coming true, and I am so fucking here for it, but my only 3 times of ever having sex were 3 minutes long and I never came to answer your questioning look."

"Devin, that practically makes you a virgin, baby." He puts his hands on the sides of my face and bends over to rub our noses together, "I have so much to show you, oh my God, so much to do to you. New goal, make you addicted to me so you can never be without me."

"Don't threaten me with my dreams Loverboy, I am warped enough to want to crawl inside you because even then that isn't close enough."

"I love this disturbing side of you, Kitten." He kisses my nose and turns to go shower. As he walks away, I reach out far enough to smack his delicious ass.

This man stands there and bends his elbows and laces his fingers behind his head and starts gyrating his hips with the lamp light illuminating him and casting a long shadow across the room. I watch his sexed out cock flop around.

The sight of him makes me giggle, I yell, "Whooo hooo, shake it for me, baby."

Oakley smacks his ass and walks into the bathroom as the last notes of 'Fire' by Barns Courtney dies out and another tune starts with the surround sound. 'Tonight You Are Mine' by The Technicolors starts playing when I walk into the bathroom, and step into the shower with him.

He rinses his hair and gives me a dazzling smile, "Kitten, I love you but give me at least an hour, ya wanton slut."

"Silly ass, I need to rinse all this cum off of me," I laugh at him, "Give me the sprayer, damn."

Chapter 29: Oakley

Devin spends forever drying all that hair. "Do you want me to remake this tea or just warm it up in the microwave?" This shit is ice cold now that she's taken a calendar year to tame her hair.

Devin walks in from the bedroom in a thermal underwear set with a very low cut, skintight top and no bra. Jesus, probably no panties too. I can see her nipple pressing through the fabric.

Oh my God this is torture.

"Uhh Devin, what are you wearing there, babe?" in voice more gruff than intended.

She gets done knotting her hair up in one of those hair ties I've been finding everywhere and looks down at herself and back up to me, confused, "I'm wearing pajamas. What else would I be in?"

"Devin, those are way too sexy to be pajamas. Did you get them from the 'How to Torture My Boyfriend' store?" Jesus Christ, I have never wished so hard that I was the type of guy who could bounce right back and go again.

Give me a fucking hour, woman. I'm not going to survive.

She snorts at me, rolls her eyes, and walks right by me standing at the end of the counter, and into kitchen.

I see, audacity is strong with this one.

I walk up behind her and push her into the counter, caging her in with my arms, I thickly tell her, "You keep it up, pushing my buttons, and I will put you over my lap and smack that sassy ass until it welts. Try me, baby Kitten." I smack her ass a good one as I walk out of the kitchen, grunting.

I get out to the living room before I remember work, I rub my chest and tell her, "Hey I have to go check my work email for a little bit, you good?"

"Yeah, I need to eat something. I'll be fine." I love when she smiles at me.

I go check my work email for a bit while she eats a snack and warms up the tea. I finish before her and hang out on the couch waiting for her.

When she has her second cup of tea fixed, she comes and sits on the couch with me. I watch her fluff the new cushions then snuggles back into them. I toss half of the blanket over her from my body. I was prewarming it for her. She settles into what's now probably her new nest and looks at me over her tea, lightly blowing on the liquid.

She rubs her hand over the woven texture. I knew she would love the blanket.

I slide my gaze over to her and ask, "Are you going to Senior night Saturday?"

She nods, and says, "Yes, Nicole said she was dragging me whether I liked it or not. I mean, I can not go if you prefer. I promised her before we were together. I don't plan on hooking up with anyone, except you of course."

I chuckle at her, "No it's fine. I trust you."

"Will you be there?" she asks me with her eyebrows up.

"Yeah, I'm a senior."

"Ok. Oo! Let's meet up and sneak off somewhere." She's so excited by her devious plan she's wiggling her toes under the blanket.

I scrunch down and smile at her and say in my most crackling old hag voice, "Anything for you my precious."

She laughs, rolls her eyes, and says, "Sometimes you are a pain in the butt."

"But I make life interesting."

"Yes, Sir." Her husky voice gives her away. Her eyes go round, and she looks at me.

Ohh darling, I didn't miss this slip of the tongue. I start crawling up the blanket on top of her. "Sir? Do you want me to be your Sir?"

She starts giggling and says, "Oakley don't you dare spill this cup of tea."

I keep moving up her, "Then you better hurry and put it on the table."

She leans over to the coffee table so fast that she sloshes the tea on the rug. She turns to look back at me advancing to her, "So, Sir. Not Daddy, or Master, but Sir. I would have pegged you for a Daddy kind of girl."

She crinkles her nose and replies, "No, Sir." She taps me on the end of the nose with her forefinger, "I want to give just as much as I receive. I think I would like to be called Mistress."

"Have I told you yet that your bossy streak turns me on?" I lean down and kiss her upturned face. I swipe my tongue in her mouth deeply and taste the honey from her tea.

When she catches her breath, she lets me know, "I want to dominate you just as much as I want to be dominated by you."

That makes a shiver run through me. I would love to bow down to her commands and do whatever she wants of me.

I sit back, facing her and roughly pull her to me. She yelps but lands in my lap.

Gruffly I tell her, "Devin, nothing was hotter than you pulling my hair and demanding me to fuck you right then. And telling me that's an order." I look down at her while she pants. "Kitten, I will drop to my knees and worship at your altar, just tell me how you want it done."

She leans in and kisses my neck. Rising up, she bites me as she removes herself from my lap.

Fuck, it's so hot when she takes over.

Devin lowers me down to the couch so my head is on a pillow behind me. She balances over top of me and firmly says, "I want your loyalty." A roll of her hips on my hardening cock through my shorts. Over top my lips she says, "I want your honesty." Another roll of her hips.

"You have it, baby. Every bit of it. Goddamn everything I have is yours."

"I want everything you can teach me so I can better serve you, Sir," she peeks her little tongue out and licks my bottom lip making me groan. That Sir makes my cock twitch. "I want to spend the rest of my life fucking you as often as I can." And she rolls her hips harder this time. "Any way that I can."

I'm so hard again it astonishing to me. "Fuck, woman." I groan. "Bottoms off, now." I snap my fingers to get her to move quicker. "I want you to ride my cock like a good little girl."

Getting off the couch, she pushes her pajama pants down and steps out of them, "Yes, Sir."

I sit up and pat my lap with one hand and hold my stiff cock up with the other. "Come here, Kitten."

"Didn't you get enough yet? You want more of this pussy?" She chides me but she climbs onto the couch and staddles my lap.

"I will never get enough of you, Devin. Now, sit on my dick baby girl."

My kitten slowly slides herself down on my cock while her moans fill the living room. My apartment is so bare it makes it sound louder than it is.

"You are soaking wet from our cum, and so warm, it's like a furnace." I love the sounds of her moaning at my words. Nothing besides her cumming, sounds sweeter to my ears.

I put my hands on her hips and push up into her, meeting her the rest of the way. "Oh my God Oakley…"

"Bounce on my dick, baby. Fuck me good. Let go and chase your orgasm."

Her hips are already rolling as she slides up and down my cock. "Yes, Sir." She is still so wet from earlier and I feel the wetness seep down my balls.

We are going to need another shower.

I pull one hand away from her hips and lift her thermal top to bare her tits. I use that hand to cup her breast and bend my neck to run my tongue across her nipple. It makes her speed up and chase harder, not to mention breathing harder.

In between licks, I say, "That's my good girl, ride this dick. Whose cock is it?"

Devin groans and says, "Mine."

"Louder, Devin, I can't hear you."

"MINE. It's my cock. You're mine Oakley."

I take her nipple into my mouth and roll the sweet bud between my lips while I groan. This sets off her hips in a rapid motion, around, up and down, as she works herself over top of me.

She puts her hand on my throat and puts pressure on it. "Be a good boy and make me cum again, Loverboy. Can you be my good boy for me?"

"Yes, Devin, all yours to do with what you wish…cum on me baby…you have all the control Mistress, use me…make me cum inside you again."

I am so close and fighting for control. I grab her hips and push up into her harder, her moans growing longer and louder. The harder I pull her down and grind into her, the more lost I get in the hurricane of emotions she conjures inside of me.

"Make your pussy purr for me, Kitten, give me what I want."

"Yes, Oakley…right there….I'm gonna cum.." Devin stiffens and throws her head back to cry out, pushing her chest into my face. I bite her left tit on the top and she practically screams.

I hold onto her, and she leans back, body riding me, fingers in my chest hair pulling, and her other hand gripping my forearm.

Devin looks divine taking her pleasure from me. An irresistible goddess.

She leans in, pulls my head back using my hair, and seals her lips to mine, panting and moaning, while I give a few hard thrusts upwards.

She breaks the searing kiss for a minute to say to me, "Oakley, cum in me….I want all of it, fill me up, Sir…please baby, I'm begging for it."

My chest rapidly heaving, all I can get out is, "Yes, Mistress." Seeing and hearing her cum, talking dirty to me, all of it makes me unleash inside her again. Her pussy walls vibrate with intensity while she milks my cock up and down. There is no resisting her any longer.

My balls tighten and that spectacular feeling climbs up from the base of my spine, outwards towards my core, and I moan into her mouth. I spurt everything I have left inside her and feel her pussy walls clamping down hard on my cock for every last drop.

I moan into her mouth, "Fuck, Kitten," and my grunts and growls fill the space around us as my climax comes back down.

Breathing hard, she rests her forehead on mine as our breaths mingle and she loosens her grip on my hair. I run my hands up the back of her head and lightly grab her messy hair by her bun.

"Never will I get enough, Devin. I could spend the rest of my life fucking you and it still wouldn't be enough."

My kitten purrs her appreciation at my words.

Making my kitten purr is now my new obsession.

Chapter 30: Devin

I feel like all I do is take showers now, but it's for a good cause. My body is sore from Mr. Beasley manhandling me last night but also from all the sex we've been having the past 24 hours.

The man is insatiable.

As I sit in my new nest on his couch with my cup of tea, covered with the the fluffy blanket and pillows he bought me, I let Oakley know I have to make a phone call to my mom. He asked if I wanted privacy and I told him I didn't mind if he heard our conversation, just don't give himself away.

I explained she's going to want to come flying up here and coddle me or drag me to her house. That's fair, she's my mom and will want to love and pet on me and make sure I'm safe. This was pretty traumatic for me and I feel like I'm coping well enough. Oakley has been a saving grace in this whole fiasco. I don't think I could have made it through last night without him.

Mom picks up on the first ring, "Hey baby, how's my little fire ant?"

I see Oakley's face light up and he mouths "Fire Ant" and smiles really big.

I wave my hand at him to stop.

"Hey Mom, I'm good. But this isn't going to be a good upbeat call. I have something disturbing to tell you, and I don't want you to hop in your car and race up here."

I tell her what happened last night, trying to smooth it over for her. It does no good, she starts crying and I can feel her nervous energy across the phone call.

"Devin, I'm coming up there to get you and bringing you home with me."

"No Mom, I'm fine, seriously. I'm at my boyfriend's and he is taking great care of me. Aside from a few bruises and cuts on my hands and face, I'm ok."

"I would feel better if you came and stayed with me."

"Mother," I try not to sigh too loud; I knew this was going to happen, "Listen, I know you want me there with you, but I have a life here I can't leave at the drop of a hat. I have to work tonight, and I cannot miss my shift again. Pam depends on me. And I want to go to the Senior's party tomorrow night with Nicole. It's all over now, the bad guys were arrested."

"Turn your camera on for me, I want to see my baby. I have to see for myself you're ok."

I hold my phone out and turn on my camera and wave to her. I know the first thing she sees is the bruise on my cheek from where I fell, and face planted from the SUV.

In a shaky voice, "Devin, my baby..." I see fresh tears fill her eyes.

"I'm ok Momma, I promise. It just looks bad." I gingerly touch my cheek to show her. "I would come home if I wasn't good. I swear."

"Oh Devy, this has been a lot to handle. How are you coping? Should we get you started in counseling?"

My mom is always the advocate for counseling, and she thinks it helps with everything. I mean, I can't disagree with her. But I don't feel like I need it at this point.

"I'm going to pass on the counseling, Mom. I don't feel I need it; I just need some rest and I'm getting it here…Sorta." Oops, I didn't mean for that last part to come out.

"Devin!" Mom shrieks. Then in a lower throaty voice, she asks, "Are you sleeping with him?"

My blush creeps up my face. I look over at Oakley and he's snickering into his hand with his eyebrows raised.

"Yes, Mother, if you must know."

"Well, I uhh, don't know what to say."

"What? My mother at a loss for words when she has words for every little thing?" I say stunned.

"I guess good for you, girl! And make sure you stay on your birth control! Use protection, Dev. Be smart."

"Yeah, yeah, Mom, that's all happening." I conveniently leave out the lack of using condoms.

"I didn't know it was that serious," she says as she lets out a sigh. "Why are you keeping him such a secret? Don't you want me to know him?"

"Mom. I just want him for myself right now. That's all. I am not keeping him secret. I called and told you about him the other day."

"But I don't know anything about him." I can hear her pouting.

"All in due time. I'm still getting to know him, and I really want it to be just me and him right now. You will get to meet him for

Christmas, remember."

"Oh God, Devy that's so far away!"

"It is not," I laugh at her dramatic response. "It will be here before you know it. Then I will get to know your boyfriend, too. You have been secretive with him also, ya know."

"Fine, touché. Well, tell him I appreciate him more than he knows, and I already love him for taking care of my baby and rescuing her again. That man was ready to kill for you, Dev, that means something."

"I am well aware, Mom. He is truly the best. He's a keeper for sure."

I chat a little more with her before getting off the phone. I look over at Oakley and he's looking at me with his intense, possessive gaze, the one that makes me have shivers, "She has no idea the lengths I am willing to go for you."

Oakley reaches over to caress my unharmed cheek, probably hoping his touch could make it go away.

"I have to call my other Mom now. You can stay for it too if you want." He looks at me confused.

I find Aunt Jilly in my favorites and hit the phone icon.

She answers with, "Devin! Do you know how worried I've been?"

"Hey Aunt Jilly, I'm ok. Promise. I just got off the phone with Mom and I wanted you to hear it from me what's been happening."

I proceed to fill in my aunt and she of course, has the same reaction as my mom. Since she lives closer, like 20 minutes from my apartment, she insists on coming over to check me out because she needs to do her 'just duty' to my mother by checking on her baby.

"Give me an hour ok, I'm not there, I'm at my boyfriend's house."

Aunt Jilly's breath catches before she says, "Devin! Your mother told me you have a boyfriend. When can I meet him? Your mother says you are torturing her by making her wait until Christmas," she laughs.

"Well, you are waiting until Christmas too, just so you know. I want him all to myself for the next 8ish weeks. Stand in line with Mom."

"Devin, you are becoming a stubborn hard ass like your mother," Aunt Jilly retorts.

"Yep. I know." I smirk to myself.

"I reckon I will be waiting, too. But if I catch you out in the public, I'm going to ask him 50 questions, from both me and your mom. There will be no stopping it so be warned."

"I know that too, that's why y'all are waiting."

"Do you know how frustrating you are right now? Ugh. Well, I hope he makes you happy. That last one was a dirtbag shit head and anyone is better than him. Fucking a potato is better than him."

I can't help but laugh at her. "Yes, I agree, now."

"Oh boy! Does your mom know you're fucking him? She's going to be so far up your ass when she finds out. It will kill her nosy ass," Aunt Jilly cackles. I love it when she and my mom get started, but only when it's someone else other than me. They are the two worst gossip hounds I know.

Facts, they have already started perusing my social medias for a piece of meat to snag and gnaw on. They will be looking for me to post anything with him. I think I will like dragging this out for them and teasing them. Torture, indeed.

"She does now. And she's already tried to drag me home with her. I have work tonight and I have a Halloween party I want to attend tomorrow night. I'm staying here and living my life. I promise to you too, I am fine." I absently pick at my hoodie while she takes a breath to preach to me. I expected no less. I watch Oakley get up and go to his office.

"I'm really glad you told her. Thank you for telling me too, Devy."

I am shocked I am not getting a lecture on birth control, self-defense, and that I should carry a gun.

"You are welcome, Aunt Jilly. I couldn't imagine not telling you."

Trying not to be sentimental, but Aunt Jilly has been in my life since the beginning of it. Her and my mom were college besties. She has watched me grow up and always been there for me. I could never leave her out of something this important.

"Can I come see you before you go to work?" she asks.

"Yeah, I have to go over there to get dressed and get ready anyways. When were you thinking?"

We agree on a time, and I finish speaking to her. I shoot off a quick text to Clover and ask her how she is and to let her know what time to expect me. I finish my tea and take my cup to rinse out in the kitchen.

Oakley comes out of his office and says, "When do you want me to take you back to your place? Not that I want to, I want to keep you here with me, safe."

I groan, "Not you too. I still have a life to live, Oakley."

He comes up to me and puts his arms around me, "I know Kitten, but I still want to keep you all to myself." He leans down and nibbles on my neck, rocking me back and forth, "Let me keep you locked up in my castle tower and let me make love to you all day, so you won't ever think about leaving."

I slap his shoulder as I giggle at his administrations, "Nope. You have to let me be a street cat and parade the goods around town."

"Like hell you say, woman." Oakley smacks my ass with a slap that stings. "Let me tie you down to the bed, let me love all over you until you can't take anymore and pass out."

"As good as that sounds, I really do have to work today. Besides, I'm sore enough and I don't think I could go another round with you," I push his head away from my neck, "So get your feely hands back to yourself and take me home. *Sir*."

"Fine, partypooper, I will let you go, for now, *Mistress*." He releases me and steps back.

"You will be fine without me." I call over my shoulder while I walk into his bedroom to grab my overnight bag. "You should probably hydrate yourself, too. I'm sure you are slightly depleted also."

"Good call, Kitten. I need to make more spermies to fill you up with."

"Eww, don't say it like that," I chuckle.

After I shower for what feels like the tenth time in the past 24 hours, my Aunt Jilly shows up. I show her all my cuts and bruises because I know she will tell my mom.

Clover comes out to see her and hug her. She hasn't seen Aunt Jilly since I moved in this past summer. Aunt Jilly was happy to pet on Clover too.

God, this past week has been a whirlwind.

My whole life has been changed. I believe for the better. But shit, I've already lived one whole lifetime in one week.

Clover is looking good. She was dehydrated and tired, but mostly walked away with cuts and bruises like me. X said she slept all night and she was still sleeping when I got there around noon.

X left when I arrived. He and Oakley talked for a bit in the living room while I was in Clover's bedroom checking on her. Her eyes were puffy from crying, so I grabbed her cold facemask from the freezer for her. It's her after party go to beauty trick, but clearly she can use it now.

Before leaving, Aunt Jilly insisted on having food delivered for Clover and I. After refusing twice, Clover finally conceded and had Aunt Jilly order from the Mexican restaurant across the street from the apartment. I knew better than to argue. I gave the lady my order as soon as she mentioned it. Clover learns the hard way. Don't argue with Aunt Jilly.

Clover and I sit at our small kitchen table, and I take a bite of my cheesy chicken and shrimp with rice, while Clover quietly says, "I didn't think I was ever going to see you again."

"Oh. Clover, honey," I get up and walk around the table to her and give her a side hug.

Clover's eyes overflow with the tears she held at bay while Aunt Jilly was here. "It was so scary, Dev. Now I know why you sat up all night."

I pet down her hair and kiss the top of her head. "It's really traumatic, and I'm here for you. Just like you were for me."

I pull back and she nods. I sit back in my seat and stare at her across the table. "Do you feel safe here while I go to work?"

"Yeah, I do. I know those guys are in jail and they can't get to me." She pushes her food around before taking a bite. "What about you? Do you feel safe going to work?"

"Yes, I do. Same with me, I know the assholes are locked away and I'm less likely to be taken." I finish up my last few bites, I didn't realize I was so hungry and I put the container in the trash.

"I'm a phone call away; I am not that far away either. Call me if you need me."

"You know I will. I think I want to lay down for a while. Just process and rest, ya know." She puts the rest of her food in the refrigerator.

I grab my purse and phone from my bedroom and tell her, "Ok then. I'm out for now, I'll be home around 11."

She blows me a kiss and I take a bite out of it, causing her to give me a chuckle. "See ya, Devy."

Part of me feels a twinge of guilt for leaving her alone, but I also know she has to process what happened to her on her own. Same as I had to. Clover is a very resilient woman, she is going to pull through this just fine, I'm sure.

We will put all this behind us.

Chapter 31: Oakley

I arrive at the Senior party late as planned. I wanted Devin to question where I was. If I was hidden in plain sight and watching her, will she wonder if I'm coming for her?

I read the second book in her series. The book I read has a masked man. No wonder she stood there staring up at me when I found her that night. I'll have to ask her about it. Wonder if my kitten has a masked man fetish now and just realized it that night?

Right now, I'm in the shadows watching my girl in her red kitty mask talk to Clover, X, and Nicole and laugh at something said. I see her quick, darting glances while she, no doubt, is looking for me. She is biding time, pretending to be in the present while her mind wanders elsewhere.

Her mask does things to me, too.

I'm waiting for the perfect opportunity to steal her away. It's been over 24 hours since I've been buried in her and I would really like to get there again.

Two guys from the football team come over and fist bump X. Another girl runs up to Sam, who is only about 5 feet away from Devin with his back towards her, and drunkenly hugs him. Clover is hanging on to X listening to the newcomers talk to X. Nicole is outright drooling over the guys, especially when two more shows up and greets X.

My poor baby is just standing there alone. This is the moment I wanted to watch.

Devin can't hide her feelings, and I've already learned a great deal about her reactions. Any minute she's going to search for me again.

I watch her eyes come up from her cup and she scans the area. I want her to want me by her. I want to see her craving my presence. I want to see my baby miss me.

She is all alone standing among friends and looks so lost. Devin looks down at her cup as her shoulders slump.

Now is perfect.

I turn on my mask and see the red glow from the lights on the car beside me.

I have on the same outfit as that night. Black V neck t-shirt, black jeans, biker boots, black belt. Chained wallet clasped onto a belt loop.

I watch her closely as I walk towards our friends' circle. I move with purpose, so she barely registers how fast I appeared. I hold my hand out, I know exactly what she will do.

"Come with me so I can go fuck you on the hood of my Maserati."

Chapter 32: Devin

Oakley holds his hand out to me. At least I hope it's him, he has the same mask, and same build. Of course it's him.

I can smell him. My body vibrates when he is near.

Everyone has stopped talking and looking our way.

One of the football players says, "Hey Oak" and Oakley ignores him, never taking his eyes off me.

I look at Nicole as my hand slips into his. As soon as his hand closes around mine, my body recognizes him, and I know I will be lost soon. My body awakens and the ripples are spiraling around my center.

Nicole is smiling at me and waving, not at all upset I'm being stolen from her. She actually blows a kiss to me as I stumble after him.

I give little resistance to Oakley as he pulls me towards the darkness where the cars are parked.

He continues to pull me further away from the fire, the darkness swallowing us up, as we come to a line of sparsely parked cars. He turns right and three cars down I see lights beep on. He is parked by the only grove of trees in the field.

The party is approximately 60ish yards away. The music drifts out to us and you can see the fire illuminating the sky.

He stops by the front of his SUV and turns around to me and takes my throat in his hand. "Did you miss me, Kitten?"

Involuntary thigh clench.

"Fuck yes I did." My breathing picks up being near him. He circles me running his hand across my chest, around to my arms, then back. He stops right behind me and brings his arm around the front of me, gripping my neck and forcing me to look up at the night sky. I feel my neck bob as I swallow under his hold.

"You look positively delicious tonight." He runs his other hand across my nipples, making them pebble. He pinches them both and it send jolts to my clit.

"Do you want to be my good girl and cum on my face?"

"Yes, Sir." My head lolls back on his shoulder as he pinches my nipples more.

"Are you going to let me put you up on my hood? You gonna squirt all over my Maserati, pretty Kitty? I want to watch it drip down my grill."

Fuck, when he talks to me like that.

He makes it feel like my body is on fire and I am content to burn alive for him.

"Yes, Sir." I whisper. I can't think straight already.

"Now be my good little slut and take those pants off; they're in my way." He smacks my ass trying to hurry me along.

He pulls his arms away from me while I hook my waistband with my thumbs and pull my pants down to my ankles. As soon as cold air hits my ass, his hand is there, fingers finding my wet slit. He sticks one finger in me, and I moan, grabbing the SUV to steady me.

He pulls his finger out and licks it clean. "Mmm, that's the finest pussy around and it's all mine." He slaps my ass again, "Faster, Kitten." He takes a breath, spreads his arms wide to the sky and yells, "WOOO, MINE ALL MINE."

All that's missing is him beating on his chest to stake his claim.

I kick my shoes off and quickly take my leggings off over my feet. I'm standing there in my black long sleeved crop top and my kitty mask.

He walks around in front of me and lifts my shirt. He groans and bites his knuckle at the sight of my red mesh bralette. I will buy every piece of sexy lingerie in his favorite color if he always gives this reaction. I opted for no panties tonight. I knew he would find me and steal me away. I practically begged for it.

Oakley moves his mask up enough to lick my nipple through the fabric, nibbling at it. I grab onto his head and hold him to me. My desire is peaking, and I want him inside me, anyway I can get him. The red glow from his mask is driving me crazy.

Putting his mask back down, he bends down and picks me up. It surprises me and I wrap my legs around him. "Don't hurt yourself."

"Woman, do I look like I'm struggling here?" He hefts me up higher and I look down as his mask is looking up at me.

Oakley walks me over to his hood and I reach back and put my arms down while he sets my ass on the hood. It's so cold and smooth on my ass cheeks.

"Devin put your legs on my shoulders and lay back baby, I don't care what happens to this hood, we'll just get it fixed." He uses his hands to spread my legs wide, "But I am about to tear into my pussy and make you scream to the night sky."

With that he slides up his mask and starts devouring my pussy. My legs immediately start shaking. He is perfect at doing this and I enjoy every dark and devious thing he does to me.

My body begs for more. I know there is so much more to show me, and I relish the feeling he has chosen me to do these things with.

Each lick and tongue caress brings me closer to climax. "Oakley...Mmmm it feels so good."

He doubles down and puts a finger inside me and slowly moves it in and out. His tongue swirls around my clit and when he sucks on it gently it makes me pant. I'm already so close.

Oakley adds another finger and curls them just how I like. He starts massaging my g-spot and sucking on my clit between his lips. It's too much as I moan loudly on the hood of his Maserati.

A second before I cum, the pressure too much, I feel the gush down my ass crack, then a powerful orgasm launches inside my body and rains over me. The fire burning in me is intensified and consumes me as I throw my arms wide and my back arches.

He's right. With abandonment, I scream his name into the stars and pray this never ends.

I chase the high as it fades but still simmers in my core. Frantically I beg, "Oakley, oh God, fill me with cock. I need you inside of me, now." I say through my chest heaving.

"Sit up here Devin, I have to put you down, I'm not that tall, baby," he chuckles as he picks me up off the hood and sets my feet on the ground.

He puts his mask on again and grabs my hand and leads me to the back of the SUV as the hatch opens. "Oakley, you can't be serious, people will see us with the interior light on." He quickly tosses down a blanket.

"I know, let them look, you're glorious. They can see how well you take my cock, my pretty little slut." He reaches into his back pocket and produces a pair of handcuffs. My heart begins racing

Oakley spins me around and cuffs my arms behind me, after he pulls on them to make sure I can't slip out of them, he gestures to the floorboard. Oakley demands, "Bend over, chest on the floorboard, Kitten. Spread your beautiful legs for me."

With his hand on my back, he pushes me down until my ass is in the air. I hear his belt come undone, and his zipper being ripped down.

My pussy is clenching, wanting him inside me.

"Please Sir, I need it now. I've been a bad girl. Punish me."

"Jesus, fuck, Devin. You're gonna make me cum before I even get inside you."

I feel a sharp smack to my ass cheek that makes the entire SUV sway. Oakley lines up to my center and slowly pushes into me. I'm so wet he slides in smoothly.

I love the feeling of being filled with his cock. I clench to make sure he can't leave.

He groans and begins to move, and it draws long, low throaty moans from me.

Oakley grabs the handcuffs and pulls, arching me back and making me cry out. He slams into me hard, "How does my baby like that?" He hits bottom, making me gasp. He pulls out slowly and rams his cock back into me.

The sway of the SUV keeps me bouncing on his dick. "Hang on Kitten, I'm going to fuck you within an inch of your life."

"Show me, Sir. Oh God, fuck me like a dirty whore."

"My dirty whore." Oakley picks up his pace but does not stop the force he enters me with.

I start sobbing at the overwhelming sensations, calling for him, begging for him to let me cum.

Oakley reaches around in front of me and rubs his fingers over my clit. "Yes, please, right there."

"Do you want to cum on your cock, Kitten?"

"Yes, Sir, please, oh God, please."

Oakley slips his thumb in my ass and does not take long for his fingers to bring me to the edge and I fall down the spiral, screaming his name again and again, while he roars my name and finishes pumping into me.

He drops my arms onto my back again. He bends over and puts his arm on my back and drops his head on his forearm. I feel his breath cascading over my back.

I feel him slide out of me and drops of cum run down my inner thigh.

Oakley catches his breath and stands up, "Devin you good, baby?" He runs a hand lightly down my spine making me shiver.

"Yes, Sir." I back up and stand, and I watch him do up his pants and buckle his belt.

He looks up at me through his lashes. He puts his thumbs to his bottom lip. Licking his lips, he says, "Devin...I have no words on how beautiful you are right now. Fucking hell. I wish you could see what I see."

He reaches out and captures my chin in his hand, squishing my cheeks. "Heavy, dazed eyes from a good fucking, flushed face, messy hair, breasts exposed, no pants and cum glistening on your thighs in the low light. The handcuffs are a bonus. All backdropped with the endless stars behind you." He leans in and kisses me.

"My Kitten is a Goddess, and I will spend forever worshipping her body."

Oakley kisses me deeply, passionately. His tongue sweeps into my mouth, assaulting my senses once again. Just as quickly as he started it stops.

He turns me around and unlocks the handcuffs. I pull my hands in front of me to rub my wrists. He turns me back around and takes my arm and brings it up to his lips. He kisses inside my wrist and whispers, "It had to be done. I needed to hear you beg."

He picks up my other arm and kisses my wrist there too. "What's even sexier than all this?" He goes over to the compartment in the the back driver's side corner, "I brought you wet wipes to clean up with."

"I could kiss you. Thank you so much."

"I mean you can still kiss me, I'm just saying." He brings me the pack of disposable wipes and I lean on tip toes to kiss him. "Happy one week, Devin."

"Oh wow, it has just been a week hasn't it. It feels like I've known you for years." I lean up and kiss him again, "Happy one week, Oakley. Thanks for my present."

I clean up and he helps me get dressed again. "Are you ready to get back to this party?"

"I should probably make an appearance to my own party, " he says as he gazes off towards the fire.

I look over at him, confused, "Your party?"

"Yeah. Every year, the Senior's assign one person to find the location and coordinate the wood, parking, and booze." He looks towards the bon fire, "The seniors gathered wood from around the community to bring here to burn for our fire tonight. We do clean up and use it for ourselves. It's been a college tradition. Last spring I was chosen to be this year's Captain."

"Wow. Why didn't you tell me?"

"I didn't really think about it. I just wondered if you were coming, if not, would you think about coming with me." He watches me intently as I clean myself up. He looks entirely gorgeous with the fire backlighting him.

"So, whose place is this?" I look around in the dark. There's nothing around. Just woods and fields.

"It's mine. I bought it back in the beginning of summer when I was notified I was the Captain." He shrugs like it's no big deal to buy land just to have a party.

"Ok Loverboy, go big or go home, huh?" I grin over at him. "It's a beautiful place, quiet, and that view of the sky. Chef's kiss, Oakley. I love it out here. Congratulations."

I see the gleam in his eye by the firelight, "Maybe one day I will build a house here. It will depend on what my wife wants." He tucks a piece of my hair back, "So be thinking how many bedrooms you want, Mistress." And he kisses my forehead and takes my hand to lead me back to the party.

I have a smug smile on my face.

I have a real life book boyfriend, too.

Chapter 33: Oakley

Sam approaches us as we are coming back from our fucking on the hood of my car session, and says, "So this is the new girlfriend I haven't been introduced to?"

Devin holds her hand out and says, "Hi! I'm Devin."

Sam takes her hand and looks down at her for a moment longer than I like, saying, "I'm Sam." She pulls her hand away as he leans into me and says, "She's gorgeous, if you're ever interested in sharing."

I growl at him.

"Ok, man. Chill. Didn't know it was like that." He holds up his hands, chuckling.

Suddenly Devin calls over to him, "What if I'm interested in sharing him?"

Sam looks over at her stunned. winks at her and says, "If you need someone to bottom, sweet cheeks, just call me."

"Sam," I warn him.

Sam smiles at me, winks at her and walks off into the crowd of partygoers out near the cars smoking weed.

Devin turns and looks at me, "Have you two fucked already?"

I dare a look at her, and I honestly reply, "No, he would love to, but no, I'm the problem. Do you think it makes me bad to want to, but I don't know if I could?"

"Honestly, I think that's first class, gold star fucking hot. Let's do it. When can he come over?" I watch her breathing pick up, signaling to me she's turned on.

I saddle up to her and press her up against whoever's truck this is, and I put my fingers around her chin, pushing he face up to mine, "Does my little Kitten want to be the naughty ringleader in her own little circus?"

She moans as she melts into me. Her body is already trained to crave me and let it overtake her. I love her this way.

"Do you want me to bend Sam over and fuck him in the ass?"

"Oh God, yes." She arches her back and moans.

I move my fingers around her clit through her leggings, slowly, in circles. "What do you want to be doing while I'm fucking Sam?"

She is panting and trying hard to stay quiet as I increase my pace and pressure on her clit. I want to see how fast I can get her off. We are still a good 40 feet from the first outer ring of the bonfire circle. I could make her scream, and they won't hear her over the music and the fire.

"I-I Want to..I want....to peg you. I want to be behind you."

That surprises me. I trip up on my rotations. Would she have kept this fantasy secret from me if we hadn't of met up with Sam? This dark kinky side of her comes out to play when I push her boundaries and I fucking love it.

"How would you feel if I said yes? I would let you fuck me in the ass. I would take every bit of it for you," I say in a low gravelly voice.

Devin sags and whimpers as the first ripples of her orgasm washes over her. Staring into her eyes, watching the tidal wave crash onto her, "Yes, that's my good little slut. You make me so proud doing all these new things with me....Good girl." Her body convulses as she has her hands on my shoulders, needing me to keep standing. I put my hand over her mouth.

Her eyes never leave mine as she tries so hard to keep her yells inside. Her pleading eyes almost roll back in her head. It almost looks painful for her not to scream. I smile under this mask because she is absolute perfection to me. She sags as her body comes down from the climax.

Pulling up my mask with one hand, the other hand I pull my fingers from between her fabric coated pussy lips and bring them up to my nose and take a deep breath in. "Devin, I love the smell of your pussy. My whole face smells like it right now, and it's trapped in this mask and I am in fucking heaven. I'm about to go introduce you to my friends with the smell of your pussy right in my face."

"Jesus, Oakley. That's fucking hot." I watch her thighs clench. My baby is ready to go some more.

"Come on, Kitten, I don't have it in me right now to go again so soon. Let's get a beer and mingle," he laughs and pulls me along. "Have you ever tried pot?"

Love struck and star gazed, I obediently follow him.

Chapter 34" Oakley

"It's getting cold out here, Oakley. Just let me catch you and be done with it already." Her discomfort is making her whiny.

"Oh no, Mistress Kitten, this is how you wanted to spend Thanksgiving. My advice is keep up and move faster, you will get warmer quicker."

We are out in the 94 acres of land that I purchased this past summer. It has groves of trees, wide open spaces, 2 creeks, and a pond. We have been out here numerous times to just talk and stare at the sky while we lay on a blanket, or we make love under the galaxy.

Who knew my baby loved the night sky so much? She is obsessed with stargazing.

Devin got this hair brained idea from one of her books. She wanted to try it out.

So, here I am with my mask on and she with her red kitty mask and she wants to chase me. If she catches me, she gets to dominate. If I catch her, well, it doesn't matter to me, I'm getting laid by the most beautiful girl in the world either way, so who cares if I catch her.

She is frustrated I keep dodging her, but staying close enough to taunt her. She only has a few more minutes to get me. Once the timer in my pocket goes off, she will get a 10 second head start to run.

Then the hunter becomes the hunted. Or I should say the huntress in this instance.

Devin stands there and pouts and I call out to her, "Is your fantasy not being fulfilled, my love?"

I stand maybe 15 feet from her in the darkness. She can clearly see my mask lit up, but she is nowhere near fast enough to grab me. I slip behind a large Oak tree.

"Don't poke fun at me!" her frustrated growl follows. "I thought this would be easy. Obviously, I underestimated how fast you were and how out of shape I am."

"You said not to make it easy for you." I hide my laughter from my words.

"Can I change my mind and just tackle you to the ground now?" she asks as she bounces on her feet. I know my Kitten is cold and shivering, but this is the game she dreamed up and wanted to play. It's going to get a lot worse for her when I yank those leggings off her and the chilly breeze hits her wet pussy.

I know my girl, she may be whining now, but don't let that fool you, she is wound up tight and wet as fuck right now. That's why she wants to catch me so badly.

Devin has learned out here she can scream as loud as she wants, no one will hear her. The nearest house is one and a half miles down the road and a hard of hearing old man lives there. No one is going to come help her. We are all alone out here. One of the better advantages to having a loud cummer. And how I make her hoarse with how loud I make her cum, goddamn I'm hard just thinking about it.

To be fair, I should just let her catch me. No more waiting. It's killing me not to be buried to the hilt inside her.

"Ok, Kitten, Let's do this, why don…" The timer on my phone in my pocket goes off.

"Oh Oo Kitten, you know what that means." I step out from behind the big oak that was hiding me from her view.

"When I catch you, it will be rough and brutal. Get ready baby. Your ten seconds starts now. 10, 9, 8,…"

Devin squeals and takes off sprinting. I have to hand it to her; she did try but she is rather slow. I watch her ripe ass bounce in the full moonlight. I can't wait to rip her pants off.

That's the deal. Primal, feral, wild sex. She wants consensual non consent in a safe environment. She wants to be hurt, but also wants to be in charge. Welp, she lost and it's my turn now.

"ONE! You're out of time, Mistress Kitten." I watch her disappear in a grove of trees near the creek.

Fixing my mask, I jog over to where I seen her last. I know if I pick up speed it will end too quickly. Devin needs me to take my time. She needs to feel in danger and chased.

Devin has the fantasy of an unknown man trying to force himself on her.

She came out to me one evening under these stars and said she had a fantasy of being taken against her will, and that's why she was in such a stupor the night we met. Apparently, I was everything her daydreams could think up and then some. Except with the whole real kidnapping thing.

I search the shadows for her. We were called back to the police station to give more details and Devin had to testify in a room with a judge on the validity of her story.

It seems the men in blue have no doubt about her story,

however the judge did. It went in her favor when a spirit conveniently popped up in the judge's chambers and it told Devin it was Judge Patterson's deceased mother.

Devin relayed message after message to Judge Patterson and he followed along, until it came down to the validation of his mother's last words spoken to him in an empty room.

He was a believer after that.

He allowed her testimony into court and Wayne Beasley was charged with one count of murder, five counts of kidnapping, and is being investigated for the disappearance of two other girls who were from a town 30 miles away.

The FBI has gotten involved since it's a suspected human trafficking ring. They need to know who he was supplying girls to.

Some of the other girls' testimony is that they've overheard conversations through the walls. Mr. Beasley was casing out students from both schools. They heard him yelling at the other two idiots that he was under contract to produce five girls every six months.

The disappearances started about two months ago, therefore the Feds believe he is new to the game, and this is how he was taken down so easily. He has no idea how to play the game.

Good for us.

The two other morons were local idiots who needed extra money and had zero morals. They were also charged with the same charges as their leader.

The other girls are safe and have been returned to their families. Devin received a $5000 reward for the return of one of the girls. The family offered the reward and would not hear of Devin refusing it. She had no choice but to deposit the money into her account.

It alleviated some of her stress. Mine too. Because if I ever needed to step in and make sure she's taken care of, I would do it in a heartbeat. She will try to stop me, but she will be cared for.

Devin has such a stubborn streak it's difficult to get her to accept help. So, if the circumstances arise, I will have to force her to accept the help.

I still offer for her to move in with me. Fuck, buy a house. Better yet, build our dream house, right here, right now.

She said she doesn't want to get married just yet.

Fine. I'll wait. But I did go to Columbia and have had many meetings with a jeweler about designing a custom ring she has no idea about.

Oh, I'm proposing. That's for fuck sure. She is not getting away from me.

I have a plan for the proposal, but I need some help. I snuck into her phone and grabbed a few contacts to use later.

"Where did my pretty Kitten go?" I sing song to her as I wade through the trees, not giving a fuck how loudly I crash through the dead overgrowth.

I hear her off to the left of me, trying hard not to make a sound as she gingerly moves, but her heavy breathing gives her away. I don't even think she realizes she's breathing that loud, I chuckle to myself.

Her excitement is palpable, and she gives off waves of fear every so often. Good, let her get her fill of her fantasy. Anything for my girl.

"I'm going to make my pussy purr so loud the heavens will tell us to shut up."

I hear a small gasp about ten feet in front of me. I like when she gets turned on by my words. I have never talked so much naughty things in all my life, but for her I've gotten creative.

We have also gotten into talks about bringing Sam in to teach her how to prep and insert a butt plug for me. I am willing to let my girl peg me, but only her. Sam is not getting near my ass with his cock. I will willingly put my ass in the air for him to demonstrate and give her lessons, but his cock doesn't touch my virgin ass.

Devin has also voiced she wants to see me fuck Sam. She's mentioned this a handful of times. She was drunk on margaritas one night when we were out with X and Clover, and Sam tagged along.

We were walking back over to the girls' apartment when her little drunk ass stops in the middle of the street and rounds on Sam, placing her hand on his chest and looking up at him with her full pouty lips on display and some heavily hooded, lust filled eyes, "Would you like my boyfriend to fuck you?"

I thought I was going to choke on my own tongue.

I think Sam did, because his eyes shot to mine and then back to her, then me again. He couldn't speak for a solid minute. My cat got his tongue and rocked him speechless. Hard feat to do because this motherfucker never shuts up. His ego knows no boundaries.

But yet, she continued, "I would really, really, and I do mean really, like to see that. And I think you would too. What do you say, Sammy boy? Do you want to fuck my Loverboy?"

Sam put his hand over hers while on his chest and said he would be delighted to make her dreams come true on one condition; she join in.

Devin in all her brazen drunken glory shot back, "Oh I plan to, I'm going to be the one behind him with a strap on."

The smile that plastered across Sam's face told me he just fell in love with my woman.

We've spent plenty of money, scratch that, we did nothing, Sam and Devin spent a bunch of money on a sex toy and lingerie site and he made sure to get her everything she needed. It arrived in a big box and all I could do was stand there and stare as she pulled one thing after another from the box, squealing with delight.

Sam is scheduled to come over tonight in a couple of hours to enact her devious plan. Once we are done here, we head home for a shower before the next shower. We stay cum covered.

What ever makes her happy.

Pussy whipped. Yeah, that's me.

Lovesick. Yeah, me too.

Irrevocably, madly, passionately, absurdly in love. Yep, guilty again.

I don't give a fuck who knows it or what they think. This has been the best month of my life, and it just keeps getting better.

In about one minute it's going to be a fuckload better because I'm done playing around. It's cold out here!

I circle around a few trees and hear her take off running into the field. Tisk tisk, babygirl, that's too easy.

I take off in a run and line up behind her, and wrap my arms around her, taking us to the ground as I maneuver me to take the hit from the hard earth.

Devin immediately screams and tries to twist out of my grasp. She starts kicking and clawing at the ground to crawl away.

I have to remind myself; this is what she wanted.

I take the opportunity while she's on her stomach to rip down her panties and leggings in one shot. I smack her hard on the ass and that stills her for only a moment. She is still trying to wiggle out from where my thighs have locked her to the ground.

I hurry to undo my pants and pull my rock hard cock out. I move to between her legs, and pull her hips up and back to me. Running my hand up her slit to her asshole, I feel how soaked she is.

I knew she was, and I also know this isn't going to take her long as excited as she is.

My Kitten, fighting until the very end as she grunts and tries to break free. I reach up to her neck and put a firm grip on her throat, "Stay still if you know what's good for you. It will hurt less if you cooperate."

"I will never cooperate." And she reaches back her tiny hand and tries to slap my head away.

While she's trying to hit me, I take my dick in my other hand, line it up, and bury myself in one push because she's so wet. Devin howls at the invasion, "Oh my God."

I grab her hair and pull her head back, "Watch the stars, baby, they want to hear you cum, too."

I have a steady pace pumping into her and I have to fight to not release my unborn children yet. Goddamn she is so tight. I been trying to break this thing in but it is still a vice on my cock. She makes me want to cum at the sight of her any other time, actually being inside her is the sweetest torture.

Across the field you can hear bodies slapping, Devin's wild moans, and my grunts as I fuck her as hard as I can. I hold onto her hip and pull her body back roughly.

"Oakley, oh God, I need to cum...please Sir," she begs. I do love to hear her beg.

I release her hair and reach around her body and find her clit. I move in the circles she loves so much and put just enough pressure that it takes roughly ten rotations, and my kitten screams her head off while clamping down on my cock with her tight pussy. Her voice breaks with the force of her guttural yells of my name.

I once fucked her so hard she lost her voice for a few days. She told everyone, including her mom, she caught a cold.

"Fuck, Devin!" I unleash inside of her as her orgasm crests, and she rides it out, her walls vibrating every last drop of cum from me.

I rip my mask off and throw it on the ground beside her while I slip out of her dripping pussy. Devin falls to the ground on her side and reaches her arms out to me. I land on the ground beside her and pull her head to my chest.

She's so content she hums and sighs. My job here is done. My kitten is content and happy. I will probably have to feed her though. Fucking her brains out makes her want all the snacks.

Good thing I have a whole basket of them in the SUV.

"Was it what you wanted?" I hope I lived up to her expectations.

Devin sits up and stares down at me with her beautiful, silky hair brushing over my face, "Baby it was perfect. Thank you. I loved it, except not being able to catch you but in the end, I got what I wanted, so that's what counts." She leans down and kisses me with her full, luscious lips. I reach up and grab her and pull her down on top of me. She lays sprawled out on my chest and says, "Everyday life with you gets better. Thank you for saving me."

I watch a slow-moving shooting star (that's what Devin calls satellites in the night sky) slowly trail across the sky as I run my fingers through her hair, "My pleasure, all the way. I don't know how I lived without you in my life. I was so lonely and depressed the night I saved you. Now I have purpose, dreams, goals, love. This was meant to be, Devin. I refuse to believe you weren't destined to be mine. I would have found you somehow."

She snuggles in tighter to my chest. "I don't want to live in a world where you aren't. I buried myself in books, school, and work to ease my own loneliness, my own sadness. I don't feel so alone now, and I feel safe with you."

"Come here, Kitten," I say as I pull her to sit up on me and straddle my hips.

"No matter what happens, you will always be taken care of. I've made sure of it."

She laces her hands through mine and holds them to her chest. "I don't know what that means, Oakley."

"It means my Kitten has five million dollars in a trust right now for her and any offspring, should anything happen to me."

She drops my hands to my gut with a thud and her mouth pops open, "No, Oakley, I don't want that."

"It's a done deal, Devin. It's my inheritance to do what I want with, and I want to make sure more than anything you are safe and want for nothing."

She puts her hands up to her face and a small sob escapes. "Hey, hey, baby, don't cry." I sit up and wrap her in my arms. She sags against my chest and sniffles a little.

I reach up and pet her hair and smooth it down, "One day you will have to live without me, and hopefully that's a far off ending for me, but I need this for me, I need to know the love of my life will be looked after. Don't fight me on this, Devin. I had my dad's lawyer set this up two weeks ago."

I remember telling my dad I wanted to do this. He fought me

for a few minutes before he realized I was dead fucking serious, and this is the girl I'm going to marry. He ended up giving me Gary's number and I met with him two weekends ago when I drove over to Columbia.

"You knew two weeks ago we were going to be together forever?" She sits back and looks at me in the moonlight.

I run both my thumbs across her cheeks to wipe her tears, then my fingers in her hair beside her ears, "Baby, I knew within the first 24 hours I was keeping you."

"Sometimes I have to pinch myself to make sure this is real, you are real. Us, we are real. Girls like me don't get the dashing, handsome knight."

"Wrong, girls like you get everything they ever wished for and then some."

I bring her down to kiss her and feel her shivering. After a quick kiss, which I feel her cold nose hit my cheek, I slap her ass to get her up. I find her clothes in the dark and help her get dressed. I stuff my cock back in my boxer briefs and zip me up.

I throw my arm around her, and we walk towards the Maserati. The sky truly is beautiful tonight. But not nearly as beautiful as her.

Chapter 35: Oakley

Sam arrives on time and in a great mood. I'm sure he is.

Seriously though, Sam is a really good looking guy. He is tall, blond, toned and tanned. He goes to the gym every day and takes care of himself. Just not his apartment.

We got home about 2 two hours ago, and Devin inserted the anal plug into me to prep my ass. That was not comfortable but oddly turned me on. She was giggling like a schoolgirl the entire time.

She told me she bought the same size cock as mine so I can feel what she feels when I'm inside her. I saw the thing. It is not my size. It's larger and now I'm intimidated.

When she finished and the plug was all the way in, she jumped up and down and clapped. That's how excited she is.

Sam is dressed in a pair of jeans and a tight red long sleeved cotton pullover. He really is handsome. The first time I saw Sam at X's apartment I was attracted to him. He returned that attraction, but was bolder with his flirtations than me.

I am not sure why I've never acted on the other side of my sexuality with him. Maybe I thought people would think of me differently if they found out. I'm not sure why I even care.

Sam does make my heart rate speed up and for some reason he has always made my cock twitch. He is the first man I've ever been attracted to.

Devin walks up to him and hugs him, while he kisses the top of her head and murmurs, "Hey sweetness."

Nope, don't like that.

I step closer to them, and he knows to back away from her. He is not here for her. There will be no touchy touchy of the Devin for him. He is aware of the rules.

"You want to go outside and smoke before we try this?" Sam asks.

Devin has tried a little pot here and there with me, but she declines this time and tells us to go on out without her.

Grabbing a jacket for the cold November night, I follow Sam out the door. When we get to the parking lot he turns to me and asks, "You sure you're ok with this, man? You seem tense."

Sam lights up the joint and takes his hit, passing it over to me. Before I take a hit, I say, "I'm not sure what to expect, I'm a little nervous for all of it honestly."

"That woman of yours is going to lay into your ass, you know that right?"

"Jesus fuck, dude, she is all about fucking me in my ass. My sweet little innocent Kitten has turned into a wanton sex fiend."

Sam laughs and says, "That's all your fault, man, you shouldn't have been fucking her every minute of the day and night. I'm surprised she isn't pregnant yet."

"Well, it's only been a month and she's on birth control. She doesn't want kids right now or else I would keep her belly full. I want a ton of kids."

We pass the joint back and forth a couple more times. I look over at Sam and grin, "Thanks for being a good sport and fulfilling her fantasy."

"You're joking, right? I been trying to fuck that cock since I met you. I am here for it and already know this sex session is going to be one for the books. I've never gotten fucked by a guy who's getting pegged from behind. This is going to be wild. I can't wait to hear you wake up the neighbors. You might as well move after this."

"I'm already anticipating the next noise warning from the complex." I roll my eyes. See, this is why we need a house in the middle of nowhere.

"She noisy, is she?"

"Wow. She is loud as fuck, and I love it. I take her out to the property and fuck her until she doesn't have a voice."

Sam adjusts his crotch and says, "That's fucking hot, bro. You are one lucky ass man."

"Tell me before we do this, is this going to heighten my orgasm or something?" I tried to do some research, but I still like opinions from people who have experienced it. Sam once told me he will top or bottom, it doesn't matter to him, guy or girl.

"Oh man Oak, this will be mind blowing for you. Once she hits that g-spot up in you with that strap on, you will wonder why you didn't do it sooner. You will love it."

I hand him back the joint and already I am feeling loose and more relaxed. Sam assesses me and asks, "How do you want to do this, Captain?"

I hadn't thought about how to start all this. I've only been thinking of the during and maybe the ending.

"I'm honestly not sure. I guess that's why we have you." I down the rest of my apple juice in my hand.

"Let Daddy get you inside and I can take over."

"No, you will not be my Daddy and don't even ask me to call you that."

Sam claps me on the back and pulls me back to the apartment complex. "Maybe you can be my Daddy after this, eh?" He walks up the stairs in front of me laughing.

We get back up the apartment and the lights are off and Devin has candles lit everywhere. I'm starting to seriously worry she's going to set the fire alarms off.

All those thoughts evaporate when she walks out of the bedroom in a red leather and mesh teddy, complete with buckles, belts, garters, and thigh high black fishnet hose. Her hair is piled on top of her head, and she is flush with desire. She has no panties on either. Fuck me.

She is stunning.

I see Sam adjust his crotch again. I can't complain or point it out because I have to do the same thing.

Sam is the first to speak, since I've momentarily lost the ability, "Devin, you are breathtaking. Wow."

She smiles sheepishly and dips her chin. She can play coy all she wants now, but I know as soon as we enter that bedroom, she will dominate the situation. I am 110% down for that.

"My good little boys, where do we start?" She puts her hands on her hips and cocks her head. Just when I think my girl can't get prettier, she tops it and knocks it out of the park.

I clear my throat and let her know, "We were just coming in to figure that out actually. Sam is going to…" I can't continue talking because Sam's tongue is sliding down my throat. I can only grab on to him and hang on.

Sam greedily takes over my mouth, French kissing me hard and making me moan. He dominates my mouth and holds my head in his hands.

The feeling is completely different than kissing Devin. I feel a little of Sam's scruff scratching at me and the fact that he's taller than me is weird. Not complaining though.

My cock is finishing hardening up nicely so there's that.

I vaguely hear Devin panting while I wrap my arms around Sam. He puts his fingers in my hair and pulls. More moans elicit from me. I love it when Devin pulls my hair.

Sam presses his erection on to mine and I rub mine back and forth over his. That gets Sam to moaning.

Devin comes to stand beside us and rubs both our backs, "Boys, you look fucking hot kissing each other. It's making my pussy so wet."

Sam and I both groan together at that.

He breaks the kiss and says, "I'm ready, y'all ready? Show me where to go before I nut in my pants standing here. Devin, you are such a beautiful distraction."

Devin squeals and takes our arms dragging us to the bedroom. Where there's more candles. She's going to burn us alive, literally and figuratively.

"Be good boys and strip for me. I can't wait to see swords crossed."

I wish I could say I'm shocked at her behavior, but who am I kidding, I am greatly turned on by her right now. As I can see Sam is too.

We are naked and standing in front of her, cocks standing out in front of us. Devin comes up to us and takes a dick in either hand.

Nope, don't like that.

I place my hand around her little baby kitty wrist and gently remove her hand from Sam's cock. It makes her laugh.

"Oakley, I can't even touch Sam?"

"Nope. That's my boundary. He can't touch you either, remember? Those are the rules."

Devin looks at Sam and says, "Would you like to suck his cock?"

Sam doesn't even answer as he drops to his knees and grips my dick in one hand and my balls in the other. I watch as my dick disappears into his hot, wet mouth. Fuck if it doesn't feel amazing.

I let out a hiss between my teeth and put my right hand fingers in his hair. I take my left hand and put it behind Devin's neck and pull her to me to kiss her.

I pull back from her while she's panting, "If I bury my face in your tight little pussy right now, will I drown?"

Sam groans around my cock and Devin weakly says, "Yes, Sir."

I suck air through my teeth as Sam sucks harder and slathers his tongue all around my cock. He gently massages my balls and works my dick further into his throat.

Devin looks up at me and asks, "Sir, do you want to be balls deep in Sam's fine ass giving him all my precious cum?"

Sam pulls off my dick and says, "Jesus Christ, you two are some of the hottest people I've ever been with."

"Oakley, how do you feel about sucking dick for the first time?" Devin asks.

"I can try, I've never done it."

Sam smiles at me and replies, "Don't worry big guy, I will let you know if it's good or not."

"Sam, go lay on the bed, on your back. I want to watch Oakley suck your cock, pretty please."

It's the please at the end that makes me melt. She is holding back her begging. I know she wants to cum already. She will be begging by the time this is over.

Sam lays down on the bed with his cock jutting out. I stand between his legs and bend over him, placing my hand around his girth.

I am really happy Sam is not fucking my ass. Who knew he was walking around with a monster cock making us all look bad? He should really be doing porn.

As I bend over slowly and Sam's cock is right by my lips, I hear Devin buckling on her strap on behind us.

I take Sam's cock in my mouth and explore his ridges with my tongue. It's not so bad. It's smooth and veiny, he has a big head, and he's stiff as a board. I go deeper on his rod and work up more spit to lube with. I start swirling my tongue all around it and bobbing my head up and down.

I hear Sam sucking in air and moaning. Sam puts his fingers in my hair and pulls gently. I shove Sam's cock far back in my throat and gag. He jerks and says, "Ok pretty boy, that's enough or I'm going to blow."

I continue to swirl my tongue up with length before my mouth pops off the head. Devin stops her slow stroking of my cock and says, "I'm ready. Oh God am I ever ready."

Standing up, I turn slightly to see her standing beside me with a red strap on tightly fastened onto her hips and groin with soft black leather. I know she showed me before when it arrived, but I'm well aware there is a fat fake cock in my woman's pussy, that is vibrating and rotating.

I know nestled on the inside on the leather is a silver vibrating bullet her clit will sit and rub on. It's going to drive her wild. I can't help but wonder how many times she's going to cum with that on her clit.

And the cock on the outside that's going in me, vibrates too. She said I would enjoy it more.

Sam has sat up and is looking at her with his mouth open. "Oak, you are officially the luckiest man alive, I hope you know that, fucker."

I reach over to roughly pull her to me by her neck so I can lay a deep searing kiss on her. While I kiss her Sam puts his lips around my cock again. I'm moaning into Devin's mouth and praying my knees don't buckle.

Devin breaks away, with labored breathing she loudly says, "Alexa, play 'Devin's List' starting with 'I Want It All'." The notes of 'I Want It All' by Omido, Mandrazo, and Rick Jensen play through the apartment.

We picked up a wide exercise stepper from the sporting goods store for Devin to stand on since she's going to be too short normally. This way she can comfortably reach me and it's a wide area to stand on. It was better than a stepstool. It seems to be the perfect height to make her comfortable. And hopefully don't hurt me more. This is helping me too.

Devin places the stepper behind me as Sam takes his mouth off my cock. I put my hands in Sam's hair and pull his head back, and lean down and kiss him. Our tongues are dancing around and wrestling. Devin is breathing so hard. You can hear mine and Sam's labored breathing over hers.

I let up off Sam's lips and he stands up right into me and our dicks touch. "When you cum in my ass, I know you're going to be thinking of her, and that's ok, I'm going to be thinking of her, too." He smiles as my eyes narrow. "Now that you're properly pissed off, fuck me like you hate me, Daddy."

Sam turns around so I shove him over the bed. Devin lays an unpackaged condom in my hand and I roll it on my cock. She hands me the lube and has her own bottle to take back there.

She walks behind me and says, "Bend over, baby, I have to take the plug out first."

Sam looks back over his shoulder, "Dude, you've had a plug in the entire time? That's hot as fuck."

Devin pulling it out was a lot better than Devin getting it in.

I rub Sam's ass and spread his cheeks, kneading them. I run a finger around the rim of his asshole and apply a little pressure. Sam spreads his legs wider and moans. It makes my cock jump.

I use some of the lube in my hand and wipe it all over Sam's asshole. I use a healthy dollop for my dick. I run one finger inside him past the rim, then two fingers.

Gruffly I ask Sam, "You ready?"

"Absofuckinglutely. Don't be afraid to hurt me, Oak. Let go. Now stick your dick in me, I've been waiting long enough."

No sooner had the last few words left his mouth I had my dick as his back door and pressing in. Sam's breath hitching. Mine is stuck in my chest. I push my dick in a little harder, making Sam arch his back and push back onto me, Sam takes my dick to the hilt.

His ass is tight and hot. His ass is not as tight as my girl's pussy, but it still feels really good.

Devin has her hands on my shoulders and says, "Are you ready?"

"Yeah, Kitten. Fuck me in my ass."

Devin groans and dips her body. "Lean over Sam, play with his dick while I enter you, fuck Sam slowly."

Devin is at my entrance, and this fake cock feels much bigger than mine. She lines up and applies pressure. I feel the head slipping past the rim slowly.

I'm moving my dick slowly in and out of Sam and it's helping Devin get the dildo inside me.

I feel the burn of my ass stretching and there is some pain, but underneath all that, there's pleasure. I find myself pushing back into Devin.

"Oakley," Devin whispers, "It's all the way in, Sir."

I moan as she adjusts and I lean up over Sam, putting my arms on either side of him. Sam is laying face down on our bed and he keeps clenching his ass. It's driving me wild.

"Kitten, you better get to fucking me because Sam's ass feels really good and I'm close."

That's the green light she needed.

Devin plows into my ass, effectively knocking me further into Sam. The sensation steals my breath. I fully stand up and reach back to Devin's thigh as she finds a rhythm.

Come to find out my baby is a ten pump chump because she cums almost immediately, panting out my name. She sags for a minute but catches her breath in no time and renews her efforts of fucking me.

Sam yelling, "Oh my fucking God Devin, that's so sexy. Fuck."

I use her momentum to fuck Sam.

Who has done nothing but moan and jack his cock while pushing back onto me.

I look down at me entering Sam, back and forth, in and out. It turns me on more to know this is not a pussy. I'm fucking my first guy, and I need to get into the present. I've been riding the pain wave but now that it's leveled out, I start fucking Sam in earnest and let Devin find her rhythm off of that.

The dick in my ass feels amazing. Sam was correct, it's hitting a spot in there I've never felt before and it's making me quickly lose my mind.

Devin rubs her hands all over my chest, in my hair, over my nipples, and whispers to me, "Do you like it?"

"Mmm, fuck Devin, it feels so good. Sam's ass wrapped around my cock feels amazing."

I put my head back and Devin runs her hands in it and pulls my head back then bites my neck. I moan out and draw air through my teeth.

I hear Sam picking up the pace of his stroking.

I moan and tell her, "Yes baby, that's it... But I really want to hear you cum.....let Sam hear you again baby. Show him....he's thinking what it would be like to be deep as fuck in that tight pink pussy of mine."

From below me Sam groans, "Fuck Oak, I want to hear her cum. I need it. Devin please."

I lean back and twist while staying in Sam's ass, and kiss Devin, "Give me what I want, Mistress."

Sam, "God fucking dammit."

Devin grabs my shoulders and picks up her pace. 'Pretty Boy' by Isabel LaRosa plays as Devin fucks me in the ass. I bend over Sam and put my hand on his throat and gently squeeze. I grab a hold of his hips and pull him back to me.

Devin feels so good back there, I would definitely do this again.

"Oakley," Devin rushes out, "Oh my God, Oakleyyyyy!" A powerful orgasm rips through Devin and her voice cracks with her release. She is digging her nails into my shoulders. Sam roars beneath me and says, "Fuck fuck fuck."

I slam into Sam a few hard times and cum in his ass as I feel him clenching my dick inside as the cum spurts out of him.

I throw my head back and yell as Devin wraps one of her hands around my throat and squeezes, while the other she puts her fingers in my mouth to suck. I mumble as I suck her fingers and unload in Sam's ass.

I'm slowly aware of Devin pulling the dildo out of my ass. It feels so empty now. Is that what women are talking about in feeling full? I really liked the feeling of being stuffed and the sensations it caused.

Devin comes around and stands beside the bed, where I'm slowly pulling out of Sam's ass. "That is one the of sexiest sights I've ever seen. Sam your ass looks good with Oakley's dick in it."

Sam has caught his breath now, turns his head to look at her and replies, "Thank you, pretty girl."

As soon as I slide out of Sam, I step back. I had such a powerful orgasm I'm dizzy. My whole body is jelly.

Sam stands up with a huge smile, and puts his hand up. I take it and grip his hand, "That was awesome, bro. I am on cloud 9 right now. Nobody can tell me shit."

He turns to Devin and hugs her..

Nope…well, maybe.

"Devin you are the most amazing woman I've ever met. You call me anytime you want me to bottom for your man again."

She giggles into his chest.

Ok buddy, I reach over and gently pull Devin back into me. Sam walks over to his clothes. "Hey Oak, can I hit the guest shower real quick?"

"Yeah, sure thing. There's soaps and towels in the closet."

I look down at Devin. She is still so excited. I smile at her and ask, "Was it everything you imagined?"

"Oh. My. God. Oakley. It was so much more. Thank you so much, baby!" She stands on her tiptoes and kisses me.

I reach down and take the condom off, tie it up and take it to the bathroom trash. Devin is out there unbuckling herself from the strap on and then I hear it hit the floor.

I come up behind her and start helping her out of her teddy too. She has one of the four clasps on the garter undone. When those are all undone, I roll her fishnet hose down her legs. I stand up and I slip her straps down her shoulders and pull the teddy down her hips and hold her as she steps out of it.

Sam appears in the doorway, staring at my woman.

I'm going to allow this considering what we all just did.

"Oak, thanks for letting me see your girl naked and in action, and double thanks for letting me hear her cum. Devin, stay in trouble, sweetness. I'm gonna head out, you two crazy kids. Let me know whenever you wanna do this again." With that, Sam is out the door.

Devin reaches up at me and I pick her up then she wraps her legs around me. Her forehead is pressed to mine.

"I love you, Loverboy."

"I love you more, Kitten."

Chapter 36: Devin

Breathe Devin, it's here somewhere.

I look one more time around my room and don't see my Kindle. I know I left it in here on charge. Or did I? Anxiety has me twisted up not thinking straight.

Losing my Kindle is like losing my arm or leg. It's an extension of me. I find comfort in it, even just carrying it around. There are worlds and people wrapped up in that machine that I am severely invested in.

Oh God, my TBR!

I will never recover from this. I clutch my chest.

Dramatic bitch. You can redownload all of it.

I cherish my paper books, but my Kindle has my heart and soul. Sure, I could buy a new one, but I can't replace the stickers or the memories and tears we've shared. Who wants to set up another electronic gadget anyways?

It's like losing a friend and my chest beats with another pang.

I hear the front door open and close, and Oakley calls out, "Devin?" Good thing we gave him and X their own keys. *eye roll. Now they think they can come over and stake claim whenever they want. In his defense, right now he is here to pick me up to go to his dad's. And I'm running behind. Of course.

"In here!"

He appears in my bedroom doorway and takes one look at my panic stricken face and says, "What's wrong?" in his concerned tone.

I'm sure he's taking in the half-packed suitcase and the pile of clothes on the bed I still have yet to fold and pack. We are going to be gone for two whole weeks to our parents for Christmas, which is in two days. So, starting today I am on my first adult vacation.

Don't ask me how I'm supposed to live without him for two weeks. It's going to be a race to see which one caves first and drives to the other.

Clover has graciously offered to babysit her god-cat Luna and make sure she isn't lonely. She also said we could video chat the cat. Oakley is very happy about that. I think this fucker is trying to steal my cat.

I literally heard him telling Luna one time last week, 'If you follow me out the door to the car, Mommy will have no choice but to move in because you chose a side. Help me with this fluffball, and I can make all your tuna dreams come true.'

"I lost my Kindle," I feel my bottom lip tremble.

"No, you didn't. You gave it to me a few days ago to finish reading one of your favorite series."

I'm dumbstruck. How could I forget?

"Oh, yeah, I forgot." Now I feel stupid. Crisis adverted. Back to packing before I lose my mind. I put my hand on my forehead and take a deep breath, whoosh let it out. God, I hate anxiety.

Oakley walks over to me and rubs my upper arms, "What's really going on, Kitten?"

I look into his eyes and see all the love he has for me gazing back. The panic claws at my chest again and my eyes tear up, I softly tell him, "What if they don't like me? What if they think I'm just after your money like the last girl?"

"Stop. You're overanalyzing again and working yourself up. Your fears are valid; however, they will accept you because I love you so very much. I don't give a fuck if they approve, this is my life and you are my entire universe, ok?"

I have never once taken for granted that he is the greatest man to ever walk into my life and I cherish every second I get to be with him. I would hate for someone, like his family, to come between us. I could never make him choose.

He wraps me in his arms so tight I can feel his chest vibrate on my cheek when he says, "Do you think I don't have the same fears? I'm meeting your whole family, too. What if they don't like me? What if they think I'm too much of a distraction for you and your degree? Or what if they think it's too soon and try to persuade you from me?"

I slip out an unrestrained click of my tongue, "Are you fucking kidding me?" I pull back and look up at him. "My mom has talked nonstop about meeting you and how she loves you already. I have given her no big details to know you, just vague comments, that highly piss her off by the way. I think she has some made up version of you in her head and I am all for it," I giggle at my mom's romantic ass putting him on a pedestal, "She is going to be so happy when her dreamed up knight in shinning armor turns out to be everything she could wish for for her daughter."

His chest rumbles with his laugh, "Fair enough." He pulls me away from him, leaving his arms draped on top my shoulders by my ears, "Does she know how hot I make her daughter?"

He sways his hips playfully. He glides his scruffy cheek across mine, and then down the column of my neck as his hands roam my body. "Does she know how often I want to throw her daughter down and fuck her silly?"

He uses his hand to push my hair away from my shoulder. He gently nibbles at my collarbone. It tickles so much it gives me shivers.

"Does she know how I make her daughter cum over," nibble, "and over," lick up my neck, stopping by my ear, "and over?" That part makes me moan.

"You want me to bend you over the bed right now, Kitten?" he nips my neck just hard enough to make my pussy flutter.

"It's not even been 10 hours, Oakley." But I know I want it. He says drop panties and I do it. Fucking Goddamn, I do it. Every. Single. Time.

He was right. He made me addicted to him. My drug of choice is him, it will always be him. I am full on slut mode for this man and no longer have shame. He orchestrated this to perfection.

My mother is going to take one look at me and KNOW. Aunt Jilly too. They are going to see everything they can't see over the phone or video chat. She will just know how in love with him I am, and how her little Fire Ant turned into a Fire Slut. And I secretly can't wait to see it written across her face.

Her little girl is growing up.

"That's 10 hours too long, Kitten."

I let him rock me and nibble on me until I say, "Ok, but be quick, we have to get on the road and I need to pack still."

He moves so fast at that green light, taking all my clothes off the bed and throwing them to the floor. He yanks me over to the bed and says, "Get your bullet, Kitten, this will be the best three minutes of your life."

I can't help but belly laugh at him as I reach into the nightstand drawer and pull out the vibrating bullet. This has been the best purchase so far. So many things I can do with this, so many ways I can cum, and it makes it great when he's behind me, like now.

He quickly undoes his belt and unzips his pants, and they drop to his ankles. And he reaches for me..

"Wait! Shut the door at least," I giggle. "I'm positive X nor Clover want to see your white ass pumping dick into me."

He hops over to the door, dick jangling around, and swings it shut, effectively slamming it. I look back over my shoulder at him and narrow my eyes.

"What? It slipped." He shrugs. "Now, where was I? Oh yeah, about to be balls deep in my favorite thing." He hops back up behind me and slaps my right ass cheek while he buries his face in my hair, "I promised you three minutes...bend over."

I do what my body is trained to do; listen to him and bend over.

Epilogue 1: Oakley

Soo, the little sexcapade set us back by 45 minutes. I blame her. She blames me. Luna blames us both.

I know because she was wailing outside the closed bedroom door, loudly expressing her displeasure at being locked out of 'family time'.

We try to keep it PG around the cat. She's a baby, we cannot corrupt her.

We stop and grab some food and eat in the restaurant because Devin insists we can't get the 'fancy SUV' dirty. I quote, "There shalln't be any soiling of the food upon thy carpet in the carriage."

Set back by another 20 minutes.

I think it's safe to assume Devin is reading a historical romance currently.

Her new interest in corsets was also a clue.

We get back on the road and I think it's within minutes, no seconds, Devin passes out and starts snoring. I turn up the music a little, so it lulls her. It's her favorite playlist, the one she labeled Devin's Playlist. She's added so many songs to it since we started dating. She says it's all the songs that remind her of me and us.

'The Devil Wears Lace' by Steven Rodriguez plays through the SUV as she starts to drool.

It's a good thing I told her to bring her pillow and blanket. I know I kept her up far too late and she got up early to go to work for the morning shift so we could have tonight to drive to my dad's. She has to be exhausted.

Honestly, I don't know how either of us hasn't slipped into a coma from lack of sleep.

We are going to stay at my dad's one night, then I will drive her the couple hours to her mom's, where I will meet all her family. I have no idea how I'm going to survive away from her.

There has not been one single day in the past few weeks I have been away from her. I see her every day. And if she's tired and been on her feet all day, I take her to her apartment and rub her feet until she falls asleep. We go back and forth sleeping at each other's place.

Our days off are spent wrapped up in each other. The outside world barely exists anymore. We stay exhausted. I wouldn't want this any other way.

Sometimes I am shaken by the profound realization I can be this happy for the rest of my life. I can have this every day. And one day I will have more.

Sometimes I will lay awake in bed late at night, with her arm resting on my chest and her leg draped over me. She sleeps soundly tucked under my arm while I can't sleep and fight my demons of depression. I refuse to let it ruin this. Her presence help quell the sadness.

There are zero reasons I have to be sad or depressed over, but my brain thinks it's time for a bout of sadness. I fight that shit back into a corner every chance I get. Devin once brought up counseling and medication to me when we discussed mental health.

Maybe it's time I do see someone. My sleepless nights and hard-working sex filled days are going to be the death of me.

Devin said her mom always said to give people a chance to miss you, then you'll see where you stand in their life. I do not need to test that.

Fuck, I miss her every second she isn't near me.

Yes, it's that bad.

She can get up to go pee and I immediately want her back right next to me. The space around me doesn't feel right if she's not right there, near me.

'Work Song' by Hozier comes on next, and I hum to the song. This is one of my favorites she put on her list. I sing it to her all the time.

I sing softly while I drive and watch the road. Maybe in these two weeks Devin will have me come get her for a few days to stay at my dad's. We never discussed that because we were too hung up on the two weeks away from each other.

This is the happiest I've ever been in my life. I hope my dad, Sarah, and Myles can see that. Devin doesn't give one shit about my money. She still has no idea how vast that wealth is.

I put 5 million back for her, but I make almost that every week on my investments. That's just mine, not my dad's for me, or my salary from working.

Devin hasn't a clue on how rich she will be.

It's been truly hard to watch her count her money and juggle her paycheck. She's pretty thrifty, I'll give her that. But I can make her life so much better if she would only let me.

She will let me spoil her with material things like sex toys, lingerie, restaurants, books, and margaritas, but will always refuse me when I want to help her with rent, or buy her groceries, or fill her car up with gas.

Devin will truly be mad when she figures out what I do. I go to her work and sit in her section. I give the people around me money to leave her as a tip. It always makes her happy when she has a 'good night'.

She doesn't know I slip 20's into all her sweater and hoodie pockets when she hangs them back up in the closet. That way she will find a nice surprise when she wears it again. So far, she's found about $120 that she 'must have forgotten about'.

I've stolen her car twice while she sleeps. I fuck her really good and then she passes out. I dress and tiptoe out the door after swiping her car keys. Thankfully Devin sleeps with music on so it makes for a smoother getaway.

I've taken her car to fill it up across town to the station that's open 24 hours. I also accidently on purpose forget her favorite snacks in the car.

But I've only stolen her car once while she was at work. Pam was in on that one and was my accomplice. She got in Devin's purse for her keys and handed them to me out the back door.

I took Devin's car to a trusted mechanic in town who enthusiastically agreed to stay open until 9 for an extra $3000 cash so he could tune up her car, change the oil, check the brakes, and install four new tires. I think she's onto me with that one.

I sent her and Clover to a spa for a girls day in Columbia two weeks ago. They spent the day getting pampered, and I spent that time with Dad's lawyer, setting up her account and making a will for myself.

I had my dad on speakerphone the entire time so he could hear first hand what my wishes are. He told me, "The pussy better be worth it, son, it better be golden and spit cash.".

I told him to watch how he talks about my future wife. Absolutely no one will disrespect her to me.

Even my dad.

Devin and I haven't talked about what happens with us. Are we going to move in together? Does she want to build a house with me? Are we waiting until she graduates college to get married? Can I marry her right now?

Would she still want to go to college if she knew she never had to work another day in her life? Would she still be worried about trying to provide for her life?

She said she picked nursing because she has always wanted to help people, and she isn't squeamish. Devin said when she was growing up, every time she said she wanted to be a pilot or a lawyer or have her own company, her father would tell her, "No honey, those are man jobs, why don't you be a nurse, or a hairdresser?"

Devin picked nursing to appease her dad who is paying her tuition. She picked it because she was conditioned to pick it.

Would she still choose nursing if she didn't have to have him pay for a degree?

I hope she would pick what her heart wants.

Her dream is to be a writer. She wants to be free to write stories about the people she sees while people watching. We see people out in public and together we make up their back stories and who they are. Of course they are outlandish, but who's to say life really isn't that strange.

I start humming 'Never Let Me Go' by Florence + The Machine. I've danced with her in her kitchen and in my living room to this song. I hold her to me as I hum to her, and she softly sings.

Those moments are what brings me back to her altar again and again. Every day I worship at her feet and try to be a better man for her.

I will do everything within my power to keep her. I know she is free to leave whenever she wants. It will break my soul for her to do that, but she's free. I want her to choose me. That doesn't mean I won't make her life as comfy as possible to keep her with me.

If she ever leaves, I hope she finds her way back home. I'll be waiting.

There will never be another Devin.

I would most likely live like my dad. The realization hits me so hard I put my hand to my chest.

In this moment, I understand my dad. I understand the magnitude of loss he suffered when my mom died. He lost a piece of his soul.

That pain was unfathomable to me, until now. Until her.

My dad never said one bad thing about my mom. He would often tell me stories of her. They took a ton of pictures and videos of each other. I've seen all of them, numerous times, too many to count.

I feel like I know my mom, and through Dad, Sarah and Myles, I have a firm grip on who she was.

Pretty soon we were pulling up to my dad's house. All the outside lights are on and it looks pretty festive. This had to be his girlfriend's doing.

I turn off the SUV and gently nudge Devin. "Hey baby, we're

here, Dev, wake up Kitten." She groans and rolls onto her back and stretches.

That's when her eyes become saucers and she notices it got dark, and behold, in front of us is Clark Griswold's house.

Oh yeah, this is going to be interesting.

Devin slips her shoes back on as I come around the front and get her door for her. She still looks so sleepy.

"Devin baby, as much as I love your sleepy, freshly fucked look, you are going to have to wake up and look alive." I sing to her. She looks up at me and seriously growls. She's like a fucking bear if you wake her up too early. "You said don't let you embarrass yourself. Just doing my duty, Mistress."

And here comes her cute as fuck pouty lip.

"Come on," I hold my hand out, knowing what she will instinctively do.

She puts her hand in mine and stands up. She wipes her face and slaps her cheeks a few times. She runs her hands through her wavy, long hair and then runs in place for a moment. She looks like Rocky warming up.

It's seriously hard not to crack up laughing.

She gives me the death stare. I'm dead.

Devin lifts her chin and takes a big breath. "Ok, I'm good."

"Yeah?"

"Yes. For the record, I'm mad at you for letting me fall asleep and not waking me up so I can look decent in time. Five seconds was hardly enough to time to get refreshed."

She crosses her arms over her chest and pouts.

I take my hand and wrap around her throat, shoving her back against the Maserati. Her eyes grow big and I hear her breath hitch in her throat.

"Mad enough to give me dirty angry sex at my Daddy's house?"

Her sharp intake of breath was all I needed. Yep, she's awake now. I drop my hand and smooth my jacket down. I hold out my arm to her, "Ready? Let's go."

My dad opens the door and yells, "Hey son!" He grabs me for a hug and drags me into the house with Devin following.

He lets me go and I gesture to Devin, "This is my girlfriend De..."

"Devin?"

Devin jerks and quickly looks over to the kitchen doorway. "Mom?"

I am highly confused right now. Devin's mom lives two hours away, there's no way this is the same neighbor my dad is fucking.

I should have looked closer at the address Devin sent me for her mom.

My dad's girlfriend runs over to hug Devin just as Devin was running to her too. They hug and the lady puts a kiss on Devin's forehead and Devin says, "Hey Mommy."

What the fuck is happening here?

My dad clears his throat and says, "I guess you two know each other then."

She lets out a throaty laugh and says, "Yeah, I made this."

I see where Devin gets her goof from.

I come to my senses and say, "Yeah, I can definitely tell. Devin, you look just like your mom. You two could be sisters, wow."

Devin has the audacity to giggle.

Dad claps me on the back and says, "Ok, well, Larken, this is my son Oakley."

She reaches over to hug me and it takes me by surprise. "It's a pleasure to meet you. I've heard so many wonderful things about you."

"My dad has told me how great you are. I can't wait to get to know you." I pull away and put my arm around Devin, "Dad, this is Devin."

Dad hugs her and she doesn't seem as uptight and stressed now that her mom is here with her. It's uncanny how much they look alike. Scary almost.

Oh God, does this mean my dad is going to be attracted to his daughter-in-law too? *Now why the fuck would you think of this right now?*

Larken looks at Devin and has a knowing smile, "I see this is what you had to do tonight and couldn't stay with me."

Sarah chose this moment to come around the corner and beeline straight to me and wrap me in one of her bear hugs.

I introduce Devin to Sarah and Myles, and Sarah immediately grabs her in a hug, too.

I'm going to say Devin passed the Sarah test.

I can see Devin visible relax after that hug. I'm thrilled to see her more comfortable.

Holy shitballs. I am still wrapping my head around all of this. Maybe if we wouldn't have all been keeping secrets and surprizes, we could have figured it out sooner.

Holy fuckity fuck, does this mean I'm fucking my step-sister wife?

Don't panic Oak. Maybe it's another woman your dad is dating.

No, it's not. My dad has already talked to me about marrying this woman. They are going to make me marry my stepsister. As fucked up as that sounds, Devin will probably find it hot. She reads strange shit and will tell me all about it while she sits on my cock. Because naughty books taught us about cock warming. Appreciative nod.

After dinner, we talked about how we met each other and Devin and I jokingly tell them in a class. They already knew. I notice my baby yawning and I tap the inside of her thigh and tell my dad we are going to bed.

Her mom says, "Well I suppose you won't need your own guest bedroom daughter."

I assured her Devin indeed would not be sleeping anywhere that's not beside me.

She gives Devin a wink and goes off to bed herself, after kissing my dad.

I see where Devin gets a lot of herself from. They have the same wicked sense of humor, and they act like sisters, best friends more so than mother and daughter.

From what I've heard from my dad, her mom is a saint. That makes sense because I swear Devin is some kind of angel. She's the same woman that snuck into the kitchen and did the dishes before Sarah or her mom could get to them.

She is the one who selflessly takes care of others. She's the one always making sure everyone is happy.

And I am the Loverboy behind her making sure she's taken care of. Making sure she eats, sleeps, orgasms, and drinks enough coffee or tea to fill a giraffe.

My devotion to her is unwavering. I give into her every whim.

In my old room, in my teenage bed, I tuck her tighter under my arm. Into the darkness, I whisper to a half sleeping kitten as I hold her, "I promise, I will never stop loving you for the rest of my life, until the Angel of Death comes for me, even then it won't stop. When I get to shine with you in the sky in our own constellation, the whole universe will see me burn for you."

"Oakley," her sleepy little voice whispers. "I love you." She stirs her arm and leg that's draped across me, weaving her fingers through my chest hair as she moves. "Oakley, come make love to me again."

I roll her onto her back, positioning myself between her legs, and look at her sleepy face. My voice low and husky, "Devin."

Her legs spread wider as a small smile forms on her face. Her beautiful eyes slowly open and she quietly says, "I will forever shine with you wherever you go. My place belongs with you."

She pulls me closer, and I sink into her.

I pray to whoever can hear me, please let me keep her forever.

Epilogue 2: Oakley

6ish months later

Devin is so excited for tonight. A little birdie, that loves and adores me by the way, told me the Fourth of July is her daughter's favorite holiday. She loves fireworks because since she was a child, they reminded her of stars exploding with love and glitter across the sky.

This birdie also told me she is very happy to see her Fire Ant so happy and loved.

I passed the family test, too.

That brings us to now.

That family has been helping me set this day up for a couple weeks now. I may or may not have hired a team of pyros who specialize in fireworks and bought a shit ton of fireworks to set off tonight in the back fields behind her mom's house, while there's barely a sunset left. Big badaboom!

We made sure that X and Clover could be here. Nicole rode with us here and is staying at Devin's mom's house.

Aunt Jilly, who is hopelessly in love with me, and you can't say one dang bad thing about me or she will shank you, she is here already and helping make food (that I catered in so they wouldn't have to cook) look good on platters, and keeping me level headed.

Aunt Jilly is a lot to take in. Wow, she really has no filter. She's as honest as the day is long and she is fiercely loyal to Larken and her kids. Aunt Jilly don't put up with shit and has no problem calling you out on your bullshit. So, when I called her for help on setting this up, you can imagine how nervous I was.

Nicole was easy to get on board. Clover said she didn't even know what I wanted but it was a yes for saving her.

Dad, Sarah, Myles and Ben are all here from my dad's house. I can't imagine not inviting them. It's going to be a helluva show.

Nicole aspires to be a photographer, so she had a good camera already and I've hired her to take pictures. I've given her a certain spot to be in, per Aunt Jilly. She was also given instructions from Jilly that she had to follow to the letter or risk wrath from Larken.

Ahh, Larken. One of a kind. Wait, she made a mini me. Literally.

Larken is a great woman and I'm truly happy my dad is going to marry her. They are planning a winter wedding. Devin was shocked her mom would marry again after swearing off marriage. My dad knew Christmas was Larken's favorite holiday when he proposed in front of the tree last December with all of us surrounding them. Devin cried for days she was so happy.

I think Larken has been a great addition to my dad's life, and I give them my blessing.

Still grumbly about them making me marry my stepsister. Devin is going to be my wife someday whether Dad and Larken get married or not, doesn't matter, incestuous or not, she's marrying me.

Devin has teased me a few times asking if I want to come home and fuck my sister. She finds it hilarious.

Home. Our home. After I graduated this past June, Devin decided she no longer want to go to college. We are building a house together in between Dad and Larken's properties. Plenty of space between all three houses and close to family. Larken is thrilled. Especially since Devin agreed to 10 bedrooms because I asked for a dozen kids.

She said we could never afford that many kids.

I let her know exactly how rich she is and that helped her make up her mind on a lot of my wishes. We will be moving into our new house this fall when it's completed. Until then, we have been staying with my dad since graduation last month. Before that I had to stay with her in her apartment for a few months because she got me thrown out of mine for noise.

It was totally worth it.

I'm walking through Larken's spacious back yard with all its flower gardens and concrete monuments, and I stop to admire the hard work Devin's mom has put into this yard. It's a complete wonderland back here. That lady definitely has a green thumb.

The backyard opens to the fields my dad owns behind her mom's house. The sky is huge out here with it's unobstructed view. You can see the milky way and a sky full of stars with no light pollution.

There was no doubt in my mind, this is the perfect backdrop to it.

The sun is setting, and Devin doesn't notice the shift in the playlist as she's talking to Clover. Good girl Clover, run the diversion as planned.

I watch Devin talk to her in the fire light. She is having a great time. She has on a pair of pink cowboy boots and a white dress that comes to her knees. She wore her hair up in a messy bun and didn't put a lick of makeup on.

The only jewelry she has on is the golden acorn necklace I had made for her and gave it to her for Christmas last year. She never takes it off. She says it will go well with all the other acrons she going to give me from her big Oak. I have her convinced to give me so many acrons and I'm so excited. God, she's fucking gorgeous. How did I ever get so lucky?

They let off a test firework right on schedule. I turn around and hold my hand out. It's like she senses my hand now because she had her hand out before she even turned around from Clover to face me.

She places her hand in mine, and I lead her out to the edge of the lawn, right before the field starts. Everyone follows us out there and stands sorta behind us.

They have places and cues.

We stand waiting for the show to start and she's dying with anticipation. She leans into me a giggles and does a happy shake and dance, she's so excited.

I lean my head over and say, "This is all for you, baby."

They start the fireworks, and I see her eyes light up and her big, open mouthed smile. She is breathtaking right now. I get to watch the fireworks in her eyes because I can't look away.

Devin points to ones she loves and ohhh's and ahhhh's at others.

If I knew this would be the reaction she would have; she's that enraptured right now. I would blow up gunpowder every day to see her face light up like this.

They are coming up on the finale in less than a minute, and as scheduled 'Scared To Start' by Michael Marcagi plays and they gradually turn it up from behind us.

As soon as Devin hears it, she unconsciously starts swaying and points to more fireworks. She loves this song.

I stand here holding her hand, watching her. She's not the only one enraptured.

From her side, I watch the beginning of the finale in her wide open eyes. I watch tears pour from the corners of her eyes.

She looks over at me smiling huge, and I reach for her face, I kiss her lips and drop to my knee.

I take out the ring I had custom made for her.

Devin puts her hand over her mouth and her eyebrows raise. I watch as her eyes fill and spill over.

"Devin, spend eternity with me, spend every day loving each other, and promise to be my best friend forever? Marry me, Kitten."

She giggles and screams, "YES! Of course, Yes!"

I jump up, grab her by her waist, and lift her off the ground, twirling her around and kiss her perfect pink lips passionately. I would be lying if I said I didn't shed a tear, too.

Ok, don't think bad of me, but I'm crying like a baby.

My Kitten said YES!

Now, I want to just runaway with her.

At least take her in the house and do that favorite thing I like to do to her.

We pull apart and smile at each other.

"You sly dog." She weakly hits my arm that's holding her and glances at her ring.

The center is a large diamond cut into a fat C shape as a moon. There is a star-cut blue sapphire in the middle of the C. There are tiny blue sapphires and diamonds surrounding the mount and the band has stars and moons stamped into the platinum.

Inside the band I had inscribed 'Forever my Kitten'.

"I told you I would chase the cat, and now I have her. I love you, Kitten."

"I love you more, Loverboy."

The end

Follow more Medium Manor adventures in the 3rd book, Cougar, available in a few weeks.

Thank you!

Thank you for continuing this journey with me! I appreciate all the support I've received. Y'all are fabulous!

Thank you to my husband Bryan, for listening to me clickity clack on the keyboard every night after I get off work. For answering my 'man' questions and letting me know which gun he would use to save me with.

Thank you to my friends and family for surprisingly reading my dirty words. That touches my heart so sweetly.

Thank you to everyone who has downloaded or purchased my books. It means the world to me!

I could have kept writing Devin and Oakley's story. I love this book so much. I have a serious book hangover from their love story.

I drew a lot from my husband for Oakley. Bryan is just as goofy and loving, and I am a very spoiled wife. These type of good guys are out there and I am supremely fortunate to have found one. I quickly upgraded him to husband and plan to keep him and the hand necklace he gives me forever.

Bryan, when we die and become stars, the world will know how much I love you by the shine I throw. ilu

ABOUT THE AUTHOR

Brandy Rife

 Brandy lives in South Carolina with her husband of 16 years, Bryan, her soulmate Albus (their chiweenie), and 4 cats, and 3 ferrets. She is originally from Chesterville, Ohio and lived there all her life until 2 years ago. Together her and Bryan have a blended family of 5 adult children and 3 grandchildren.

She has a full time muggle job she works during the day and at night she likes to write, create her taxidermy art, or read on her Kindle.

Since Brandy was a child she has had Medium abilities. She has done many house clearings and home visits to speak to spirits.

It was always a dream of her's to write a book. One night she sat down to her laptop and just let a story spill out of her and Songbird was born. That story is still going strong with many others in her head.

Be kind to one another, you never know what someone else is going through.

BOOKS IN THIS SERIES

Medium Manor

Medium abilities run in the family? Find out when spirits start showing up begging for Larken and her children to help them solve their murders.

Songbird

Larken needs a fresh start after divorcing her husband of 22 years. Moving 2 hours away to an old Victorian in the middle of nowhere South Carolina, she finds herself smack dab in the middle of a murder mystery from the ghost that's haunting her house. Being a Medium has it's perks...and drawbacks.

Meanwhile, the sexy new neighbor is taking up a lot of her time and energy. Not that she minds at all. Does all that flirting back up what he's packing? She certainly hopes so! She's trying to find her inner kinks and maybe he is just the man to teach her what her body craves.

Quinn wants to dominate his new neighbor and make her his new toy, but she ruins all his plans. He finds himself wrapped up in his new obsession, making her sing. And damn, is it beautiful! He feels compelled to help her solve the murder and keep her safe while doing it. He has to keep his hands and lips off her long enough....

Larken and Quinn try to solve a murder together while having their own dark and steamy romance.

Kitten

Larken's daughter, Devin, gets dragged down a dark hole of human trafficking and murder. She needs to find out who is behind this, because they've already tried to abduct her once.

Oakley is just your average guy, until he saves a kitten in a dimly lit alley. He falls hard for his new obsession and will do everything in his power to keep his Kitten safe.

Together they will take on human traffickers, because now one of their friends has been abducted.

Meanwhile, they can't keep their hands and tongues off each other. Be sure to check out this highly steamy book 2!

First class, 5 star smut being served up with twists and turns.

Made in the USA
Monee, IL
14 November 2024